Losing Control

Henrietta Bond

Published by
British Association for Adoption & Fostering
(BAAF)
Saffron House
6–10 Kirby Street
London EC1N 8TS
www.baaf.org.uk

Charity registration 275689 (England and Wales) and SC039337 (Scotland)

© Henrietta Bond 2012

British Library Cataloguing in Publication Data
A catalogue record for this book is available from the British Library

ISBN 978 1 907585 50 0

Project management by Miranda Davies, BAAF
Designed by Helen Joubert Design
Cover design by Lucia Reed
Cover photography by istock.com
Typeset by Fravashi Aga
Printed in Great Britain by TJ International Ltd.
Trade distribution by Turnaround Publisher Services, Unit 3, Olympia Trading
Estate, Coburg Road, London N22 6TZ

FSC
www.fsc.org
Paper from
responsible sources
FSC® C013056

Acknowledgements

Once again there are so many people I want to thank – and apologies to anyone I've forgotten. As ever, a very big thank you to everyone at BAAF: Miranda, Shaila, Michelle, Jo, Ruth and Charlie.

Big thanks also to those organisations and care leavers who have been so supportive of *Control Freak* – especially Jonny Hoyle and Maxine McDermott at A National Voice, Janet Rich and the Care Leavers' Foundation, Martin Hazlehurst and colleagues at NCAS. Thanks, too, as always, to Ena Fry and Benni-Jo Tyler. And I want to give a special mention to Pasche, Jade Aitken, Kevani Kanda, Hope Daniels and Matt Langsford.

My huge gratitude goes to my incredibly supportive and encouraging friends: Hilary Rock, Clarinda Cuppage, Lesley Turney, Sarah Wragg, Sarah Algar, Shelagh Coghlan, Penny Craufurd, Algie Gray, Sarah Shankster, Katharine Radclyffe, Leigh Chambers, Will Thornton, Chris Dowd, Jude Tavanyar and to my very dear Warren House friends. A big thank you also to Ewan, Michelle, Jamie and Caspar Wright for making me feel slightly less old than I look. And to my beautiful god-daughter, Keresha Stupart, and Dylan and Naomi. And to the inspirational and broadminded Cannonesses of the Holy Sepulchre, who make me feel that there is always a calm, safe place for me.

The last year has also brought me the support of some new and very special people (many of them met through Twitter): Naomi Stolow, Noel McDermott, Isabel Jana, Gregory Dolecki, Theresa Gallacher, Vivienne Tuffnell, Gordon Johnson, Shani Solomons, Paul Whitelegg and Sharon Worrell. And I want to thank those highly successful authors, Marika Cobbold, Elizabeth Buchan and Louise Douglas for their kindness and support.

About the author

Henrietta Bond recently moved to the rugged beauty of the Yorkshire/Lancashire borders and spends many happy hours walking on the moors. She is grateful to all those friends who make it possible for her to return frequently to the bright lights of London, Essex and Hertfordshire. Henrietta lives with her husband, two elderly cats and a very young hamster. Her horse Dingbat now lives in retirement in Barnet, London.

To earn a living, Henrietta works as a freelance journalist and media consultant specialising in children and family issues. A former press officer for BAAF, since becoming freelance she has worked with Barnardo's, Fostering Network, The Who Cares? Trust, A National Voice, and many other children and young people's organisations, and local authorities. She has also written for *The Guardian*, *Community Care*, *Care and Health* and *Children Now*, as well as authoring several BAAF books, including the highly successful *Control Freak*, first of a series of three teenage novels on the theme of leaving care.

Note

Losing Control is a work of fiction. The book's characters are the product of the author's imagination and any resemblance to real people, living or dead, is purely coincidental.

Dedicated to my amazing husband, Frank, and to the
memory of his mother, Avis, and my mother, June

Stupid diary thing for English

My name is Ryan Richards and this is my diary. I am 14, nearly 15. I am this handsome, popular boy who is good at everything. My life is dead perfect and I have this perfect family and we live in Fairmount, which is this posh bit right out on the edges of Corrington. We have this big house and a swimming pool. Today my dad is taking me to football and tomorrow me and my mates are going scuba-diving. My girlfriend Beyoncé is coming too.

THE END (for today anyway)

What would Mr Stephens say if I handed that in? I bet he wouldn't dare say that's a pile of crap Ryan Richards, and you don't have a dad to take you to football. You've got a foster dad called Martin, who's a decent enough kind of bloke and comes to parents' evenings and stuff, but doesn't know one end of a football pitch from his bum. And while we're on the subject, Ryan Richards, I know your foster parents have a biggish sort of house, but it's not what you'd call posh or anything, now is it? And I'd say, 'How do you know that Mr Stephens? Have you been spying on me or something?' And he'd not be able to say in front of the whole class that he's my "designated teacher" coz that would give away that there are other kids in the school who are fostered too, and he's the one that keeps an eye on our education. Coz it's a legal requirement or something.

He might say, 'Do you really have a girlfriend called Beyoncé, Ryan Richards?' And I'd say, 'Just what are you insinuating, Mr Stephens? Are you saying I'm gay or something?' And then he'd go a bit red coz he knows about that stuff in my file and he'd say, 'No, Ryan Richards. I wasn't saying that – and it would be OK if you was anyway – but what I was saying is that I find it hard to believe you are dating a mega-star like Beyoncé Knowles.' And I'd say 'Beyoncé Knowles, Sir? Isn't that some singer off the telly? My bird's called Beyoncé Windsor and she's a member of the royal family.'

And then Mr S would say, 'You have such an imagination Mr Richards – I wonder that you haven't fallen down a rabbit hole yet,' and some of the girls in the class who fancy him will laugh and the boys will just groan coz we know he's an idiot.

I don't believe I just typed that stuff. Anyway, I'm going to delete it all on Sunday night before I hand it in.

Saturday 3 July

Dad and me went to the match. Corrington won 3 nil. Dad has this private box thing because of his job. We sat with this guy who is a managing director or something, and this supermodel who is his girlfriend. And after the match Robin West, the manager of the Corries, came in and said hello. And he brought that Rashan Gayle with him, who is their best player. And we chatted about this and that and Rashan asked me and my mates to his BBQ, which is next weekend.

THE END (of Saturday)

If I hand this in Mr Stephens will go mental. Like the Corries ever win a game he'll say! And he'll have a good point.

I don't even know who my real dad supports. He used to support some team up north but they were rubbish. My dad's rubbish as well, so I don't really care. My first dad supported the Corries but he's in America now and he's probably into American football or baseball or something. He doesn't write any more. I know he's not my birth dad but he was like a father to me when I was a little kid and I thought he was my real dad. Till he left coz of Mum's problems. And that's when she introduced us to "Uncle David". 'Cept he wasn't my uncle or nothing like that. He was my dad coz Mum had gone with him when she and the man I thought was my dad split up.

When Mum got taken into the long-stay mental hospital they said I would go and live with my dad. And they meant David. They didn't ask me or anything – which they're meant to. Kids who are fostered have to be consulted and they said they did, but if they did I don't remember. I wasn't that old then. If they'd asked me properly I'd have said I wanted to be with Holly, coz she's my sister. And she was the one who looked after me when Mum wouldn't get out of bed and stuff, and when she thought she was getting all those messages from the Queen.

Dave might be my biological father but he's a right idiot. He never hit me much but he didn't need to. His mum and his sister did plenty of that. I was only a little kid and they didn't know what little kids are like. So if I, like, got a bit dirty at school or I broke something, they would hit me with this belt they kept on the back of the door. And they wanted me to go to church all the time – like on Saturdays as well as Sundays, and they didn't like it when I asked to go and play with my mates.

There was this older girl at school, called Josie, and her mum was the dinner lady. And she often walked me back from school. And if my aunt and Evil Granny were out at a prayer meeting then Josie would take me back to her house. I think it was Josie's mum or the school or someone who told social services about me getting beaten all the time. And that's when I got sent to my first foster carers, who were OK, but not as good as Jane and Martin who I live with now. And I get to see my sister more often. Though I don't know why that's a good thing, coz she's a moody old moo most of the time.

Hey, I've written loads of this diary. Pity I'm gonna delete it all tomorrow night, but it's not like I want to end up in the bookshops, *Diary of an Abused Kid* or whatever those books are that all the girls at school read. Not that I wouldn't mind the money or anything, but I don't want them all looking at me and going, 'Ah, isn't that sad?' and all that kind of crap.

Sunday 4 July

My sister is dating this singer in a band and he's mega-famous and he's written this song for her. He didn't say her name but he said he wrote it for his girlfriend the last time they broke up. I heard it on the radio after me and Beyoncé and the lads came back from scuba-diving. We had crispy-crust pizza for supper with the spicy meatballs and four cheeses.

The end of my perfect weekend.

There you go Mr Stephens – and I bet you'll say, 'Since when has your sister been dating a rock star, Ryan Richards?' and I'll say, 'Since forever, Mr Stephens. And anyway he's not a rock star, he's an indie frontman and he plays guitar as well. And she's had this on and off thing with him for years and he's this really decent bloke called Sean and she treats him like a mug. But he loves her like he's crazy and when he first went off to uni I swear he was like crying down the phone every ten minutes. But now he's in this band with some of his uni mates and they are starting to get some airplay and stuff. I say to her, sis, you got to watch out coz there'll be loads of girls wanting him now he's like some famous dude, so you better start treating him right. But she's that arrogant my sister Holly, she never listens to no one.'

And you still don't believe me about this Beyoncé, Mr Stephens? Yeah well, what would you say if I wrote in my diary that I don't want a girlfriend, now or ever? That I knew since I was about 12 that I was gay and I had this crush on this older guy at school, but he left and I heard he got this girl pregnant, and when I saw him down the shopping centre he had this baby in a buggy and he wasn't that good looking any more. And no, I don't have a boyfriend or a crush on anyone at the moment, Mr Stephens. And no, I don't fancy my best mate Luke or anything, though all the girls fancy him. Not that it's any of your business, anyway. And my therapist says that's probably coz of what those paedos did to me last year when they drugged me and all that stuff. She says it's OK for me not to know what I want at the moment, and that's it's OK to be mixed up after what happened to me. And I guess she might be right, although she's not right about everything. And I do know what I want, but I can't see Rashan Gayle giving up that supermodel girlfriend just yet. ☺

SUNDAY 4 JULY

Why do 14-year-old boys think that 11.45pm is an OK time to go calling people? Some of us need our beauty sleep, especially after a hard day's work at the garden centre.

And he came out with all this rubbish about me being the girlfriend of an indie frontman.

'You what?' I asked him, trying not to sound as irritated as I felt.

'You know that programme on the radio – where they like play new bands and stuff...'

I didn't but I made an uh-huh kind of noise coz I didn't fancy a long explanation. Ryan takes his music really seriously and he can go on and on if you don't stop him.

'Anyway sis, Sean's band was on. Well, one of their tracks – that one with the quiet bit at the beginning and then that guitar bit in the middle which goes...'

Yeah whatever, I thought. Very likely. My boyf is the singer in this band of people he met at uni. I mean they're not exactly rubbish but they aren't exactly brilliant either. Well, not to my ears. But then I'm a bit of an R&B girl myself.

Ryan noticed I wasn't saying anything. 'You don't believe me, but god's truth sis it was The Static. There was this interview – it was like a pre-record or something. And Sean was talking. About the band and what inspired them an' all that.'

I was beginning to wonder why Sean hadn't told me about this.

'And Sean was like, "I wrote this song when me and my girlfriend broke up." That's you sis.'

I remember Sean reading me the lyrics when we first got back together. It was quite touching really – and kind of funny at the same time. He's got quite a way with words has Sean.

'Then he was, like, but we're back together now, and the interviewer said was that a good thing if he wrote such good stuff when his heart was broke. And Sean says, yeah well, you were like the best thing in his life and he didn't want to go there again... It was dead romantic sis.' And then my charming brother made throwing up noises over the phone.

'Some of those people clearly don't have enough stuff to fill their programmes,' I said, feeling my cheeks going scarlet.

'Nah, the guy said that The Static was bound to be huge.'

'They always say stuff like that. Doesn't mean anything.'

Ryan chuckled in that really mischievous way he has. 'Hey sis – don't you want your boyf to be a mega-star? I mean I thought you two were loved up. Or are you scared the groupies'll get to him or what?'

But that wasn't it. I know Sean loves me, he's never left me in any doubt how he feels about me. But I'm a private person. I don't like everyone knowing my business. I wasn't crazy about the idea of Sean mentioning me on the radio.

'It's not like he said your name or anything,' Ryan protested. 'C'mon sis, most girls would be well pleased to have a boyfriend saying stuff like that 'bout them.'

I reminded my brother that I wasn't 'most girls'. And also that it was getting on for midnight and I had to be up early.

Ryan said he'd go but only after I promised him I'd get the gossip from Sean and tell him what was going on. 'If he's like playing at Reading or anywhere this summer I want free tickets,' Ryan informed me.

So I said it was time he went to sleep and he said he couldn't coz he still needed to write some diary project for homework. I said he should have done it sooner but he said he had – but he'd written stuff that was made up, and then stuff that was too real for anyone else to read, and he still hadn't written anything that he could hand in to his teacher. I said I'd like to read his diary and he said 'As if' and I said 'Sleep well little bro. Love you,' and he said 'Love you too old bag of a sister.'

MONDAY 5 JULY

I texted Sean to ask what was going on. I got this reply saying he thought I already knew, coz he'd put it on Facebook and he'd sent me an email and some texts. Apparently it was all a last minute thing which had been set up since I spoke to him on Friday night. I felt a bit embarrassed to admit I hadn't been online for a day or two and I'd only glanced at the top line of his text where he'd been saying stuff about missing me, loving me lots and all the usual. I've had loads of my own things to do this week, what with my first year project having to be handed in by Friday and all that. But I still felt a bit guilty. So I texted him to say:

Soz babe, think I got some probs wiv me interweb. Hope u got copy coz I v to hear this. Stardom here u come!

I was proud of myself writing something that nice. The old Holly would've chewed his ear off for talking about her without checking first. But these days I'm a grown-up, chilled-out 18-year-old who lives and lets live. And who channels all her negative energy into making brilliant art. Sometimes I hardly recognise myself coz I'm that laid back.

Then I did some of my coursework but it wasn't working out like

I wanted it to. So I've kind of scrapped some of my drawings and I'll have to start again tomorrow. Sorry, diary – not going to have much time for you this week.

Keesh just got in and she's crashing around like a madwoman out there. She's trying to be quiet coz she thinks I'm asleep but Keesh doesn't do quiet. She's like the most outgoing person you could ever imagine and she's really loud with it – but everyone loves her. Even the kitchen is under her spell and it's like the cutlery drawer just has to fall at her feet every time she opens it. LOL. Suppose I might as well go and join her for a quick cuppa. She may not be the quietest flatmate ever, but she's always good for a gossip!

Monday 5 July

No, Mr Stephens, I am not turning into a diary writer, and you're never going to see this anyway so don't start thinking of any of your pathetic questions to ask. You know you're not as clever as you think. When you read out that bit where I'd written that I spent my whole weekend trying to do some stupid project for English, and you said that you were surprised by that because you couldn't imagine how even I could spend 48 hours writing three sentences, the girls only laughed coz you've got those baby blue eyes and they think you look like some guy in *Hollyoaks*. Personally I don't see it. He's got muscles and you're a bit of a wimp.

I am not writing this because I'm worried, which I bet you'd like to think I was coz you did all that stuff about diaries are a good way of letting out our inner emotions. But did you honestly believe that after a whole period of the girls reading out what they bought at the shops and the boys reading out what they watched on telly that we're pouring out our hearts in diaries? No way. Diaries are so last century, Mr Stephens.

And no, I do not really believe a kid has nicked my memory stick on purpose. I'm not *that* paranoid. If someone has it, then they've picked it up by mistake. There are hundreds of random homework things on that stick and they won't go looking at everything that's on there coz that would just be weird. Tomorrow some kid will come up to me and give it back.

TUESDAY 6 JULY – 1am

Sean seemed dead pleased with my reply and sent me this link where I could hear his interview on the radio station's website. So I did. And it was OK. There's loads of bits of him giving these really pretentious answers to the presenter's questions. 'So Sean, who were your early influences?' and him saying how he used to listen to his dad's music in the car, like Bob Dylan and Jimi Hendrix and stuff. But no mention of that Steps album his mum bought him when he was eight coz he wrote a letter to Father Christmas asking for it.

But the bit about me was sweet. And makes me sound a bit mysterious and kind of dead glamorous. Sean told the presenter that he wasn't going to say my name coz I'm such a private person and the presenter sort of assumed I was a celebrity or something. And Sean kind of played along with that and said I was like an artist – which is true. But then the presenter starts calling me Lady X and Sean picked this up, and dedicated our song to me – calling me his Lady X. If he was in a boy band his agent wouldn't let him do stuff like that coz they all have to pretend they're young, free and single. So the ten-year-old girls don't cry their little hearts out.

But I guess indie isn't like that. And besides, as far as I know The Static don't have an agent. Unless you count the dad of the boy who plays drums, and personally I'd rather not. ☺

The project is nowhere near like finished and it didn't help that I spilt tea on some of my drawings, but I think the final thing is going to be OK. I am cool, calm and collected. As Keesh reminded me (when I stopped hyper-breathing), I am not someone to panic.

Tuesday 6 July

No memory stick, but I'm not worrying. They probably just stuck it in their bag and they haven't needed to use it yet. Tonight they'll go to do their physics project and they'll go, oh no, I've picked up Ryan Richards's memory stick and I need to take it into school tomorrow...

I've kind of finished my art project today, but I'll still check it through again tomorrow. I might do one of my drawings again, but I'll see how I feel. I'm that proud of myself for getting so much done.

I rang J and M this evening coz I haven't spoken to them for ages. Since I got my new flat I meant to see them at least once a week and ring them every couple of days, but it never worked out quite like that. Martin got them FB accounts coz Jane went on this course that said foster carers need to keep up with what kids in their care are doing. I mean, I think that's a good idea but honestly, most kids know how to block adults from seeing stuff, don't they? But Martin uses his about once a week to say how he had a nice time at the model train club or how he came third in some quiz at work, and Jane just likes stuff about child care and fostering. Of course, I don't let them see all my stuff. It's not that I'm not careful or anything, but what if one of my mates got on there and...? Martin and Jane might not realise that I hadn't actually shown my boobs in public or whatever it is that some joker thinks is funny.

Martin sounded really pleased to hear from me. But then he

always does. Martin is like one of those big St Bernard dogs, which is always wagging its tail. He's big and playful and cuddly, but you know he'd always dig you out if you fell in a snowdrift. We talked about this and that and then Martin said that Simon was standing nearby and he had something important to tell me.

Simon doesn't normally say much – sometimes he doesn't speak for days – but today he had this big news he wanted to share with me. 'I'm getting adopted,' he whispered to me down the phone. And I said that was terrific, although I already knew about it, coz Jane and Martin have been talking about it for a while and were just waiting to see if the local authority would support them to do it. But the social workers were glad about it coz they know that Simon's family are a bad lot. I don't like to say mean things about foster kids' families coz most of them do their best but screw up a little bit, but Simon's family are these really evil people. Half of them seem to be in prison for GBH or robbery, or doing something vile to people or animals. When he first arrived at J and M's he was swallowing paper clips and weird stuff coz that's what they used to force him to do. But then his little brother drowned in the bath coz nobody was watching him, and after that, social services was clear that no kids would be allowed to live in their family again.

Jane and Martin didn't really mean to adopt any kids coz they've got their own grown-up children, and what they used to do is foster kids for short times. Except they kept me till I was old enough to go to college and now they have my brother living with them on this residence order thingy. And then there's Lucy and Nathan and baby Ruby. But I guess they don't count as living in the house, coz J and M had the over-the-garage rooms converted into a little flat thingy for them. So they could have their own door and be their own little family. 'Cept it seems to me that Lucy spends half her time in Jane and Martin's bit asking her mum how to cook stuff and Martin spends half his time in Lucy and Nathan's bit wanting to hold his granddaughter. Jane loves seeing her grandchild too of course, but she's always doing stuff, like arguing with Ryan and Simon's schools, or having a go at the health authority about some foster carer or kid who isn't getting their rights. If Martin's a St Bernard, then Jane is probably a terrier. Once she gets hold of something she never lets go. ☺

Simon needs a lot of special support coz he's not exactly a normal kind of kid, and the local authority was taking forever finding the right people to adopt him. So J and M decided it would be best if he stayed with them permanently coz he fits in their home really well. When I lived with them we had all sorts and shapes of kids with all kinds of problems and baggage. So nobody thinks he's strange or weird or laughs at him coz he puts his clothes on back to front some days and is dead picky about what he eats. And if Simon says he saw a pterodactyl in the garden, then we just say 'That's nice,' and nobody makes a big fuss about it. There was one time when he tried to cover Boots in green icing sugar, but the old cat wasn't having none of that and scratched him on the arm. Since then Boots sleeps on the bottom of Simon's bed every night and they're the best of mates.

When Si hands back the receiver I ask Martin if he's seen the baby today, and he says, 'You bet!' Then he tells me proudly, 'Ruby has another tooth.'

'Is it any different from the other three teeth she's got so far?' I ask, and Martin says no, but Lucy will still tell me all about it when she sees me. And then we both laugh, which is OK, coz we both totally love Lucy to bits.

Wednesday 7 July

OK Mr Stephens – maybe you're just a teeny bit right about being careful what you put on FB. But only a little bit. It's not like I called Natalie a fat cow or anything; it wasn't that rude. But she's asked me out three times now and I keep having to say no, which is a waste of my breath. And it's not like I named her or anything. I thought she'd know who I meant and she'd get the hint – so she doesn't keep embarrassing herself. It wasn't my fault that Luke went and named her when he made that comment...

There was no need for her brother to send me all those texts calling me a **** and a ******* (See I'm censoring this coz I did listen to some of your advice, Mr Stephens). And that stuff that Natalie's best mate put on FB about me is well out of order.

THURSDAY 8 JULY

This afternoon me and Lucy went swimming. Since she had Ruby, Luce has been struggling to lose the weight she put on when she was pregnant, and nibbling her way through all those choccies the midwife told her she shouldn't have. She's always been on the curvy side and she looks fab, but Luce says that she feels like one of those giant walrus things that find it hard to move around. So she left Ruby with Nathan and we got to spend a girly afternoon together.

I miss Luce if I'm honest. We shared a bedroom for ages and she's probably my best friend in the world.

'Ruby's teeth are getting really sharp,' Luce told me as we finished our sixth length of back crawl. Both of us were a bit puffed so we stopped for a rest coz neither of us had been in the water that much this year. 'She got another one on Tuesday... it was really hurting her as it came through, but it's only a tiny one, bigger than that first one, but not so big as...'

'I thought babies didn't get teeth till they were about a year old,' I said, not wanting to hear every tiny detail about Ruby's molars.

'Babies can be born with teeth,' Lucy told me and I guess she knows what she was talking about coz she's read every baby book, magazine and website ever published. Lucy could do Mastermind on pregnancy and childbirth and get the highest score ever. 'And believe me they hurt!' She winced as she crossed her arms across her boobs.

'One more reason not to have any myself,' I replied.

'But you must have children – you always said you wanted children!' Luce insisted, 'They are like the most amazing thing ever...'

'Creating paintings is like the best thing ever,' I told her, but I didn't expect her to believe me. Luce was one of those girls who found art lesson boring, unless she could make a nice Easter card with fluffy cotton wool chicks or something with lots of pink to hang on her dressing table. And the more sequins and glitter she could stick on it the better.

'You could be an artist *and* have children,' Luce suggested, hopefully. 'Just think how nice it would be if you had a little girl too – she and Ruby could play together. Or maybe if you like had a boy, then maybe when they got older they could like marry or something...'

'Lucy-Poocy just listen to yourself!' I scolded her. 'I haven't even thought about having any kids and here you are marrying my imaginary son off to your poor little daughter. Anyway, wouldn't that be like incest or something?'

'The Egyptians married their sisters,' Lucy reminded me.

'Only the pharaohs,' I corrected her. 'And some of the Roman emperors married their sisters or nieces or something.' But I'm not completely sure about this as history was never something I was that interested in.

'Wasn't there that emperor who ate all his children coz he didn't want them to be more famous than him?' Lucy always enjoyed history more than I did and she likes a good costume drama on the telly. Romans, Spartans, Victorians or the Middle Ages – Lucy loves them all.

Then she shook her head. 'Oh no – that was a Greek god. Not a real person.'

'I really hope so,' I replied. 'Eating children isn't very nice. Unless of course they're really well done and you cover them with plenty of BBQ sauce and you have them with a really nice crisp salad with some of those crunchy little toast squares on the top.'

Lucy was appalled but she couldn't help but laugh. 'Would they be high in calories?' she asked me.

'That would depend on the child,' I replied. 'And how many fizzy cola bottles and doughnuts and sugary snacks they'd eaten. Of course if they'd been very good children and eaten their five-a-day then they wouldn't be too fattening.'

Luce sniggered but then straightened her face. 'Holly that is horrible,' she said, going all proper on me. 'Is that the kind of stuff you talk about with your art student friends?'

'Definitely,' I said, 'But it's usually much worse than that. We talk about things like how vampires reproduce and what would happen if you swallowed a razor blade, or how long it takes a body to rot if you leave it in an acid bath...'

Lucy squealed. 'That's disgusting!'

'And when we're not doing that we cut up eyeballs, or steal dead men's fingers from the morgue... Our tutors say we have to do that kind of thing coz it's the only way we can really "feel" our art!'

My foster sister gazed at me in horror for a moment and then the penny dropped. 'You're winding me up. Sometimes you're so horrid Holly,' and her bottom lip jutted out into that cute little pout she's never grown out of. Men go wild for that pout and several lads messing about a few feet away from us had noticed, and were starting to edge closer.

'Race you to the end,' I said and we swam away in a frenzy of thrashing arms, purposely splashing each other as much as we could.

Afterwards we headed into town for a coffee. Well, a milkshake actually, coz that's Lucy's favourite. She went off them for a bit when she got really bad morning sickness and she started fancying celery and coffee powder and the smell of furniture polish and all sorts of truly weird stuff, which fortunately she never got round to tasting. But now she's chocolate milkshake queen again. 'I'm still eating for two,' she told me as she asked for extra marshmallows on top of the whipped cream.

I reminded her that we'd just been working out at the pool to lose some calories. 'Like you really need to lose calories,' Lucy glared at me accusingly. 'You could eat Big Macs every day for a year and you'd never put on a pound.'

'But I'm not the one who announced she was going on a diet...' I reminded Lucy and she glared at me again. But it's hard to be mean to Lucy. 'C'mon, enjoy your shake – I think you've burnt off millions of calories with all that swimming.'

'I did ask for skimmed milk,' Lucy reminded me. And I wasn't gonna spoil her fun by saying that there's no point in skimmed milk when the shake's made with two scoops of Cornish ice cream and half a bucket of whipped cream.

I guess breastfeeding takes it out of you. Reason 247 why I don't think I'm going to have any kids. Well, not in a hurry anyway.

'You could bottle feed,' Lucy said but wrinkled up her nose at the idea. She's one of those people that thinks depriving babies of breast milk is almost as bad as abandoning them on a hillside to starve. 'But there's like all this special nutrition stuff in boob milk and it helps babies to build up their immune systems and...'

'Does that make the babies more fattening?' I asked, and I got another Lucy pout. But then she giggled – the little girl Lucy inside the grown-up sensible mum. 'Guess so! Specially if you eat them with chocolate fudge sauce.'

Friday 9 July

Been up all night. I'm that wound up and it's your fault, Mr Stephens. If you never started that stupid diary thing then I would never have written that stuff and there'd be nothing on my memory stick 'cept biology homework. I should have wiped all that stupid stuff off and not left it on there. I was never going to show it to Holly anyway. Thank you, Mr Stephens. Thank you very very much indeed. You have very probably ruined my life.

FRIDAY 9 JULY

I woke up to find a text from Ryan being all mysterious. He seemed to have sent it some time round 3am in the morning. He said he needed to speak to me – urgently – and needed my advice.

Now my brother is a right drama queen and has the imagination of a thriller writer, but he's also pretty good at getting himself into real trouble. So when I get a message like that I get worried.

I tried Ryan's phone but I guess he was in school by the time I rang back. I was having a bit of a lie-in so it was quite late. I sent him a text saying he should call me when he's free.

I tried him again round lunchtime but there was no answer. I guess it's hard for him to talk from school and maybe the problem has gone away. I hope so.

Anyway I had stuff of my own to think about. I handed in my coursework and bumped into some mates of mine. Dan was there and he made this big thing about how he'd missed me, coz I haven't been around all week. He'd texted me during the week to say he was thinking of splitting up with Rani and it seems like he's finally done it. I guess he's done the right thing. She may be dead pretty but she's far too straight for him. She's got no S.O.H whatsoever and she always looks fed up when me and Dan and the others mess about. He said he'd seen her in the corridor earlier and she'd just ignored him, like he didn't exist any more.

'She takes everything so seriously,' Dan told me, drawing patterns in the foam on his cappuccino. 'If I'd drawn this,' he put the flourish on something that possibly could have been a bit of stick and two cherries, 'she'd have told me it was rude and I should learn to grow up.'

'Well, it is a bit childish,' I said, but you can't help but love Dan. He's a bit like an overgrown teddy bear in some ways – especially to look at. He's a little bit on the hefty side but attractively so, with fluffy blonde hair that sticks out at all angles, like those football players the girls all fancy in the American rom coms. And he's got this really boyish face, like a kid that's just done something a bit naughty and hopes that if he smiles hard enough you'll forget all about it and not be cross with him. But in other ways he's like this guy who is solid through and through. You would trust Dan with your life, if it ever came to it.

I do feel a bit sorry for Rani if I'm honest. I was like that before I came to college – always dead serious about everything and so focused. She's got this father who's a professor and he wants her to be a teacher or something, and he makes it very clear that he doesn't like it that she's doing art. So she's got this thing about always having to prove herself.

'Yeah, but she needs to lighten up,' Dan started, slurping his coffee and leaving a big blob of foam on his nose. 'If you can lighten up Hol, then anyone can. I remember when you first got here and...'

'Yeah, yeah – no need to tell me that again,' I said, interrupting Dan before he started going back over old ground. But I was grateful to Dan for sticking with me through those early days. I was still trying to be Little Miss Perfect and Dan had this way of teasing me gently, and although I made it that obvious I didn't want to hang around with him, he kind of stuck with me until I got used to him. I think he maybe had a teeny bit of a crush on me back then, or he'd have got fed up with me much sooner. But in the end I started seeing how much fun I was missing out on and I began letting my hair down just a little. These days I'm that laid back I'm almost horizontal.

Tonight I got a reply from Ryan. It said:

Don't worry im fine. C u 2moro. Luv u sis.

Now I can't sleep coz I know something is very wrong.

SATURDAY 10 JULY
evening

I was nearly late for Jane this morning coz I wasted an hour deciding what to wear and Keesh was having coffee in the kitchen with her boyf, so I couldn't get her expert eye to check me over. It's not that I keep secrets from Keesh (coz she's care experienced like me) but the boyf was bound to ask questions. He's a DJ and he's kind of into fashion, which is good coz Keesh is trying to set up her own design label. But how do you tell a man you've only met a handful of times that you're going to visit your mum who lives in a loony bin? (I never call it that myself but that's what he'd call it in his head. Holly's mum is a psycho, he'd think, and he'd be really nice to me for a while but he'd probably be freaked and wondering when I was going to attack him with the carving knife or something.)

I'm not ashamed of my mum. It's just kind of hard watching people's faces when you tell them your mum thinks she's controlled by a central computer, and that she sometimes screams when you visit her. Coz she thinks you've come from the central maintenance department to close her down.

I wanted to look smart for my mum, coz she is my mum after

all. But not official kind of smart coz that scares her. So in the end I just wore my jeans and this purple crocheted tunic that I got in Oxfam. It's kind of 70s retro stuff but it goes fab with the colour of my hair.

Of course Ryan had something rude to say about it. 'Whose granny knitted that then? S'not very indie chick is it?'

He thinks he's such a comedian my brother but I wasn't going to let him irritate me. I knew how nervous he felt about the visit.

I was glad that Jane was driving us. She'd come with us on the last two visits. She's brilliant Jane, coz she always knows what to do or say when something freaky happens. Like it did today.

It's not that the hospital is a dreadful place. I think the staff care about their patients and there's been a real effort recently to brighten the place up with fresh paint and plants and lots of pictures on the walls. They're mainly painted by patients doing art therapy and they're a bit weird some of them – like the one with the woman with the exploding head. I'm not sure I'd want to pass that every time I needed a wee. But you can tell it's well meant. (Maybe I'll bring them one of my pictures next time, so they'll have something decent for people to look at.) And they open the windows a lot and have little bowls of pot pourri and stuff about the place but you can still smell the disinfectant underneath it all. And it's well depressing.

Mum has her own room coz she's been there for about three years now. She was on this locked ward for a bit before that but then they changed the policy and moved most of the patients to this place. They said that Mum would probably be able to go and live in the community but it hasn't happened yet. She won't even go outside her room – which is why she's got her own shower unit and toilet. "En suite" they call it and they had to install it specially for her after they realised she wasn't going anywhere unless they sedated her so much she could be moved on a trolley. And they don't like doing that to people. Not these days anyway, and not in this hospital. Mum says that if she leaves the room 'they will pull the plug'. And she can't risk it.

The staff had tried to prepare Mum as much as possible for our visit. I s'pose it's coz we only come every three months and they know that Mum is likely to freak if they don't warn her. The nurse who met us in the corridor explained that she'd been talking about us to Mum all week but we needed to be prepared for her to have no idea who we are.

'Like that's anything new,' Ryan said bitterly, giving the nurse his best drop-dead look. Which isn't fair really. He's the one who wanted these visits. After he had his crisis thing last year and got all that counselling, he said it very clearly – that he wanted to start seeing Mum again. Whereas me, I'd kind of given up on that coz it isn't that nice an experience, not being recognised by someone you love.

Mum was huddled against the pillows when we went in. She was dressed in this sweatshirt and jeans but she had a blanket wrapped round her, although it was well stuffy in the room. Maybe it's coz she's so thin and she feels the cold more than the rest of us. I don't think she ever eats much, coz she's afraid that someone is trying to poison her. Last time it was the Prime Minister or the Queen or the President of the USA or someone like that who was out to get her, coz the computer tells her things that are international secrets. One time she said it was the woman in the next room, who was an agent for MI5.

She looked us up and down for a few minutes and said nothing. Ryan and me just stood there kind of uncomfortable, but we know that if we move too quickly she sometimes panics and pulls the emergency cord. But Jane is so good in these situations. She just nodded at Mum and said, 'I've brought you flowers. Where would you like me to put them?'

'There's a vase in there,' Mum said, pointing at the bathroom. 'But be careful when you put the water in. It's best to use the water from the shower. They can't do much to that.'

Jane disappeared into the poky little en suite and we could hear the sound of cellophane rustling, vase-like clinking noises and water running. Me and Ryan went on standing, getting more and more awkward. I knew from the past that it was no good trying to approach her or anything. Once I made the mistake of being all breezy and kissing her on the cheek. She screamed so much I thought she was going to have a panic attack, so I'm careful these days.

'You can sit down if you want to,' Mum said eventually, plucking obsessively at a loose thread in the blanket. 'But I don't think you'll find it very helpful. I've already put all the details in the report I sent to your boss.'

I can't get my head around that. How can she imagine a 14-year-old boy and an 18-year-old girl are agents for a government department? And why doesn't she remember we're her children? But the psychiatrist tried to explain it to me once. She said that Mum kind of projects things onto people – like she has this scenario in her head and whoever comes through the door becomes the person she's imagining.

Fortunately Jane came out of the bathroom then, carrying the vase of flowers. 'Where'd you like me to put this?' she asked Mum, like it was all dead normal.

'Have you checked it for bugs?' Mum asked and Jane said that she had. I don't think any of us knew whether she meant creepy crawlies or those device things for listening in to people.

'So how are you Brenda? As you can see I've brought your children to visit you,' Jane said all matter-of-fact as she placed the flowers on a bedside table. And for a moment this look of recognition comes over Mum's face. And she looks from Ryan to me and back again.

'He's taller,' Mum said after a few minutes. And for a moment I feel that jealous that she's talking about Ryan not me but I guess it's most noticeable. Ryan has been growing so much this year. He's nearly as tall as me now and I'm not that far off six foot. Mum used to be tall, but she's kind of shrivelled up recently, which is sad coz she's not that old really. I think she's only about 40.

'It's what we feed him,' said Jane and laughed. And Mum laughed too. Like it was really very funny, which it wasn't. Then Mum offers Jane some toffees from her bedside cabinet – but advises her to test them first. Jane says she will do that, and passes the bag to Ryan and me.

Ryan is putting a toffee in his mouth when Mum started to scream. She screamed so loudly that the nurses came running. Mum was semi-hysterical by this time and it was hard to make out what she was saying, but it sounds like she's accusing Ryan of trying to poison her or something. Something really wild, like he'd slipped some poison in the bag but is taking a toffee himself to try and fool her that they're OK. Or whatever mixed up stuff goes on in her head. She was yelling and pointing at him and she kept saying 'that man from the agency'.

Jane ushered Ryan outside and I stayed for a minute to see if Mum would calm down. But when she stopped yelling she started crying, and she sobbed and sobbed. It was heartbreaking to listen to that and I was in tears too. But she clutched at one of the nurses, begging her not to leave her and the nurse sat down on the bed stroking Mum's hand. Then Mum whispered something in the nurse's ear and the nurse was speaking very low to her coz she clearly didn't want me to hear, but I understood what was going on. Mum wanted the 'strange lady' to go away. So I did.

I didn't cry again after that because it was like a shutter came down over my heart. I find that sometimes, when things are too painful, I can kind of cut off my feelings and pretend that everything is normal. I think Ryan was doing the same thing too. He was dead silent for part of the journey back but when Jane tried to get him to talk about what had happened he just made a joke of it – some stupid comment about Mum needing re-booting.

So of course it wasn't a good time for me to ask what he was worried about. And later, when I was round at supper with Jane and Martin, and Lucy and Nathan and Ruby were there too, and Simon wanted to sit next to me, so it wasn't easy getting time alone with my bro.

'You wouldn't understand, sis,' he told me, when I finally managed to get a few private minutes with him in the kitchen.

So why did you bother texting me in the first place, I nearly said. But I didn't. Teenage boys are delicate creatures. You have to humour them.

'Well, if you do want to talk to me, you know where I am,' I assured him, rather lamely. And he just rolled his eyes at me and went back to doing something on his phone.

But enough now, I really need some shut-eye. When I got back, Keesh had some friends over, and like her, they really know how to party! They brought some rum and juice and other fancy drinks with them, and they asked me to join them. They made these cocktails with lots of fruit and sugar and stuff. Very refreshing indeed.

MONDAY 12 JULY

I'm writing up two days coz I forgot to take you to Sean's in London. Sorry, diary. That's not like me. But then it's not like me to nearly miss my train – and I did. Well nearly miss it that is. I just got on as the guard was about to blow the whistle.

I had really weird dreams on Saturday night, about being part of a computer. Not run by a computer like poor Mum but I was the human bit of the computer and I had this special code inside me that was needed to save the world. Except I'd forgotten the code and nothing I did would bring it back. And people were threatening me with all sorts of horrible things if I didn't remember. Fortunately I woke up before they poked my eyes out with burning sticks but it left me feeling that upset I was nearly sick. Well, the tequila was maybe part of it but I didn't drink that much, honestly.

I'd meant to get up early and pack my bags and put in some of my best things – like my lovely red boots and this slinky black dress with a halter neck, but I ended up shoving the first things I could find into a bag and rushing out of the house. If you don't get the early bus on Sunday morning you're doomed coz they only come about every three hours. And Sean said he'd meet me when the train got into London coz the dad of the boy who plays drums in the band was taking everyone to a posh Italian restaurant to celebrate the band having been on the radio.

I managed to make myself look half decent in the toilet on the train, with a lot of hair gel and plenty of lippy and eye liner. It's a big responsibility being the girlfriend of a wannabe musical legend – especially when you're also going to be a great artist yourself. You want people to look back and go 'OMG – I remember the first time I met her. She was like this really awesome person and such a dedicated artist. I always knew she'd be bigger than Van Gogh.'

Well, something like that.

Actually I don't know why I bothered coz my 'budding artist' look was a bit wasted on most of the band members. Kyle, who plays guitar, is pretty cool and I'd met him before a few times, but the drummer and his dad were total nerds. So was this boy who played keyboards, and his mates. They spent the whole meal trying to look down my cleavage and nobody asked once what I did or what I was going to be.

Kyle's girlfriend, Alicia, was OK but she didn't seem to like it much that Kyle spent ages telling me about his holiday in Australia and all these "chicks" he hung out with – although, as he explained, it was way before he met Alicia. Sean said afterwards that Kyle was flirting with me something rotten but I don't think that was true. Anyway Sean seemed to like it, coz I think he was quite pleased that the other band members fancied his girlfriend. He's not the jealous type, which is good, coz I'm not the kind of girl who likes people getting possessive.

After the boys had stuffed their faces with pizza and pasta and enough garlic bread to feed an army, they all ordered the cheesecake or these massive ice creams with sparklers and cream. But I said I wanted the zabaglione – and everyone stared coz I don't think they knew what I was talking about. But it's this cool dessert made with cream and wine – which I saw some famous chef make on one of those cookery programmes and everyone that tasted it went 'Ooh' and 'Aah' and said how sophisticated it was. No word of a lie, it was that full of wine that it didn't taste much like a dessert. But I ate all of it because it's a pity to waste things.

We drank cappuccinos and then the drummer's dad wanted us all to go to the pub. But that's not my idea of how to spend a Sunday afternoon, so I said thank you for the lovely meal but me and Sean had things we wanted to do. We don't see each other that often and I wasn't spending it with a middle-aged man with bad breath and some stupid boys whose names I can't even remember. I think Alicia felt the same but Kyle said he could murder a pint or two so she went along. She should put her foot down more or that boy will walk all over her.

Me and Sean went for a walk in Hyde Park which is this massive green space right in the middle of London. We went to the Serpentine River and we sat and held hands and talked about our plans for the future. Then we went back to Sean's flat and it was brilliant because all the lads he shares with were out. So we had some time to ourselves, and we made good use of it. Then we showered and got ready to go out to this party that some of Sean's mates were throwing. And that was good coz there were some dead interesting people there (as well as the usual nerds and people that are so into themselves that they can't be bothered talking to you) and people kept coming up to Sean and congratulating him coz they'd heard him on the radio. Or someone had told them he'd been on the radio. And some of them thought he was already dead famous and one girl even asked him for his autograph. Cheeky mare – she wanted him to sign her thigh and Sean said he was flattered but he'd rather sign a piece of paper. So she got this paper plate and asked him to write 'love from Sean' which he did. But then she dove in and planted this big smacker on his lips – like she thought she was irresistible or something and he was gonna kiss her back. I was trying to decide whether to scratch her eyes out or pretend I wasn't one bit bothered, but he wriggled out of the way and said he charged for kisses – and only his girlfriend got them for free. I was proud of him then and glad I was with him. But I hope that won't start happening all the time – girls throwing themselves at him in public places. I will have to learn to be an ice queen all the time and I think that could be hard. I like to let my hair down and have a laugh and I don't want to stop doing that when I'm around Sean.

This morning I woke all snuggled up and cosy in Sean's tiny little bed with his arms wrapped round me, and I felt really happy. And I didn't feel at all guilty that Sean was skipping his lecture to be with me and I was missing an end-of-term supervision thing at college. My tutor knows I've worked my guts out all term and she said that nobody would think the worse of me if I didn't turn up, and I took her at her word. The old Miss Perfect Holly would have had to be there, but the new Happy Holly isn't so hard on herself. Me and Sean don't get to see each other so much and he's got this summer school thing which is part of his course, so he won't be home for a couple of weeks.

We had such a brilliant day together. We went up to the West End and looked round the big fashion stores. Neither of us had any money so we had nothing to spend, but Sean pretended he was designing a new look for The Static (and they certainly need it – they could start by giving the drummer a decent haircut) or appearing at some award ceremony or something, and I was just looking at all those designer frocks I'm gonna buy when I sell my first painting for a cool million.

It's good being with Sean because we know each other so well. We've had our ups and our downs and we split up for a while last year. But we know what each other is into and we make each other laugh. Sean is more laid back than me and he's someone who doesn't mind sitting back and letting life happen to him. Whereas me, I'm always out there looking for all the opportunities, making sure that I don't miss out on a single one. Which is why I told him I had to come back today. Coz there's this thing going on at college tomorrow – with this famous local artist coming to give a talk and look at some of our work, and I'm not going to miss that for anything.

At the station Sean told me he loved me. He's been saying that almost since our first date, but the weird thing is I know he means it. He says that the moment he saw me he knew I was the only girl in the world for him and that no matter how I behave (and I haven't always been the perfect girlfriend) he will always love me. And you know what, I actually believe him. Not coz I think I'm the greatest person in the world or anything but coz he acts like it's true and that makes me feel good about myself.

And today I said it back coz I really do love him, although sometimes I wonder if it's a bit more like a brother or best friend instead of a boyfriend. I mean I really fancy him these days (coz he scrubs up really well and has this cute haircut that really does it for me) and the physical part of our relationship is fantastic. But do I really love him in the happy ever after, let's-get-married- and-have- three-kids-and-a-semi-with-a-mortgage kind of love? Well, I'm not so sure about that. I'm not really a forever kind of person and the thought of just one person for 'better or worse' makes me panic a bit. But something I have learned is to enjoy the moment and not fret too much about what's round the next corner – coz you never know what's going to happen. So for here and now I do love being with Sean and I like to make him happy by telling him what he wants to hear.

So I'm back in Corrington now, and Keesh is making us supper. Her cooking is fantastic and she's a real laugh to live with – even if

I hardly ever see her coz she's always out partying. Then I'm having an early night so I will look wide awake for the talk tomorrow. My tutor said the artist is a man in his 50s and he's spotted a few really talented young people and helped them to get into the art market. I wonder if it's too tacky to wear my short denim skirt and sit in the front row?

Later

Did I really write that? Oh no, I can't believe I did. Maybe my denim skirt is just a bit too short for attending a lecture, but I could wear those designer jeans I got from the Sue Ryder shop. They fit me like a glove and make my legs look longer than ever.

Holly Richards you are becoming a scheming minx. And I kinda think I like you. LOL.

TUESDAY 13 JULY

Well that will teach me for making assumptions! Of course the guy turned out to be gay and my extra efforts with blow drying and extra length mascara were pretty wasted on him. But my tutor told me later that when he was looking round the exhibition he stopped at my work for a bit. 'This one,' he said, 'shows considerable promise.'

But of course, I'd have rather been James – the guy he singled out for real praise. Whose work he said he'd like to take some photos of so he could show a friend of his. Personally I think James's work is a bit rubbish – just some squiggly black marks that look like spiders have tipped over the ink pot and run around in the mess, but a lot of the tutors like his stuff so I guess he must be good. That's the problem with art really – it's all in the head of the people who look at it. You just need enough people to say 'that's brilliant' and you end up selling for a fortune in some flash private gallery or getting your pictures exhibited somewhere like Tate Modern. Which is hard on the other artists who think their own work is as good, or even better, and can't understand why nobody realises.

Dan told me I should be thrilled that this artist guy noticed my work. 'You expect too much Hol,' he told me. 'You could see he thought the rest of us were just crap. You're probably the most talented of any of us, and you know it.'

'Yeah well, I'm not that keen about being second best,' I told him.

'Now who's sounding like Rani!' he teased me. Rani had looked mortified ever since the artist's visit. He'd not glanced once at that painting of hers the tutors had all said such nice things about. I did feel a bit sorry for her coz I'd have felt the same myself if my stuff had been overlooked.

'Surely everyone wants to be the best?' I asked Dan, thinking it a bit of a no-brainer.

'Ah Holly,' Dan shook his head, 'Now that's where you are so wrong. Some of us know we could very easily be tenth, or twentieth, or possible a hundredth. So the idea of being second... Well, that seems pretty good to someone like me.'

'Someone like you! Don't make me laugh. You work your socks off to get a good pass on every single one of your assignments. Don't tell me you don't care how you do...'

'But I do care,' Dan assured me. 'I care an awful lot about passing assignments and not getting chucked off the course, but that doesn't mean I expect to do very well.'

'That's defeatist,' I told him. 'If you don't have aspirations, and work for them, you're never going to achieve your best!'

'Oh Hols, you sound like one of those sayings that people have on their fridge magnets,' Dan is grinning as he shakes his head at me. 'Stand on your tippy-toes and reach for the stars, and the whole freakin' sky will be poured all over you... Just be careful not to get the planets tangled in your hair.'

'OK, OK,' I said, getting his point. 'I admit it's a bit of a cliché, but surely we do need to have things to aim for.'

'Aiming for stuff is one thing, but it's this always having to be top of the ladder stuff that I don't get. What's wrong with settling with being halfway up?'

'Yeah, but why would you settle for that?' I asked, genuinely puzzled. Dan is like one of my closest friends but sometimes I just don't understand what makes him tick.

'Coz for some of us it doesn't seem like settling, Hol. We get to somewhere we like being and we're happy to be there. It's called contentment Hols – but I guess it's not something you know much about!'

'Or laziness,' I said, but instantly regretted it. 'Sorry, that came across a bit harsh. I'm not implying that you're like that Dan, but some kids … they just don't aim high enough.'

'Yeah well, there's ambition and there's making the best of what you've got. Take me, for example. I was like the kid who none of the teachers much bothered about. And my parents weren't much into education. Both my mum and dad were grafters and they were always doing stuff. When other kids went on holidays we went down to my uncle's in Norfolk and helped with the fruit picking … And before you say it, we weren't "poor but happy". We got along OK, but we had our problems like other families.'

Family problems I know about. I've got the T-shirt and read the book. And I joined the FB Group.

'And it was like, if I did well at anything at school it seemed to embarrass my parents. Like I was showing them up or something – they'd say stuff like, "Where did his brains come from? It can't have been from us" … so I didn't make much of an effort. Correction: I made no effort at all.'

'But that's good,' I reassured him. 'Not the not-making-an-effort stuff, but the fact that your parents loved you unconditionally. That they weren't constantly trying to push you, like Rani's parents, who are never satisfied with anything she does.'

'But it wasn't that brilliant, if you think about it, coz I needed a bit of pushing. Then I got this new teacher who was different to the others. He had this thing about making everybody feel like he cared about them. Not just whether you got good marks, but about whether you were trying. So if you failed but you'd really tried hard, he'd make you feel good that you were getting better. But if you failed worse the next time he'd seem so disappointed. And you ended up wanting to get things right – just for him.'

I could understand that. Mrs Wilson, my art teacher at school, was like that. She was really encouraging. But at the same time she used to push me quite hard. She told me that she wouldn't settle for work that was "good enough". It had to be my best – or she didn't rate it. She was the one who made me think I had it in me to get great marks in art – if I really put my mind to it. I told Dan this.

'Yeah but that's coz she knew you were capable of it, Hols,' Dan said. 'But if my teacher had pushed me *that* hard I'd probably have given up. Coz I'm a different person to you. He said it was better to have small goals and work towards them than have great big goals you can never hope to reach.'

And I kind of understood what he was saying. But personally I think Dan undersells himself. He's got plenty of talent but he's a bit timid about really going for it. In my humble opinion.

Talking of people who've got no ambition, Lucy really annoyed me this evening. She was going on and on about Ruby on the phone and she never once asked about how the artist's visit went. She's turned into this earth mother who wants to do nothing but talk about babies and frankly it's dead boring.

Lucy always had this obsession with little kiddies, which I don't get at all. One of the worst things for me about living in foster families was the small kids. I mean the older ones were a real pain sometimes but the little ones who came in all whiny and snot-smeared, they really got on my nerves. Jane says she'd never have realised it coz I was always so good with them, but that's coz I'm a practical person. I'd have them settled with a heap of toys or something educational on CBeebies before you could say Bob the Builder. Coz I never much wanted to talk to them or coo over them or whatever Lucy used to like doing.

Anyway, Lucy was going on about Nathan not doing the cooking, and that's not on. Nathe's doing his sports course at college and he's always trying to get bits of work and stuff. And he does loads of the housework and washing up and stuff. (I taught him well when he was my flatmate.) But Lucy's got this thing about them having to share everything for the baby. She's been on too many parenting websites in my opinion. She should spend more time looking for courses.

It's not like Ruby is even Nathe's kid or anything. She's not even the same colour (Nathan says it's not the baby's fault that she has a 'Stupid White Dad', which might be kind of racist if it was the other way round, but Ruby's dad was the worst boyf Lucy ever had. He says he never wants to see the baby and that's not fair on Ruby really, but with Nathe being such a good step-dad I don't think she's going to grow up damaged or anything. I don't see my dad at all these days and it's not done me any harm. It's not like I miss him that much.)

This evening Sean sent me a couple of messages and I sent him some messages back telling him I was really looking forward to seeing him when he gets back. It's a pain he's got to do that extra-course thingy but absence makes the heart grow fonder and all that stuff, so it will be really special when I do see him again.

WEDNESDAY 14 JULY

About 9am, Marje called to see if I could go into the garden centre. I was meant to be going into college, but I really needed the money. I don't mind the work but it's a bit of a trek getting there. It's right on the edge of the city – where the suburbs turn into fields and farms and stuff. I wish we had trams or an underground system like they have in London, but we've just got stupid buses. It's only two and a bit miles as the crow flies from where we live now, but coz the traffic is really bad round here the journey goes on like forever.

Anyway, coz I was going in a bit late the bus journey wasn't so bad. I got a seat by the window and I like looking out. I like watching how the city changes. How it's all roofs and front doors, and small shops and narrow streets when I first get on. Then it's wider streets and dual carriageways as you get out into the area around the industrial parks, and there's the football ground and there's trees and greenery, but kind of neat and tidy sort of greenery. Then as the bus gets nearer to Werryn, where the garden centre is, everything changes again. It's one of the older parts of the city and hasn't changed that much since it was a tiny little village, which kind of merged into the city as it grew up around the Industrial Revolution (we did it in history at school). Well, that isn't strictly true of course, because I don't think they had TV aerials or telegraph poles in the 18th century. But you get the feeling that you'll go round the corner and some characters out of a Jane Austen novel will be there, taking a walk round the lanes or riding out in their carriage or something.

Werryn is really different from Fairmount where all the footballers live. The houses in Fairmount are massive – dead swanky, with swimming pools and stuff. Not that I'd say no if someone offered me one of them – especially the really cool ones with those huge glass fronts – but I kind of like the houses in Werryn as well. Dan says they'd all be dark and pokey inside and you'd bang your head on the beams. He also says he'd have died of boredom if he'd grown up in Werryn. I pointed out that most of the kids who grow up in Werryn get sent away to boarding school anyway, but he said that's a bit of an exaggeration. There are small houses in Werryn too and probably a council estate if you look hard enough. But all the people who come to the garden centre seem to be rich.

Marjorie Ivy was in a real muddle when I got there. (I love it that a person who runs a garden centre is called Ivy. I wonder if she married her late husband because of his surname.) There'd been a big delivery from one of the suppliers and Marje was convinced they'd sent the wrong stuff.

As ever, that useless son of hers was nowhere to be seen. Funny how the lovely Kevin is always out somewhere when there's any kind of work to be done. Anyway, I told Marje I'd sort it and she said, 'Would you mind, petal?' So I suggested she go and sort out the indoor plants which seemed to have been left in a bit of a mess by yesterday's staff. I pulled one of the new girls off the tills and she came to give me a hand. Her name's Nessa and she seemed nice enough.

I never much fancied working in a garden centre but it's not a bad kind of a job. It's quite hard graft and there's some lifting and carrying and some girls wouldn't like it coz you get dirt under your nails, but I like it better than being in a supermarket or a shop. And the money's not bad. There's always something to do with your hands but you can just switch your brain off and think about other things. During term time I normally do Sundays only, but this time of year there are always staff off on holiday so I do a few days here and there, whenever they need me.

Eventually Kevin got back from wherever he'd been all morning and did his usual thing of hanging around and staring at my legs, while me and Nessa did the hard work. He's a slimy man and it's no wonder his last girlfriend ran off to open a bar in Spain. He's always making comments about these 'fit birds' he's dating but nobody really believes him. I saw him out once with this woman who looked like an escort, and I guess that's the only female company he can get these days.

Pity that Nessa, the new girl, isn't more his type – though to be truthful I wouldn't wish him on anyone. She's a quiet girl with a pale face and her mousey brown hair cropped short, to show off her great bone structure. She's got flawless skin, so transparent you can almost see her skull underneath it. She's beautiful really, in a gentle sort of way, but that's not the kind of looks that Kevin goes for. Maybe I need to stop wearing shorts for work and get myself some dungarees or something. And start wearing my hair scraped back and absolutely no make up.

'We missed you on Sunday,' Kevin told me as he bit into a Danish pastry. 'You with that bloke of yours, then?'

I nod but keep on with what I'm doing. I don't really want to tell Kevin about Sean but it's useful letting him know there's a man in my life. Kevin's the sort of bloke who could turn into a pest.

He offered me half of the pastry but I refused. 'You need a proper man – nice car, some real money, someone to take you out to restaurants and posh clubs. A girl like you shouldn't be hanging round with a penniless student.' I know what he's suggesting – that I'd be better off with a toe-rag like him.

I'm not sure how he knows that Sean is a student. He's probably been eavesdropping when I was talking to one of the other staff.

'Actually my boyfriend is a singer in a band,' I told him. 'He's not exactly skint – and he can get into all the best clubs.'

I don't know why I lied about it. I guess I wanted to get Kevin off my case once and for all. He's the last man I'd ever go out with. I feel sorry for Marje having such a slob of a son. She doesn't always know what she's doing but she works hard, and she's nice enough to her staff. But Kevin just hangs around doing nothing much and criticising the younger lads who work for his mum. And always seems to be taking money out of the tills, to get petrol for his car or something.

This evening I went round to Lucy and Nathan's. They've got this little front door of their own, round the side of Jane and Martin's house, where the utility room used to be. They've done a decent job with turning the place into a proper home, I'll grant them that.

I thought Lucy would want everything pink and fluffy but that girl's got a bit more taste than I credited her with. There's some sari material draped over her mum and dad's old sofa, and she got some embroidered cushions, which she bought from one of those Indian stalls in the market. She'd got rugs and curtains and stuff from a closing down sale at one of the city-centre stores. It's maybe a bit bright for my liking – lime greens and pinks and turquoise, all mixed up together – but you can see she's made a real effort. She's even got one of my early college pictures framed and hung up above the telly – the abstract one with blobs of clouds that Lucy says look like sheep. And there are literally thousands of photos of Ruby – framed ones hung on the wall, pinboards full of them in the tiny kitchen, even mobiles made up of pics, hanging in the bathroom. And there are photos of her mum and dad, and both her brothers and their families. And loads of me, some of which I'd much rather she hadn't put up. And there are montages of all the foster kids we've ever had in the house – although I think you're not really meant to do that coz of "confidentiality". Lucy says that she doesn't care, coz every one of those kids was part of her life and each of them deserves to be remembered. (She has their names and the dates they were with us written in a little notebook somewhere.)

There's hardly room for Nathe's collection of signed photos of football and ice-hockey stars. He's got a little corner in the bedroom – and even that's hemmed in all round by pictures of his stepdaughter. But I don't think he really minds. Nathe never had that much in his bedroom when we shared a flat in the "independent living" place. I don't think he has any photos, even of his sister. Or maybe he's got loads of family pics in an album somewhere. He never talks about his family so it's not something I've ever liked to ask him.

Lucy met me with a big hug and led me upstairs. In their little sitting room Nathe was lying flat on the floor with the baby curled up on his stomach and a book held above his head.

'Hi Hols,' he said. 'How's your arty farty course goin'?'

'Better than your boring one,' I told him, though I doubt that's true. Nathan really loves his sports psychology course.

Nathan taught me more than I ever wanted to know about football during the time we shared a flat. One of the first questions he ever asked me about Lucy was what team she supported. Although you could tell he wasn't really going to mind even if she supported a team he totally despised. To start with, Luce wasn't that interested in him coz she was getting over Ruby's father who was a right idiot. But Luce just loves to be loved and after a bit she started getting used to having Nathe around and she started falling for him a bit too... all very sweet. And then she found she was pregnant and most guys would have run a mile then – especially when they realised it wasn't even their kid. But the brilliant thing is that Nathe stayed with her through it all. The morning sickness, the labour, the sleepless nights... I think that's why Jane and Martin have supported their relationship. Nathan may only be 19 but he's got a very wise head on his shoulders, and Lucy is really still a big kid herself. She needs looking after, however much she sees herself as Super Mum.

'So what's this job Luce tells me about?'

'Man, this is like the coolest job,' Nathan said with the biggest cheesy smile. And then told me how brilliant it was going to be keeping lots of pesky kids happy at a summer sports camp. While Ruby wiggled like a little tadpole on his tummy. And although Nathe was talking to me I could see that all the time he'd got his eye on Ruby, just in case she wiggled just a bit too much... Maybe if I had a bloke like Nathe I'd think about having kids. A kind of house husband, who would stay home and do all the mumsy things while I painted in my studio or went to meetings with A-list celebs who wanted to commission a painting. But then my man would be there – all hot and hunky to greet me with a large glass of wine when I came home from a long day. Hmmm, I quite like that as an idea.

I can't really see Sean in that role, but maybe if he became a bit of a mega star, then took early retirement... If he loves me as much as he says he does then surely he'd be happy to be the house husband while I have my shiny career? Or is that asking a wee bit too much? If I wasn't a balanced, sensible kind of person I'd be really tempted to ask him – just to see how he reacted.

'How's my badass sis?' Nathan asked. It's hard to remember

they are related sometimes, coz they are so different. Keesh is so fabulous you have to meet her to believe her. She doesn't need to do anything to be noticed – well, apart from being gorgeous and bubbly and wearing the most amazing outfits that she puts together from stuff from charity shops and market stalls.

Nathe, on the other hand, prefers a night in with a rerun of the World Cup. You couldn't get sibs more unlike each other but they get along fine really. They just like to give everyone the impression that they fight like cats and dogs.

I told him about the DJ she's dating, and some of the famous people Keesh has met through him.

'Yeah, but is she doin' any studying?' Nathe said, passing Ruby, who was now hungry and mewling like a kitten, over to Lucy. 'She'll get chucked out of college if she don't do no coursework.'

It's not my place to tell Nathe that his sister dropped out of college at the start of term. Keesh's reasoning is that she was wasting precious time on a course that she didn't really like, when she could be doing what she really wanted to do, which is getting into the fashion business. She says she never specially wanted to do hospitality and it was her leaving care worker who suggested it. I can't imagine anyone pushing Keesh around, but she said at the time she just liked the idea of going to college and she didn't have the proper qualifications to do the fashion course she wanted. But Keesh has proved herself a wizard with a sewing machine. She's already sold some cute little tops and dresses to some of her boyf's wealthier friends. But Keesh's got her feet firmly on the ground and it's not like she's sitting back and waiting for things to happen. She's just got this waitressing job in a club, and she's always looking for shift work in restaurants and pubs. People love employing her coz she's so outgoing, and she charms all the customers.

I reassured Nathan that his sister is working hard. I just didn't say where she's working.

'Dat girl,' Nathan shook his head. 'I tink the only thing she knows how to do is party...'

Before I could jump to Keesh's defence, Lucy announced suddenly, 'You, me, Keesh – we should have a girls' night out! You won't mind me going if I leave some milk for Snugglebugs, would you Nathe? I need a bit of a social life to stop me getting all frumpy,' she says, beaming into the face of her suckling baby.

Nathan and I exchanged a look. We both remember the last time Lucy announced she needed a girls' night out. We made this plan to go see a movie – one of the late-night ones. And maybe have a cocktail or two. But by the time I got round to their place, Luce was fast asleep on the sofa. So I ended up spending the evening there, watching TV while Luce snored gently on a heap of cushions and Ruby slept peacefully in Nathan's arms.

I organised supper while Lucy fed her baby. Nathan flitted between me and Lucy, trying to look helpful, but clearly too besotted by mother and child to leave them alone for any time.

'Are you going to apply for that college course?' I ask Lucy, when we're sat round with supper and Ruby is tucked up in her cot. She's been saying forever that she wants to be a nurse, but since she had Ruby she doesn't talk about that any more. Lucy hasn't even finished her GCSEs and if she doesn't finish her education she won't have a chance of getting any kind of career.

'Oh that,' Lucy waved a vague hand. 'Mum keeps on at me about it, but I don't think I'm ready. I mean there's just so much to do here, what with the baby and everything...'

'You could at least apply,' I told her. 'If you get a place you can always defer it for a little while. You need to become a nurse Luce – you'd be brilliant looking after people. People will always need nurses; you will always be able to get a job.'

'That's what I keeps telling her,' Nathan joined in. 'Man, you got to make somethin' of yourself, coz money don't grow on trees.'

'I don't care about money. It doesn't buy happiness,' Lucy replied primly.

Nathan rolled his eyes at me, then addressed her directly. 'That's coz you never bin without money.' And of course he's right. Jane and Martin aren't what you'd call rich but they are quite well off, so all through her life Lucy's always been OK. And even now they're giving her money towards bills and clothes and food and extra stuff for Ruby. Nathe earns a little bit of money here and there with his weekend job at the supermarket, and as a care leaver he gets some support with his course and his living expenses. But if Jane and Martin didn't help out they'd be living very close to the breadline. Except Luce doesn't seem to realise that.

But Lucy just giggled. 'When you're England manager, Nathe, we'll be richer than the Beckhams.' And snatching up a sausage in her fingers she got up from the table. 'Just gonna see if my little munchkin is sleeping,' she said, going off to check on Ruby.

'I guess she still in love wiv bein' a mum,' Nathe said quickly as I shook my head. 'She's not a lazy girl – you know dat. She'll go to college when she's ready.'

You have to take your hat off to Nathan, he's a very loyal guy. I just hope he's right.

Middle of the night - OMG!

I was fast asleep when Ryan rang. It was about four in the morning. He said he couldn't sleep because he was too churned up about stuff. I asked him what the matter was and he sounded like he was about to burst into tears. But he didn't. My brother likes to play macho on the outside – even if he's got a soft centre.

Apparently it was a bit complicated and he couldn't tell me over the phone. Anyway, his credit was about to run out. I said I could phone him back but he said it would be better to talk face to face.

He said to meet him in that small park, a few roads away from Jane and Martin's, tomorrow evening, about 7pm. No one much goes there except the occasional tramp and retired people walking their dogs. What he really meant was that none of the kids from school hang out there and that seemed important to him.

I'm writing this down so I don't forget the time, but to be honest I'm wide awake now and ready to get up. I've got this book about the life of the artist Botticelli by the bed and I need to read it for a project I'm doing next year, but it's that boringly written. When I'm a famous artist I hope somebody will write an interesting book about me – or maybe I'll have to write it myself. Anyway, reading that Botticelli book should help me get back to sleep.

'You be sure and tell us when that boyfriend of yours has a gig coming up,' Kevin said, appearing suddenly from behind the bushes I was watering. 'I like a bit of a night out me'self. We could get a little party together...'

Kevin will be top of my list if Sean ever gets to do a gig somewhere famous and I get to put my friends on the guest list. Not.

'Is he always that much of a pest?' Nessa asked me later, when we were eating our sandwiches. Like most new staff she's quickly found out about Kevin's nasty ways.

'Sometimes he's a lot worse,' I told her. 'Has he stood at the bottom of a ladder when you're climbing up to get something from the shelves, yet? Pretends he's being Mr Helpful but you know he's just looking up the legs of your shorts.'

Nessa shook her head. 'Actually,' she said, a pink colour creeping across her very pale cheeks. 'It's kind of the other way round with me...'

For one terrible moment I imagine Nessa lying awake at night whispering Kevin's name into her pillow ... but the image is too incredible and it instantly vanishes.

'He heard me on the phone to my partner, Bea, and he asked me all these nosy questions afterwards. "What does this bloke of yours do? He an archaeology student like you, or something fancy?" he kept saying. And finally he started on this, "Don't tell me he's a rock star, like Holly's fella?" ' Nessa's cheeks were getting redder and it was hard to tell whether she was more angry or embarrassed.

'You should just ignore him.'

'That's what I did – or at least what I tried to do,' Nessa assured me, looking really flustered. 'But he wouldn't let it be. Eventually he started saying I must be ashamed of my boyfriend if I didn't say what he did... So was he in prison or something? And I kept ignoring that too...'

'Yeah and I bet you've been fantasising about running him through with the garden fork ... We've all had those thoughts about Kevin,' I said, trying to put a smile on that worried face.

'If only...' Ness attempted to smile but it didn't get any further than her mouth. 'Then, of course, he started guessing all sorts of stuff and that's when he suddenly got it. And when he asked me if my "boyfriend is actually a bird" I could feel myself going red... And he thought that was hilarious – although you could tell he was a bit shocked. He just stood there going, "Well, well – who'd have believed you were a lesbo?".'

I admit I hadn't realised at first, but after Nessa talked about this girl called Bea and I saw that look in her eyes – that shiny look people get when they're really crazy about someone – that's when I got it. And I have two lesbian friends at college, so I was pretty cool with it. Anyway I can't imagine Ness freaking anyone out, she's far too quiet and gentle.

'And I know he's told some of the other staff, ' Ness explained anxiously. 'Two of the girls have started whispering and giving me dirty looks if I go anywhere near them … and a couple of the men are behaving a bit strangely… it's like I've got two heads and they're trying to pretend they haven't noticed… And Kevin's making comments when he knows I'm going to overhear.'

'He's such a freakin' idiot! – I'll kill him for you if you like,' I volunteered. 'Or I could have a word with Marje if that helps. She thinks the sun shines out of Kevin's bum but she's quite a kind old lady, and I'm sure she would tell him to shut up…'

'But not everyone's been horrible,' Nessa told me quickly. 'Rhonda who works in the store room – I heard Kevin saying something to her the other day, and she had a go at him. She said he was to let me be – and it was no wonder that some lasses preferred other lasses when there were men like him in the world!'

And we both started laughing, but Nessa's laughter soon turned into tears. I sat her down and gave her a tissue, and put my arm around her. She was sobbing against my shoulder when the door opened…

'Oh sorry – didn't realise I was disturbing a special moment' … I looked up to see Kevin's piggy-eyes shining with mischief and malice. 'Always knew that "rock star boyfriend" was a cover for something. Don't worry girlies – your secret is quite safe with me.'

'Now he'll start on you too! Oh Holly, I'm so sorry,' Nessa burst out, the minute Kevin closed the door.

'To be honest, that's probably not such a bad thing,' I reassured her. 'Now Kevin will tell everyone that you and I are partners and I made up Sean or something – but I suspect almost everyone cept Kevin has seen me with Sean… Ever since that time he dropped in to see when I was working and he brought me that bunch of flowers…Yeah, to a garden centre! Can you believe it! So, anyway, what we do – you and me – is that we play along with it, we make this big joke about how we're together but really over the top. So everyone will know we're having a bit of a laugh at Kevin's expense.

That should take the heat off things.'

'Would you really do that?' Nessa gave me a look of the deepest gratitude. 'You wouldn't mind? But I mean, what if someone thought we were really together?'

'Then they'd admire my good taste,' I said, giving Nessa a friendly pat on the arm. 'Now I really must get on with those bedding plants or Kevin will say I have to work late. And I've got to get away on time today, coz my little bro is having one of his dramas.'

It rained in the afternoon so hardly anyone came into the centre, except a very confused woman who wasn't sure about the difference between indoor and outdoor plants, and had a long list of things her sister had told her she must buy for her new house. The bus seemed to take an eternity and there were lots of grumpy standing passengers, sticking wet umbrellas into each other and letting them drip onto anyone who managed to get a seat.

It was still soggy by the time I reached the park and Ryan was skulking under some trees, trying to look like he wasn't getting wet. (Don't you just love that word skulking – it's sooooo what 14-year-old boys do when they stuff their hands in their pockets, kick a few stones and try to look cool?)

'We could stand in the bus shelter,' I suggested, as a breeze rustled the leaves and a spray of cold drops pinged onto our shoulders. But Ryan shook his head. 'S'nothing,' he said, glaring menacingly at the overhead branches, like he was daring them to drop more water.

So we stayed under the trees and he told me what had been going down. Or at least he tried. My brother could confuse a brain surgeon.

What I think was going on was that my idiot brother had gone and written something about some girl called Natalie on Facebook (coz she'd dared to ask him out or something equally harmless).

And then got all surprised when this girl's friends started saying nasty stuff about him. Then this girl called Tiffany had cornered him at breaktime and said she'd scratch his eyes out if he ever did that to her mate again. So what does my stupid little brother do but go and put this up on Facebook as well! At which point everything went pear-shaped and Ryan has since been deluged with comments and texts calling him all kinds of names and threatening him with some dead nasty stuff.

'I don't think they'll actually do any of this,' I told Ryan as I scanned my way through the messages he'd received. 'Dentists' equipment isn't that easy to come by and I don't think anybody owns a poker these days...'

Ryan snatched the phone out of my hand. 'I'm not that stupid,' he said, rolling his eyes at me. 'It's this bit sis, this bit here... what's bovering me.'

It was a text from the very fierce Tiffany. It said quite simply:

We know all bout u, Ryan. We got the evidence. U v no secrets

'That doesn't mean anything – anyone could say stuff like that,' I told him.

'Yeah but it does!' my brother snapped at me, 'You don't know the half of it!'

And that's when he told me about the lost memory stick – and the really honest diary he'd written for that school project.

'But I thought you were deleting that stuff? You said you were going to print it out for me, and then delete it,' I reminded him.

'Yeah. But the printer was out of paper. So I thought if I took it into school... Well, I didn't think anything was gonna happen to it.'

'Maybe they're making it up and they don't really have anything... they don't actually say anything about the memory stick. It could still be in some kid's backpack, who doesn't know they've got it.' I was rabbiting on, trying to reassure us both.

Ryan didn't look convinced. 'And pigs might freakin' fly,' he said, taking an anxious bite out of his thumbnail. Something I haven't seen him do for nearly a year.

'Look, I think you just need to let this blow over,' I suggested. 'Try and apologise to this girl or something... just ignore all these messages. Maybe stay off Facebook for a while... don't use your phone except if you really have to.'

Ryan looked at me like I'd suggested he cut his own throat.

I walked back to Jane and Martin's with Ryan. Jane was at her yoga class but Martin was making supper and asked me if I wanted to stay. I was about to say I needed to get back to my place as I have a painting to work on, but Simon appeared just as I was about to make my apologies. He didn't say anything (which isn't unusual) but he looked at me in the way that only Simon can manage.

I think I like Simon coz he's not the type of kid most people would like. He's a funny looking boy with big sticky-outy ears and a little runt of a body. You'd think he was about six if you looked at him but he'll soon be nine. Jane says that's probably coz he wasn't fed properly by his family and one day he'll no doubt have a growth spurt. But that's not going to happen fast coz he's that picky about food. Apparently this week it was the shape that bothered him. Jane was having to serve all his meals in regular shapes like oblongs, squares and triangles and stuff. He won't eat anything with curves. When he first came to them the only thing he would eat was spaghetti on toast – and white bread. Just plain white sliced that he used to break into little bits and roll into balls in his fingers, before he put it in his mouth. But then he discovered biscuits and fish fingers and chips. But the only vegetable he would eat was peas. Then at Christmas he ate two small roast potatoes, half a parsnip and a little bit of turkey and Jane said it made her Christmas.

'Simon wants to ask you to his party,' Martin told me as we

tucked into egg, chips and beans. 'He's going to be nine on Sunday 25th and we've heard that his adoption order is coming through soon – so we're going to have a double celebration. That's right isn't it, Simon my man?'

Simon nodded very seriously. He'd carefully pushed all the beans to the side of his plate (depite Jane arranging them in a neat triangle) and he didn't look very happy about the fried egg which was as square-shaped as Jane could make it. But the chips seemed to be acceptable and he was eating them slowly with his fingers.

How could I refuse? I wrote the party date down then and there. 'What are we going to eat?' I asked.

'Yellow cake,' Simon whispered. 'Crisps 'n sausage rolls.'

'Some of my favourite food,' I told him, and Simon smiled.

'I hate sausage rolls,' Ryan said. He'd hardly touched his food and I could tell he was still fretting about that text. 'But lemon cake is OK, so long as Martin doesn't make it.'

'You have the ability to cut a man to the quick,' Martin said, clutching his heart. Ryan raised his eyebrows, exasperated. 'Man, you are so not funny,' he said, but it was the cheerfullest I'd seen him all evening.

FRIDAY 16 JULY

Today I was at the garden centre again. It rained so there were even fewer people than yesterday. I hope Marje doesn't decide to lay any of us off, coz what with the recession and everything this isn't being the best summer for selling plants and outdoorsy things. We keep telling Marje she should expand a bit – sell some cards and traditional sweets, and those fancy-smelling candles, like the really big garden places do, but she says she doesn't know about that stuff.

She's a bit stuck in her ways, is Marje. The story goes that she comes from Oakington or one of the not so posh areas near the reservoir. Nobody seems to know if she was actually married to Kevin's dad, or whether he was ever around at all. She met Reg Ivy when she came to work in his garden centre. They got married when Kevin was about ten and Mr Ivy was in his fifties or something. Maybe the shock of bringing up a right little tyke like Kevin was too much for him, coz he keeled over and died not long after they were married. But Marje inherited the garden centre and all of Mr Ivy's money and if she had any sense she'd probably sell it. But she says that it's 'Kevin's inheritance' so she's got to keep it going.

I made a point of being really busy today and looking dead useful every time Marje came anywhere near me. I even made this man buy this little tree in a pot he wasn't that sure about. It was nearly eighty pounds but he looked like he could definitely afford it. I said I really appreciated that he probably couldn't afford something that expensive – what with him probably having children or something, and would he like me to show him some cheaper plants. But he's like lots of the middle-aged men round here – big egos. He kept staring at my legs while I was talking to him and in the end he said something like 'Dammit! What's 80 quid!' and hoisted the tree into his trolley. I made sure I was near the till when he took it through so that everybody knew I'd sold it to him.

I got some news from Sean tonight. His band's got a gig booked here in Corrington for next Friday night. It seems his dad is doing some building work for The Bullfinch (which is one of those pubs that's quite famous for its live gigs) and some band from the States had to cancel coz their lead singer got arrested, so there was this gap at the last minute. Sean's dad said, 'My son's band could do that,' and somehow talked the guy into it. (I like Sean's dad. He's cool. He likes me too. Not like Sean's mum who thinks I'm not good enough for her son coz I've been in care.)

Sean said that playing to a home crowd could be quite cool. I think it's coz he wants to stick the finger up at all those kids at school who thought he was a bit of a loser coz he did his own stuff and wasn't part of the crowd. I said that I'd tell everyone I know and get them to come along. It's one of those places where you pay a bit on the door to get in, but they make most of the money from selling cheap beer at expensive prices.

SATURDAY 17 JULY

I put a message up on Facebook about the gig and texted everyone I knew. And Keesh told everyone she knows, which is like the entire city, and she says that she'll definitely be coming and bringing the whole posse. She says she'll try and make sure her DJ boyf is free to come with her. And there's this photographer guy she knows who is really into taking pictures of new bands. Good old Keesh. That girl's a superstar. I was dead lucky she asked me to move in with her after her friend Mel got that club job in Greece.

When I texted Dan he said I should go along to this party his mate's cousin is having tonight. This cousin is on one of the degree courses at my college and it's her birthday. I could go along with him and his mates and we could tell everyone about Sean's gig. Sounds like a plan to me.

I got a message on Facebook from Ryan who says he 'def wants to come'. But I know The Bullfinch has a pretty strict over-18s only policy. I tell him I'll see if Sean can smuggle him in backstage or something, by pretending he's his little bruvver. Ryan texts back *Fanx sis* and then another text follows almost immediately saying:

They started dis rumer. Dat me and Luke is 2gvr. Luke ded

frekd, not spekn 2 me.

I feel sick when I read this. This is very bad news. This mate Luke, from everything I've heard from Ryan, is definitely into girls. Whereas my brother isn't into anything or anyone at the moment. Ryan suspected he might be gay for some time, but then last year he got drugged and abused by these older men, which seems to have put him off physical relationships big time. He still sees a therapist sometimes, but he doesn't make a big deal of it. I think there's a footballer he fancies coz he's got several posters of him on the wall, but then again Ryan is a really big football fan, so it's hard to tell.

'Does Luke know – about you?' I ask as soon as Ryan answers my call.

'Dunno,' Ryan replies, 'S'not somethink we ever talk about. I mean we talk about girls sometimes – mainly the girls he likes. And I just sez if I think they are fit or not. But Luke's the big man, he does the talking – and you know me, I'm just the joker.'

Yes, I knew that. But this time my brother had really got himself into a mess. And I had to try and offer him a bit of comfort.

'But I guess nobody else at school knows either? Could be that it's just one of those obvious things... you know, suggest someone's gay coz it's a way of getting at them.'

'Maybe.' But my brother doesn't sound too sure.

'It doesn't mean they know anything for sure. Doesn't mean they got hold of that memory stick,' I try to sound like I mean it, but I'm not exactly convincing myself.

I tell Ryan he should try to ignore it and it'll probably blow over in a few days.

'Yeah, but what do I say to Luke?' my brother asks me.

'You know Luke better than I do...' I reply lamely.

'Gee, thanks, sis – that's *really* helpful,' Ryan says irritably, and disconnects the phone. But I can't feel too mad at him, he's having a bit of a rough time.

Must stop writing now and get myself ready for this party. Wish I wasn't having such a bad hair day.

SUNDAY 18 JULY

OMG – I feel wrecked this morn! But it's not coz I drank that much, I'm not someone who gets rat-faced. It's more like a guilt hangover thing. Coz of what happened at the party.

Dan's mate had a car and I got a lift to the party. It was OK except I had to sit in the back with this idiot friend of the driver, who kept trying to chat me up. I'd done my best to look like 'girlfriend of soon-to-be-mega indie star – and aspiring artist in her own right'. I wore my tightest black jeans with this top, which is kind of chiffony but with lots of floaty bits. It's a dirty pale pink colour with kind of like smudgy black patterns on it. I found it in the Oxfam shop and Keesh customised it for me. Keesh also lent me her black ankle boots with the leather fringe. (In return I lent Keesh my red ankle boots, coz she really loves them. She'd got this hot date with her DJ bloke. He's taking her to some radio awards where there's going to be celebrities and TV cameras and champagne.) But that did not mean I was available for some bad-breathed guy who fancies himself as the next Robert Pattinson.

I hung around with Dan and his mates for a while but Mr Halitosis was getting on my nerves. And Dan was on a mission – to chat up this girl he's had a thing about for a while. Fortunately the girl was with four mates, who I vaguely recognised from college. Like me they were hanging around trying not to get in the way of the Romeo and Juliet stuff going on between Dan and their friend, and didn't seem to know many other people. So when they went off to dance I went with them, which just happened to be when Mr Halitosis was getting himself a drink so he wouldn't see where we went. After the dance, me and those girls made our way out into the garden and did some chatting. I waited a little bit till everyone was relaxed and I just sort of slipped it into conversation that I was promoting my boyfriend's gig. To my amazement one of the girls had actually heard Sean on the radio and thought the band were 'kind of like the Arctic Monkeys'. She said she'd put something on her FB page and get some mates along to hear them.

It might be summer but the weather wasn't much cop, and after 20 minutes we were all shivering, so we headed back into the house to warm up. As we squeezed back into the house, some guys were heading out. I felt a hand on my shoulder and looked round, expecting it to be Mr Halitosis.

Instead it was James – of the spider paintings. He seemed a bit off his face to me coz he just grinned and said, 'Hello Beautiful.' I think that's one of the first times he's ever spoken to me, coz we hang around with different crowds. To be honest, I've never noticed him that much till the artist's visit, so I couldn't really say.

I said hello back but went over to join the girls I'd been hanging out with. He followed me over. 'This is James – who's on my art course,' I told them. 'He's, like, getting quite a name for himself. We had this artist come to talk to us and he said that James was pretty amazing.'

I don't know why I said those things. Maybe I was feeling in a generous mood or maybe I did really want to get on the right side of James. I mean the guy's all right but he's a bit too in love with himself if you ask me, which is OK if you're really good looking or something but he isn't. He's just an average kind of guy but really skinny, who wears interesting clothes and has dyed-blonde hair, cut kind of spiky. And a nose stud which I'm sure he thinks makes him look really interesting.

James just smiled this really smug smile while I was introducing him and I found that dead irritating. But the other girls seemed to like him. This girl with long straight blonde hair was immediately saying, 'Yeah, we heard about you James. Our textile tutor showed us some of your stuff,' and finding reasons to rest her long purple fingernails on his arm.

After a while James turned to me and said, 'Wanna dance?' (I don't think he even knows my name.) I was about to say no when he grabs my wrist and kind of pulls me onto the floor. But it's OK when we get there coz he dances like an art student – closing his eyes and hoping that everyone is watching him... There's no touching or anything so I think it's going to be OK. I'm not going to have to explain that I have a boyf. He's just wanting someone to pose with. Maybe he is gay like some of the girls say.

After a bit, I say I have to go for a wee, which is true. But I'm just walking towards the toilet door when I feel this hand on my arm. James is following me.

He doesn't say anything but he seizes me around the waist, and pulls me towards him. He looks me full in the eyes for a moment, before kissing me on the lips. I go to struggle and push him away but then I realise I'm actually quite enjoying this. Nothing this exciting has happened to me for ages. I know I shouldn't be doing it coz of Sean, and it's not like I even fancy this James bloke. But that's half the pleasure of it. And I find myself wrapping my arms round his neck and kissing him back.

I've no idea how long we kissed for but it felt like a long time. And his hands were roaming everywhere, under my clothes and everything, and I meant to push them away but somehow … In my head I was saying, Holly Richards you are a slut. But just for a little bit I didn't really care. It's not like I'm married to Sean or anything. And anyway this was just a one-off thing, probably coz I'd had just a bit too much to drink. I had no plans to repeat the experience.

As I'm following James back into the main room to get another drink, a very peed-off-looking Dan appears. 'All that – and then she says she's got a boyfriend in Australia,' he mutters, sounding dead miserable.

'Oh Dan, that's awful,' I say, giving him a big hug. I can feel James's eyes burning into my back, but I couldn't care less. James is a jerk but Dan is my friend, and I hate it when he's upset.

Dan wants to go home, and I don't blame him. Mr Halitosis wants to go too, but their mate with the car isn't ready yet. Fortunately one of the girls I've been hanging out with also wants to leave, so we club together and order a taxi. I stay close to Dan who looks like he'll burst into tears any moment, 'cept he's a bit too macho to do that in front of strangers.

I pass James on the way to the front door. He gives me a little shrug and that smug little smile, and walks away. I know what he was thinking – next time. But there won't be a next time. Definitely not.

So why do I feel so bad this morning? Like I betrayed Sean completely. Nobody saw what happened between me and James and it was just some stupid dare thing with myself. I don't fancy James and I certainly don't like him. I don't think he really likes me or anything. It was just a bit of excitement and too much alcohol. Something I wanted to do coz I knew I shouldn't. Not coz I wanted to hurt Sean or anything. He's so good to me and he treats me with so much respect.

I've decided I'm going to paint my feelings. I know it sounds a bit pretentious and the kind of thing that James would do, but I don't care. Some artists do all kinds of things just for the experience – so they can use the feelings in their paintings. I'm not the kind to do drugs or anything like that, so I guess what I did was safer than that. So I shouldn't waste this experience but make something positive out of it. That's the best way to deal with it.

Anyway, Lucy and Nathe and baby Ruby are coming over for tea – so I've got real stuff I need to think about.

3am

I'm writing coz it might help to put my thoughts down. Sean rang me after Luce and Nathe and Ruby had gone, and he wanted to know whether I was looking forward to his gig. To be honest I'd hardly thought about it at all, I was trying so hard not to think about *what happened last night*.

'Sure,' I told him, feeling guilty as anything. 'I've been passing the word round – big time. Lots of my college mates are coming and Keesh has asked absolutely *everyone*.' And I babbled on a bit telling him about some of the people who are coming, and trying not to mention the party where I met some of these people.

But Sean's a sensitive kind of guy, he picks up on things. 'You alright, Hols?' he asked me after a while. 'You sound a bit stressed.'

So I told him this horrible lie – that I was worrying about Ryan. Sean knows I've been through a lot with my brother in the past, so he totally believed me. He tried to reassure me, telling me all the kind of things I'd said to Ryan myself earlier. But the truth is that I wasn't really thinking much about my brother. I was just wanting to confess everything to Sean there and then on the phone – about Spider Boy and how I hadn't meant to kiss him.

But of course I didn't tell Sean anything. I read this answer once by an agony aunt to some girl who was asking if she should tell her boyfriend about the one night stand she'd had on holiday, with a guy she was never going to see again. The agony aunt said that so long as she was "safe" and got herself checked for STIs then she didn't have to tell her boyfriend anything. It was up to her to decide what she'd gain by telling her boyfriend. If she wasn't sure about their relationship then maybe it was time to tell him about her doubts, but if she really did love him and it was just a silly drunken mistake then maybe it was better not to tell him about the other guy. Coz there's always the risk you are confessing something just to make yourself feel better – but at the same time you might be hurting the other person really badly.

Instead, I told Sean about Simon's birthday party and said I really hoped he would come. Everyone in my foster family likes Sean a lot and he's always been good with the younger ones. Ever since he taught Simon how to ride a bike, Sean's been one of that kid's favourite people. Sean said of course he'd come, he likes being round my foster family as much as they like him. His own mother is such a stuck-up woman – she spends all her time going to the gym, having manicures and driving around in her Range Rover (although she never goes anywhere where there's any mud). They don't have parties at Sean's house coz his mum worries about people spilling things on the carpets. But to make up for that Sean's dad takes the family out to some posh places – Sean had his 18th birthday in the Regency Hotel – so I don't exactly feel sorry for him.

When we said goodnight I told Sean I loved him – before he told me. I could hear how surprised he was. Now I'm worrying that he'll be really suspicious. Stupid, really, coz I don't know what I'm worrying about. He forgave me for dumping him before, so he's not going to be dumping me just coz he suspects I might have looked at some other bloke, is he? Just coz there are one or two girls throwing themselves at him now he's in a band, doesn't mean he loves me less than he used to.

So why can't I sleep? I'm going to listen to my ipod for a bit and see if that helps.

MONDAY 19 JULY

It rained so hard the garden centre got a bit flooded. It's no joke moving great big, muddy pots around and all those soggy branches dripping over your clothes. Today I wished I was working on the till at Morrisons.

This evening I took a look at my brother's FB entries. It seems he's taken my advice and not been on there since the other night, but there are lots of messages from other people, some of them nasty stuff from people who were definitely taking that Natalie's side. But also a couple of messages from friends who were trying to act like nothing was happening. Even a few who were brave enough to tell him to 'ignore the witches'. But what really worried me was a link I saw to a new website. I didn't want to look but I knew I had to. I had to see what those losers were saying about my brother.

It was sickening stuff. There were some pictures up there taken from somebody's photo album – clumsily photoshopped to make them fit. Pics of my brother and Luke, clearly just doing normal stuff like watching a football game or hanging out together but made to look like they were snogging or something. And they'd added really pervy captions, stuff like "the happy couple" and a lot worse.

It was nearly midnight but I rang J and M's house straight away. A groggy Martin answered. I apologised for waking him up but he said it was OK, he knew I wouldn't call them unless it was something important. I told Martin everything I knew about my brother's situation, and I gave him the URL for the site. He hung up for a bit but rang me back as soon as he'd booted up the computer.

'Not good, Holly,' he said after a period of silence. 'Not good at all. Has Ryan seen this?'

'I have no idea. But even if Ryan hasn't seen it himself I bet some of his mates have told him about it.'

Martin agreed with me. 'And no doubt that boy Luke knows all about it. That would explain things. I asked Ryan at supper if he wanted to ask Luke over on Sunday and he mumbled something about Luke not speaking to him.'

Poor Ryan. Not only was he getting bullied by a whole load of people, but now his best mate was having nothing to do with him.

'We have to get this taken down,' I told Martin. 'We must be able to contact someone about this.'

'I think it's the website supplier, whoever that is. But I've no idea how you can tell that. There's nothing recognisable about this website.'

'If it's Facebook or Google or someone like that I think you just contact them but it isn't that easy, so I think you have to tell the police or something,' I responded lamely.

Martin wasn't sure either. 'I'll talk to the people in our IT department tomorrow,' he told me. 'See what they advise. And I'll get Jane to talk to the school tomorrow morning– maybe they can just get the people who put it up to take it down.'

'Maybe. But I guess it's whether they can find out who they are.'

'Surely they'd be kids in Ryan's class... I mean it can't be that difficult to find out, can it?'

I explained to Martin that it probably wasn't that simple. If the girl's got mates at another school, or older friends or something... I mean anyone really could have created the website.

'I see what you mean,' Martin agreed. 'But I think we'd better tell the school anyway. This is really nasty stuff and it's definitely bullying by anyone's definition. I can't see Jane standing for this.'

'Yeah, but tell her to go softly, softly about this,' I warned Martin. 'Jane is brilliant and everything but she could end up making things worse for Ryan if she makes too much fuss about it. There's bound to be kids who haven't seen this website and if the head goes and says something about it in assembly...'

'Surely the school wouldn't be that heavy handed?'

'Yeah – you wouldn't think so, but that new head is a bit of an idiot, from everything Ryan says about him.'

'Jane did say this Mr Hammond was a bit of a plonker – I think she's already got the measure of him.' Martin reassured me. 'I'm sure she'll find some way to make sure he handles it really discretely.'

I told Martin I had every faith in Jane's ability to get this man doing what she wants him to do. People don't mess with my foster mum coz she's a real force to be reckoned with.

'And now I suppose we'd both better get a bit of shut-eye,' Martin said, and I could hear him suppressing a yawn. 'I've got a meeting with the man from Roundabouts in the morning, and I suspect you've got something far more exciting to do – which requires you to look bright-eyed and bushy tailed.'

'The garden centre's hardly what you'd call exciting, but I do like to look my best for the conifers... And late-flowering shrubs are always pleased when you bother to put on a bit of mascara.'

Martin laughed and said, 'Night night Hollybear,' which is the nickname he gave me when I first went to live with their family.

'Sleep tight, Big Bear,' I said. Which is what I used to call him when I was about 13. I think it's the nearest I'd ever come to calling him Dad.

But I don't feel ready for bed yet. And I'm not sure now whether it's worrying about Ryan or guilt about Spider Boy. I miss Boots sometimes. It was good to have his big furry, purring body ready and waiting to curl up on my ankles as soon as I got into bed. It didn't make it easier to turn over but it kept my feet warm and it was always cheerful somehow. But I'm glad he now sleeps with Simon. He's such a lost little boy and Boots is such a big, confident kind of cat.

TUESDAY 20 JULY

Keesh arrived home just as I was preparing to leave for the garden centre. She was grinning like a madwoman and happier than I think I've ever seen anyone. She'd met this posh couple at the fancy awards, and it turned out the woman used to be a famous model or fashion editor or something, who just happens to be launching her own designer boutique in Corrington! Boutique lady invited Keesh and the DJ boyf to join them at a club. Then they'd all had breakfast at a swanky hotel near the bus station – before boutique lady ordered a taxi to take Keesh home, as the boyf had to go to his day job. And before Keesh left the woman had invited her to meet for lunch next week, to talk about the possibility of Keesh managing the boutique!

'Girl, I am just soooo made up,' Keesh said, spinning around the kitchen in her silver mini-dress. 'Roll out the red carpets and hand out de decorations – coz Miss Keesha is comin' through…'

That girl was born with a lucky streak but you couldn't be jealous. Keesh has such a big heart, she'd rejoice just as much if it was me having the big break.

'We'll celebrate tonight,' I told her, as I grabbed my raincoat.

'Hold ya to it, girlfriend!' she called after me as I rushed out to catch my bus.

It was a bit of a freaky day at the garden centre. Every time I turned round Kevin seemed to be there. I mean he wasn't exactly hassling me or anything but wherever I went, he was just sort of there. When me and Nessa were having our sandwiches in the store room he started talking really loud to Bert, the delivery man. He was boasting to him about this new car he's buying. And all the "hot" girls he's seeing. And I knew he was doing it for our benefit, to impress us or something. But we had better things to talk about.

Nessa told me about her uni course. She's doing a degree in archaeology because she's mad about ancient history and she'd like nothing better than to dig up some ancient temple, or discover the secrets of Atlantis. But she says there's no money in archaeology and it's hard to earn a living. And if that doesn't work out, she really wants to be a garden designer – which is what her girlfriend Bea is doing. Good for her, I said, though it's not a job I'd fancy. I couldn't be bothered to wait so long for something to take shape. If the plants hadn't all flowered in a week and the hedges hadn't grown to four foot, I'd find that frustrating. That's why I love painting. You get real results in a few days.

This evening Martin rang to update me on what's happening. The IT guy at work was off sick so he didn't get any info there, but Jane had spoken to the school head who had promised they'd make some "discrete enquiries" and ensure the website was closed down. He'd asked Jane not to involve the police at this stage coz he was sure it was something that could be sorted out without a lot of fuss. I think that's daft coz what if it's not kids at his school? And Martin said that Jane wasn't that convinced either. She told him she'll wait till next week and if it wasn't closed down by Monday then she was definitely going down to the police station.

I asked Martin how my brother was doing. Martin said he'd had a bit of a chat with him about the whole thing and Ryan had tried to give the impression it wasn't a big deal or anything. Ryan had said he wasn't going to let "them" think they'd won so he'd carry on as normal. Anyway, he still had a couple of old school mates who were sticking by him, so it wasn't like he had nobody to hang out with. And it was only a few days to the end of term and the Luke web thingy would probably blow over in the holidays.

'Do you believe that?' I asked Martin.

'I'd like to,' Martin replied. 'But what about you Hol? What do you think?'

I told him the truth, which was that I had an uneasy feeling about the whole thing. 'I think it's not knowing whether those kids have got his memory stick or not, with all that personal stuff on it. I mean, what with Ryan not wanting anything to do with his family at the moment... What if they put some stuff up about that? What if his family got to hear of it or something?'

'Lordy! I hadn't really considered that,' Martin responded, sounding dead worried. 'I'm really a bit of an old fogey when it comes to this technology stuff.' He then promised me that he and Jane would keep a really careful eye on my little bro. We all know that when the pressure was on the old Ryan had this habit of running away. But that was before he came to live with Jane and Martin and had people he could talk to. So to be honest, none of us knows what he's likely to do this time around.

So I sent my brother a message:

Am here 4 u little bruv – whenever u need me. Call me anytime. Big Sis xxx

I was down the shops when this text arrived

Hey Beautiful, fancy a coffee sometime?

For a horrible moment I thought it was Sleazebag, Kevin – which was too creepy for words. Then I realised it was Spider Boy and for a moment I was relieved – and a tiny bit pleased. But then I started to feel awful – and quite irritated. I'm nobody's 'Beautiful'. So I texted back:

Soz – really busy at mo

Most boys would get the message from this but SB has the arrogance of the devil. He texts straight back saying:

Nobody is busy all summer. I got free tickets 4 that exh at city gallery

Now that was tempting! I knew exactly which exhibition he meant. It's this really amazing collection of some absolute masterpieces from places like the Tate, the National Gallery and some really valuable paintings over from France and Italy and Spain. People like van Gogh and Cezanne and Gauguin. My tutors had been talking about it all term but the tickets sold out months ago. Besides, no one on a student budget could really afford them. Some staff tried to get funding to take a group of us but the department head said the budget was way too tight.

How on earth had James got free tickets? Maybe that artist guy had arranged it for him. Or maybe he'd got his parents to buy them for him. Someone told me his dad was in banking, but then this other person told me that James's dad was a miner who got made redundant back in the day, and the family were living on benefits. I guess that probably neither is true. James seems the sort of guy who likes to come across a bit mysterious, and I wouldn't mind betting that he starts all the rumours himself. There was this one that he was having an affair with his middle-aged female tutor. But then there was another one which said he was having an affair with the history of art lecturer, who's young and fit – and male. I didn't believe either of them at the time and personally I don't think James is big, or funny or clever.

But I do want to see that exhibition something rotten, and if James can play games, then so can I. There's nothing wrong with just going along with him. It's not like I fancy him or anything, so there's no risk I'm going to fall into his arms in front of van Gogh's *Sunflowers* or anything. (I think it's actually one of the less famous van Gogh paintings that's coming to Corrington, but a girl can live in hope.)

So I texted back, sounding really casual:
OK, maybe. When u thinking of?
And he texts back saying:
Tomorrow or Saturday
It can't be Saturday coz Sean will be back and he's not going to like it when I explain I have to rush off to meet this other boy. Coz I know I'm going to look a bit guilty and he's going to suspect something. And I can hardly say, 'Look, sorry Sean. I did snog him at this party but he's a wally and I won't be snogging him again. Although I think he thinks that maybe I would. So you don't mind if

I just go and look at some pictures with him, do you?'

It's not like Sean owns me or anything but I couldn't do that to him. So it's going to have to be tomorrow – or not at all.

I'm supposed to be working tomorrow but I can't miss this chance to see the exhibition. I hate lying to Marje so it's quite a relief when Kevin answers the phone. He's as sleazy as ever when I explain that I have an urgent doctor's appointment tomorrow as I'm not feeling at all well.

'Catch summat nasty from that "*boyfriend*" of yours?' he sniggers.

I assure him that it isn't anything like that – and besides, it's none of his business. I say I'm really very sorry but could I come in Friday instead – if the doctor thinks I'm well enough to work.

'S'pose so,' Kevin says. 'Mum probably won't notice anyway. She's a dotty old bird and I can just tell her I swopped round the rota...'

This makes me feel really uncomfortable. It's like Kevin knows I'm lying and he's making it clear I owe him a favour. 'I can come in really early on Friday and give a hand with loading the lorries or help with the stocktaking if that's useful...'

Sleazebag makes a suggestive comment about what we can do in the store room – and maybe I can bring Ness along too – which I ignore. I know Rhonda will be around and he won't try anything funny with her there. Anyway, nobody messes with me. I'm quite capable of looking after myself.

So tomorrow I'm meeting James at the gallery at 1pm. He says we can have something to eat before we go in and we've agreed to see each other in the café. That's good coz it means I won't be hanging around outside feeling like a spare part if he's late. But I'm going to make my own sarnie and eat it on the bus. Then I can get there a bit before him and pretend I've already eaten something coz there's no way I'm paying the prices they charge in that place. I might treat myself to a cappuccino, or if I'm sneaky, I can let James buy me one. I can always sit at a table where there's an empty cup and pretend I've just drunk something. And if he arrives late he's bound to offer, isn't he?

OK so that's a bit naughty, but that's what people like James do to you. I'm not the one who pounced on some girl he hardly knows at a party and pinned her to the wall. If he gets fleeced by me for a frothy coffee and an exhibition ticket, he's only got himself to blame.

I've had a few texts from Ryan today and it all sounds normal enough. But I know he wouldn't be texting me quite so often if everything was really OK. I took a quick look on Facebook and a few people are still leaving pretty nasty messages on his page, but nowhere like so many as before. And when I checked that horrible website, it's still up there – so the school head hasn't succeeded in getting it taken down yet. But maybe that sort of stuff happens all the time among Year 9s and sites like that are two a penny. It's a nasty thought, but it would mean my little bro wasn't the only one getting it in the neck, and the fuss really will die down very quickly.

And it's not just that. As I said to Martin, I worry about stuff getting back to Ryan's real dad. What if he somehow got to read things Ryan had written about him? Ryan says he wrote some pretty direct stuff on that memory stick. I don't know Ryan's dad that well coz he only hung around with Mum for a short time but I remember he's got a nasty temper on him when something winds him up. Though he's nothing compared to that crazy aunt and the demon grandmother. I met them once – and boy! You wouldn't want to meet either of them on a dark night. I don't wonder that Ryan doesn't want any contact with any of that lot at the moment.

It's sad when kids have such screwed up relationships with their families. I think Simon misses his family – although from what I gather they're all total psychos. The court said that until he's older he mustn't have any contact with them, coz they might hurt him or he'd start having those awful nightmares again, where they were doing horrible stuff to him, but I still think that makes him a bit sad. Every kid wants their parents to love them, don't they? Even if they're horrible people, you'd kind of keep hoping they'd change somehow, wouldn't you? Even when you know it's not very likely.

Funny really, what with Ryan and Simon. They've both got these dead nasty families who are like desperate to see them. But my dad – who used to be this really decent bloke – he doesn't want anything to do with me any more. Not since he got his new family in the USA. Maybe he's afraid I'm gonna turn out like my mum, and drive him spare, like she did. Or demand to go and live with him, or something. But he should know I'm not like that. I think sometimes that I could try and track him down on the internet or something, but I'm not gonna do that. I have my pride. He knows my number if he ever wants to call me.

This afternoon I texted Sean to say I was dead excited about Friday night and couldn't wait to see him play. Come to think of it, I've never seen him do a proper gig, just a few rehearsals and a really small performance in a pub. But this feels much more like the real thing. I might not like the music much but it will be quite cool to watch my boyf in action.

Sean texts back to tell me how much he's looking forward to seeing me and telling me to be sure I get to the venue early, so I can go backstage and spend some time with him. His parents will be coming too and various of his cousins, but if I get there early he says we can have a little time to ourselves – and he's missed me so much, and loves me more than he can ever say. Aw that is soooo sweet. Who says men aren't romantic?

I really will have to get into the garden centre early on Friday or I'm never going to get off work in time for the gig, let alone a bit of TLC with my boyf. I may have to get the symptoms back of whatever it is that I'm going to the "doctor" about tomorrow. OMG I'm turning into this enormous fat liar but it's just for a day or two. And it's all for my art … And then I'll go back to being St Holly the Very Good.

I'm almost too ashamed to write anything tonight. What is it with that James? He's nothing special and he's not that good looking. He just thinks he is. And it's like when he's around me I feel so mixed up, like I really loathe him but I'm kind of drawn to him at the same time. And he's so maddening, coz he's so totally in love with himself.

He arrived dead late and wasn't at all sorry. And he didn't offer to buy me a coffee, just glanced at the water bottle on the table like he was assuming I was drinking that. (I'd taken some tap water in one of Keesh's Evian bottles. She's got this thing about not drinking water in the city coz of the chemicals they put in it, and she buys all this bottled stuff, but I think that's just a waste of money.) Sean would never behave like that. I mean he'd always ask if I wanted anything. Not in a old-fashioned sexist kind of way but nice and polite, because he thinks about other people a lot of the time.

James gave me this peck on the cheek when he arrived – like he knew me really well or something. And he started talking about himself as soon as he sat down. Some really boring stuff about this friend of his he'd met on the way, which was presumably why he was nearly half an hour late. I put on my best very cross face but he didn't seem to notice. I think he's about as sensitive as a brick. I almost thought about walking out then and there but I kept reminding myself how much I wanted to see the exhibition. Instead I just played Ms Ice Queen and kept looking round the café like I was looking for someone more interesting to talk to.

Spider Boy talked at me for a bit and then took a call on his mobile. (I checked mine at the same time to show him I was busy too. There was just a message from Ryan saying, *What o'clock 2moro, sis?* And I realised I'd forgotten all about getting my little brother into the gig. But I couldn't turn him down now, not with all the stuff that's going on around him. I'd have to contact Jane and Martin and ask them really nicely – and promise to supervise my brother all the time we were there. So much for drinking champagne backstage, all romantic like with my doting boyf!)

When Spider Boy hung up, he simply got up and said, 'C'mon then.' Like I was a dog or something! So I just sat and fiddled with the strap of my shoe for a bit, just to make him wait.

Admittedly, the exhibition was pretty amazing. I mean you see all these paintings in books but you never imagine that they'll be so large or the colours so powerful. And you don't expect them to have this effect on you – which they do. And it's some of the simplest pics that have the biggest effect. I mean the van Gogh was really good and the Gauguin and the Picasso were awesome, but the picture that got me the most was this drawing by some artist I'd never heard of before. Just a very simple portrait. Nothing fancy and only small, showing a woman, maybe a farmer's wife. She had a scarf over her hair and a bundle of something in her arms but the look on her face – well, it's hard to describe, but it was like she was haunted or something. It got me somewhere deep inside and I couldn't stop looking at it. And it was about five minutes or so before I realised that she looked like my mum looks, really vulnerable and in a world of her own.

Spider Boy wandered off quite a lot while we were looking round. It was almost like he didn't want to spend too long looking at the really famous paintings coz he thought that wasn't very cool. But that meant I got some time on my own to really study them. And I made a few notes and sketches in my project book.

While I was looking at the picture of the farmer's wife this friendly looking older man spoke to me. 'Wonderful isn't it?' he said. 'You feel like she's going to say something to you...' And I was about to say yes, I felt the same way too, but then I realised SB was standing beside me. 'Some people have a very unsophisticated take on art,' he said loudly to me, and shot the older man a drop-dead look. The man just shrugged and walked away.

'Why'd you do that?' I turned on James, I couldn't help it. 'That man was just saying what he thought. It's not harming anyone...'

'Oh Holly, you are so adorably naïve...' SB said, and lent forward and kissed me on the lips. I meant to push him away, I swear it, but somehow I just didn't. I can't really explain myself. And after he'd detached himself from me and wandered off to look at some other pictures, I was still standing there with my heart leaping in my chest and feeling all breathless and stupid. And quite angry with him but angrier still with myself.

And all the way round the rest of the exhibition I was waiting for him to do it again. Part of me waiting so that I could slap his stupid, smug face but I'm sorry to say that a tiny part of me really wanted to feel his lips against mine, the way his hair brushed against my forehead as he leant into me. And it meant that after that I couldn't really concentrate on the pictures as much, which was that irritating.

When we got to the last picture before the exit door he

appeared beside me. 'So what do you think?' he asked as cool as a cucumber. And I realised he wasn't asking about my view of him kissing me like that, but what I thought about the exhibition.

'Amazing,' I said, because that's what I really thought. It was amazing to be that close to such wonderful paintings. And I saw this amused little smile cross his face, like I'd said something really stupid, like he pitied me because I was impressed by all this famous art. But maybe when you draw stupid squiggles and everyone thinks they're the bee's knees (or the spider's legs) then you start to think you're bigger and better than some of the Great Masters.

'It's amazing,' I said again quite loudly this time, not caring a toss about what he thought. 'It makes you realise what utter rubbish some of us produce as art students.'

The older man and this woman, who looked like she could be his wife, were passing by as I said that. He raised his eyebrows and gave me this friendly little smile.

I was still fuming inside when we got to the bus stop. I was promising myself that if SB tried as much as to lay a finger on me, he'd regret it for a very long time. But just as my bus was approaching and I started to move towards it, he put out a hand and dragged me back towards him. He's tall and skinny but also surprisingly strong. Or was it simply that I was being weak willed and silly and I didn't put up enough of a fight? Anyway, by the time my bus stopped he had me pushed up against the shelter wall with his tongue down my throat and his hands all over me. And instead of pushing him away, all sorts of hormones were rushing round my body and making me want to tear his clothes off. But of course I didn't. I'm too sensible for that, and besides it would have given the pair of bird-like elderly ladies who turned up to wait for the next bus, even more to look shocked about. But he had made me miss my bus and I knew there wouldn't be another one along for 20 minutes. I had to get away from him before I agreed to something stupid.

But a few minutes later another bus pulled up. And just as suddenly as he'd grabbed me, he pulled away and leapt onto the bus. He called back over his shoulder, 'I'll bell you' and left me standing there, feeling like a prize fool. What was worse was that the two old ladies were now eyeing me up and down with the most judgemental looks on their faces. And who could blame them? I'd just behaved like a complete tramp.

Instead I did something really stupid and really naughty. When my bus turned up I smiled sweetly at the disapproving ladies. 'It's OK. He's my brother-in-law,' I said as I boarded. Well, they nearly died!

What was I thinking!!! Holly Richards doesn't behave like that. Holly Richards is a sensible, together person. She doesn't go around snogging boys she doesn't even like. Especially not in art galleries and bus shelters. And HR is usually very nice to old ladies – except when they wind her up, of course.

This has to stop, it's getting out of control. So I text James to say:

Thanx for exhibtn but we cant meet again

And can you believe this – the arrogant pig just texts back saying:

Yeah really?

But I'm not going to think about him any more. I've been looking up lots of info on the internet about the pictures I saw today. The guy who painted the farmer's wife died in the First World War. That's so sad – he was only 24. Just imagine what a talent he'd have been if he'd lived to, say, 60 or something really old.

I was just going to put this diary down and get some shut eye, but then this text comes through from my bro. He writes:

Itz all kickn off Hols – rely need to c u

I'm in my pjs and it's much too late to go round there tonight, so I text back saying:

Talk to J and M – now! But we will talk b4 the gig – Jane sez u can come wiv me

Ryan texts back and says he thinks it will be alright. It's the last day of school tomorrow and what can anyone do to him? So, of course, I worry and text back to say, why does he think someone might do anything to him?

Then he forwards me this message someone sent him. It says:

You have such an imagination Mr Richards – I wonder that you haven't fallen down a rabbit hole yet

Ryan answers on the first ring. 'What the heck is that all about?' I ask him.

'It's a bit from the diary thing. From that freakin' diary I wrote for Mr Stephens – the bit I was definitely going to delete...'

'So it means...'

'Yeah, it means that those kids have got my memory stick...' Ryan sounds like he has the cares of the whole world on his shoulders. And I can't really blame him.

'But who sent it? Don't you recognise the number?' I demand. 'Have you tried ringing this number back?'

And he snorts and says: 'Yeah, that would be a *really* sensible thing to do. Show them I was worried like... They'd see my number and know I was calling them.'

'Yeah, but they wouldn't recognise my number,' I said. 'Look, text it to me and I'll call it... I'll pretend I'm delivering a pizza or something. There's got to be some way I can find out who they are.'

'I guess there's no harm in trying,' Ryan sounds unconvinced but he texts me the number anyway.

As I dialled I was regretting that I hadn't taken more time to think it through. I hadn't even made up a proper name for the pizza company. I was starting to hope that maybe it'd go onto answer phone and there'd be someone's name on there and...

The person who answered wasn't what I was expecting. At
all. He sounded kind of Canadian, and older than I'd expected. I
managed to mumble, 'This is Poppy's Old Time Pizza Company, we
have a delivery here for you...' but I heard how utterly pathetic it
sounded, and I put down the phone.

I was just wondering if it was some parent who'd answered his
kid's mobile, when my phone rang back. A quick glance confirmed
my suspicion. It was the last number calling back. I had to pick it
up, coz this could be a vital clue to who's persecuting my little bro.

'Hey, who's that?' the man on the other end demanded, trying
to sound laid back, but clearly quite cross. I couldn't think what to
say, so I just hung on.

My caller let out a bored sigh. 'If you're one of my pupils playing
tricks then guys this just isn't funny. My mother-in-law's been very
ill and my wife's worrying that the hospital's trying to get through.'

The word 'pupils' registered with me. 'Are you a teacher or
something?' I asked quickly.

'As though you don't know,' my caller said. 'Now look, young
lady...'

'No,' I said firmly, 'No – it's your turn to er...' and I was running
out of steam. But I wasn't giving up. So I said, 'You have to tell me
who you are. Coz your phone sent a threatening message – and I'm
calling to find out what's going on.'

'I'm not falling for that one,' the man at the other end told me,
sort of laughing as he said it. 'I wasn't born yesterday. Admittedly
it wasn't that long ago, and a lot of people tell me I don't look my
age...' This man clearly thought he was a really smooth talker.

'Personally I don't care whether you're 14 or 147,' I snapped
back. 'But I do care that someone is bullying my brother – and
they're using your phone!'

I think my anger got through to him because he stopped

cracking some pathetic joke and started to listen. 'Is your brother a boy in my class?' he asked eventually.

'How would I know? If you won't tell me who or where you are! You could be on a mobile in Siberia for all I know.'

'I think you'd find that phone codes in Siberia...' he started to say but then stopped. Yep, this man sounded like a teacher.

'So what's your brother's name?' he asked.

'Ryan,' I replied before thinking.

'Ryan... Ryan...' he said, rolling the word around like a marble in his mouth. 'Now I believe I have at least three of those in my classes.' And then it was like a penny had dropped. 'That wouldn't be young Mr Richards, by any chance?'

'Well erm... ' I didn't know what to say. I didn't want to get my brother into trouble.

'Quite the bright spark, that young man... Most amusing,' his tone was laden with sarcasm. 'And you, young lady? Are you sure this isn't some elaborate joke he's playing on both of us?'

Now I was really irritated by this man.

'You sound like a very sensible girl,' the voice at the other end continued. (This man was soooo patronising.) 'But I can't understand why you think this is coming from my phone...'

'Because your number is on the text,' I explained, trying to stay calm.

'Really? That's strange because it's been by my bedside since ten o'clock. And it's now gone midnight,' he insisted. 'Maybe I accidentally reached out in my sleep and sent an offensive message to your brother ... or maybe it was one of those incredibly literate mice we've been having a few problems with recently...'

'I can't believe you think this is funny! I thought teachers were meant to take bullying seriously.' I said, using my best ice-princess voice. This joker was really getting on my wick. 'The text was SENT EARLIER ... round about 7.30. My brother didn't find it for a while because his phone had run out of juice.'

There was a big silence during which I could hear the cogs whirring in this stupid man's head. I wondered if he was about to hang up, but eventually he spoke. '7.30 you say... We had the *Twelfth Night* dress rehearsal then, so I was in the gym and I definitely had my phone with me... '

'In your pocket? Every minute?' I prompted.

'Yes... No. No it was in my gym bag. Hang on a minute... Come to think of it, I do remember thinking that the stuff in my bag looked a bit messed up. Like my Speedos were on top of my towel when...'

Oh purleaase! I did not want to hear about this man's Speedos.

'So someone could have "borrowed" it for a bit? Put it back without you noticing?'

'I suppose that's possible. But I mean it isn't very likely now is it?'

'We're talking text bullying here,' I said. 'And anything is possible. Look, why don't you check your phone and see if there's anything unusual. I guess you could get rid of the record of a phone number if you knew how to, but who knows...'

'It's worth a try. I'll call you back,' the man with the Speedos said, and disconnected.

I was starting to suspect he was bluffing to get rid of me, maybe reporting me to the police or something. Then the phone rang.

'Hello ... er... This is Andrew Stephens here. We were speaking only a few minutes ago. I think I may have found something. I realise I don't even know your name... '

'Holly. Holly Richards,' I told him confidently. After all I wasn't the criminal here. 'What have you found?'

'Well – it's not that I've exactly found anything obvious, but there is something a bit strange... I had this sent message I was saving. And it's not there any more. I just can't seem to locate it.'

'So you're thinking that if they sent a text and pressed 'delete all' or something by mistake? Then maybe...'

'To be honest, it does look like someone's deleted *all* my sent messages from today. Well, from before 7ish, although of course that could just be a coincidence and my phone is playing up... I have had a few problems with my provider recently and...'

'I thought you might just know that my foster mum has been down to the school and the head knows all about this bullying stuff!' I cut in quickly. Before this silly man came up with any more waffle. 'And yes, my brother is Ryan Richards.'

'Right. OK. I see. Not one of Ryan's little pranks then... I'm his English teacher, by the way.'

And a little light went on in my head. 'So you're the one who made him write that diary thing. Which started this problem.'

'Sorry? Are you saying my homework project led to this? I don't see quite how...'

So I put him in the picture. With all the info I knew. And to give him credit he did listen. Without interrupting too much.

After I'd finished he told me he'd speak to the head in the morning. 'And, of course if he thinks we should notify the police... Well I'm sure he will. We take bullying very seriously in schools these days...'

'Glad to hear it,' I said, before hanging up.

FRIDAY 23 JULY
Big Gig Day! (on the bus)

I have to scribble this really quickly and the bus is really bumpy today, but I'm so mad... I've just got to get it out of my system. Otherwise I won't be able to enjoy the gig later... I got to the garden centre super early, and I helped with the unloading and stock taking. Marje said it was really good of me and I asked her if it was OK if I left ten minutes early – coz my boyfriend's band were performing this big gig in town. No point lying to Marje any more than I need to (I felt guilty enough when she asked me if I was feeling better) and besides, I wanted that toe-rag Kevin to hear me say this. Marje said of course it was fine and I could go 20 minutes early if things were looking quiet at the end of the day. Sleazebag muttered something about 'taking the Michael' but I pretended I didn't hear it.

But that didn't stop Sleazebag from hanging around. He was there again today every time I turned round. And then there was this incident on the tills, which was like the last thing I wanted him to overhear. I was serving a customer who was taking forever to get their stuff out of the trolley and onto the counter. I offered to help but of course it was a man and he couldn't be seen to have a girl helping him out. And while I was waiting for him to do this, these two people were talking loudly near the checkout.

Person One was Mrs Trumpet-Voice (well, that's my name for her). You know the type – cheeks all flushed and indignant, great big bosom just made for heaving up in disgust. Always looks like she's got a bad smell under her nose. I've seen her in here loads of times before and she's always complaining about something. Today she was going on about some plan the council had for a development on her road. I didn't exactly want to eavesdrop but it's hard not to listen to her ultra-loud voice.

Person Two is Mr-Anything-for-an-Easy-Life. He's clearly bored to death by Mrs Trumpet-Voice but he's much too English to say so. And I bet his wife plays cards with her or something, and tells him he has to be nice to her. So he just stands there going, 'Yes. Oh indeed, quite, quite...' though you can see he's really thinking about his miniature shrubs, or what he's going to watch on telly this evening.

Anyway, I soon get the gist of what Mrs T-V is saying. She's ranting on about a house near her being converted into flats. 'For young hooligans who've been in care!' she exclaims, opening and closing her mouth like a guppy. 'They call it an "independent living scheme" or some such poppycock but we all know what that means. There'll be drug-taking and loud music and all kinds of carrying on – and we won't be able to sleep for the noise. And worrying whether they are breaking into our homes...'

'Yes indeed,' says Mr A.F.A.E.L. 'Yes, yes indeed.'

'Because everyone knows what sort of young people end up being fostered. Tearaways and thieves, and the children of prostitutes – I hardly have to tell you...'

'Yes, quite so. That's awful,' says Mr A.F.A.E.L. but I can see he's eyeing up a potted Pyracantha.

'Yes, isn't it?' says Mrs Trumpet-Voice, getting the bit between her teeth. 'I can't imagine what it will do to the house prices in the area. Allowing young thugs and criminals to live here...'

That was it. I thought of the Independent Living flats I'd lived in until very recently, and all the kind, decent people I'd shared living space with. How dare someone label them as "thugs and criminals"! It was totally outrageous.

'Excuse me,' I say very loudly, breaking off from putting a sack of compost through the till. 'What evidence do you have that these young people are going to be criminals. Or thugs?'

Mrs T-V stares at me like I've just told her to show us her knickers. 'I really don't think this is any business of yours, young woman...'

'Well, I think you're wrong there,' I reply quickly, conscious that people are turning round to stare at me. 'I am one of those "criminals and thugs" you are talking about. Has it never occurred to you that some people get fostered coz their parents are ill or neglected or hurt them or something? Most kids in care aren't there coz of what *they* did, but coz of what someone did to *them*.'

I felt dead proud of myself at that moment. Especially when I saw the effect on Mrs T-V. She just didn't know what to say. She tried a sort of harrumph noise but knew she was in the wrong. So holding her head up as high as she could, she pushed her trolley out of the shop. Mr A.F.A.E.L. shot me a rather feeble smile, but trotted out after her, saying something hurriedly about 'the garden show tomorrow...'

'That told her, luv!' The man I'm serving hands me his credit card with a great big grin on his face. 'But you're never from foster care, are you? A bright, smart girl like you?'

I think he meant this as a compliment but it's almost as insulting as Mrs T-V's comments. 'Yes,' I answer, putting his card into the machine. 'I've been fostered for most of my life. And my foster carers taught me to respect myself and where I come from.

Now, if you can just enter your pin number.'

'Ah-ha, that would explain it,' he says, winking at me. As though he thinks that's an appropriate reply. J and M may be wonderful but that doesn't mean I was some kind of scumbag they had to save. I'd always been proud of who I was, and Jane and Martin knew that.

Nobody says anything more about my outburst until I'm getting ready to leave. It's gone a bit quiet so I'm taking Marje at her word and leaving 20 mins early.

'Go around insulting customers often, d'you?' Kevin leers at me as I'm collecting my things from the pegs outside the office. He's doing something on the computer which I bet he'd like us to think is work. But it looks like some kind of girly website from where I'm standing.

'No,' I say, 'I don't insult customers. I just put them straight when they get their facts completely wrong.'

Kevin laughs that horrible dirty laugh of his. 'Did you learn that attitude of yours from the other kids you met in foster care?'

I tell him that my attitude is nothing to do with anyone else – and I'm just proud to be who I am. And Sleazebag just shakes his head and says, 'Pride comes before a fall luv. Don't say I didn't warn yer.'

I don't know what that's supposed to mean. It's obviously some kind of threat but you can't let people see you are afraid of them. 'Goodnight Kevin,' I say very politely as I pass the door. 'I hope you have a wonderful evening – whatever pond you are wallowing in.'

He cackles with laughter like I've said something really funny and makes some nasty comment about screwed-up girls with too much imagination. I make a big effort to look as though I haven't heard him.

Nearly there now and I need all my concentration for what I'm gonna wear tonight… You get this look in your mind but you can't make it work with what you've got in your wardrobe. Sometime I'm going to start drawing some of my ideas... maybe see if Keesh will help me make some of them. Wish I could sew like her...

SATURDAY 24 JULY

Last night was really cool and though I say it myself, I was looking pretty hot. I found this amazing stripey top in Keesh's room and put it with my black jeans. When you're the girlfriend of the lead singer, you've got to look good.

I had to go and collect my brother from the bus stop near J and M's so I could take him to the gig.

Of course Ryan made a comment about me looking like a zebra crossing. How very witty, how amazingly original. So I said that he looked like an underage boy who was hoping to be smuggled backstage by his sister and he'd better be nice to me, or it wasn't gonna happen.

On the bus he told me what had gone on at school that afternoon.

It was mid-way through the first period of the afternoon when Ryan became aware that people were whispering – and he got the sense that it was about him. Then one of the girls who was still speaking to him passed him a piece of paper, telling him to check his phone.

Under cover of his desk Ryan opened a text message which said:

*Make sure 2 say bye bye to Ryan Richards. Coz you wont be
seein him next term*

Ryan had to wait til the end of the history quiz before he could
check with his mates. It seemed that most of Ryan's class had got
the same message. And the number was the same as the one from
Thursday, i.e. sent from Mr Stephens's mobile. So Ryan (and I'm
proud of him for this) excused himself from the lesson and went to
the head's office.

The school secretary tried to tell my brother that the head
was very busy but Ryan said he would go fetch him himself, if she
didn't. Eventually Mr Hammond was fetched and Ryan explained
what had happened. The head then sent the secretary to get Mr
Stephens out of his class, and Mr Stephens arrived looking dead
flustered.

'Couldn't find his mobe anywhere at first,' Ryan explained.
'Never seen that idiot look so discombobulated before…'

'So what? Oh never mind… Forget the big words and just tell me
what happened.'

Apparently Mr Stephens had left his mobile where he normally
left it during class, in his bag in the staff room, which (can you
believe this?) has a broken lock at the moment! But it wasn't there
any more.

'Then he found it. Lying on the floor near the coffee table… Like
someone might want to make it look like he'd dropped it earlier.'

This was turning into one of those crappy TV dramas where
a hundred people in the same village get murdered in this one
house, and someone's left blood on an axe in the drawing room.
Which made me think of something.

'Couldn't you have demanded Mr H get the police? They could
have fingerprinted the phone or something?' I asked.

My brother gave me that exasperated look of his which drives
me mad. 'They only do that in films. Fingerprints are no good

unless you got the prints of all the possible suspects on file. An' they're not exactly gonna have all the school kids on file are they?'

'Well, they could have taken them – if they'd got up there quick enough,' but I knew this was a feeble response.

'Yeah like twenty minutes before the last day of term, the head is going to keep all the kids locked in the gym while we wait for the police to arrive … '

'OK. OK. I get your point…'

But it seemed that the head had been in to have "a word" with all the classes in Ryan's year. He'd warned everyone that sending threatening texts and setting up or posting to abusive websites can be illegal and he'd be reporting the incident to the police.

'Yeah and they all looked terrified,' Ryan told me, sarcastically. 'Like someone is going to stand up and say, "Oooh, it was me, sir, please sir, I've been a naughty boy sir"…'

'Well it's better than doing nothing. At least it shows the school's taking it seriously…'

'Yeah but what if it's not one of the kids in my year – what if it's another year or whatever… '

I had to agree that the school wasn't exactly pulling its finger out on this one. That horrible website's been up there a while now and from what I hear, Jane's spoken to the school several times now.

'Oh – and get this – Mr Stephens and Mr H have both given me their mobile number! Aren't I the lucky one? They say that if I have any problems during the holidays I'm to call them… which I'll be doing. All the time. Not.'

Anyway that's enough of my brother. I've got to be ready for the party in 50 mins. And I've got to wrap the dinosaur picture I've made for Simon (purple dinosaur with yellow background – his favourite colours at the moment). So here goes with an instant report on the actual gig.

Later

Last night went back in such a flash but these are the main bits of the gig I remember.

7.30 ish

Backstage with Sean and his parents and my bro. Sean's mum worse that ever. She doesn't think I'm good enough for her son. But his dad gave me a really big hug. It wasn't what you'd call rock'n roll with parentals and little bruvvers hanging around but that was OK. The atmosphere was still good and there was free food and booze. Yes Jane (I know she'll never read this but I want to put it down), I did supervise my little brother really carefully. He had one small glass of fizzy wine when no one was looking – and no more. I promise!

8.15 pm

Me and Ryan go and stand in the wings. Fortunately nowhere near Sean's mum. Wow – there was this totally amazing atmosphere. Everyone was dancing and jostling and you could feel the excitement coming off the audience. People were jumping and yelling by the time the lads came on – and then the whole space erupted when they started their first track. The clapping went on for ages. If that's what a bit of publicity on the radio does for you, bring it on...

Ryan loved the concert coz he's deeply into that kind of music, but it's not really my thing. Still I did get quite a huge thrill watching all those people going loony about my boyf. There were girls holding up banners saying 'We luv u Sean'. Sweet!

10 ish

Gig finishes. Keesh and her mates come round backstage and

then we go mingling with the audience while the band are being photographed and interviewed by a couple of local journos. And at the bar there are these girls talking about Sean.

One of the girls is saying to the others that he picked her up after the last show. Several of the girls are saying she's lying but this girl is swearing it's true. I don't know what to think. And when I get close enough I give the girl a good looking over, but she's nothing really special. I mean she's pretty enough and she has long, darkish hair like me but she's smaller, plumper, not as tall as I am. I don't think she'd be Sean's type. And I know girls will tell all sorts of stories about lead singers in bands. But I felt really uneasy about it for the rest of the night.

I mentioned it to Sean, after we'd dropped Ryan off and he was giving me a lift home. I was really casual, like I thought it was a big joke. And Sean seemed cool about it. He just laughed and said it was amazing how much girls had started throwing themselves at him – and that I'd better watch out. Which was kind of reassuring coz I don't know that he'd have joked about it if it was true. He'd probably try and reassure me or something.

But then I kept thinking about the thing with Spider Boy and how I'd do almost anything to make sure Sean didn't know about it.

And now I need to stop writing and wrap that dinosaur. And it's time to stop having stupid thoughts. Tomorrow is Sunday and some people say that Sunday is the start of the week. So from now on I'm going to put behind me everything that happened last week and make a new start. And make myself utterly gorgeous for my rather amazing boyfriend...

SUNDAY 25 JULY
or is it really Monday morning?

I guess it's about 3am and I can't sleep. Maybe I just ate too much birthday cake or had one too many glass of bubbly... I just can't get back to sleep. So, dear diary, I might as well tell you all about Simon's party.

It was a proper kid's birthday party – which is just how Simon wanted it. He hardly ate anything of course, but he'd had his heart set on a traditional birthday tea – ever since he'd seen a birthday party that J and M held for some twins they'd fostered around the time Simon first joined them. I think the twins were about four or five but Simon had never seen a birthday party before and he'd become obsessed with the idea of having one. He even wanted a pink and white iced sponge cake and nine pink candles – until he remembered that he didn't like pink. So Jane did it all – sausages on sticks, rice crispy cakes in paper cases, iced buns with flower patterns on top, sausage rolls, orange squash and coke and gallons of Martin's homemade lemonade and jelly and blancmange and strawberry ice cream. And when Jane closed the curtains and turned out the lights and Martin brought in the lemon cake with lighted candles on top, I don't think there was a dry eye in the room!

Simon has only two friends. A very shy boy who is deaf and this little girl who is very tiny and uses a walking frame to get around. He doesn't get on very well with any of the kids in his class but he met these two at the club he goes to sometimes in the holidays. It's a club for all children but they do have a few kids with special needs and Simon seems to feel more comfortable hanging out with them. Jane says the little gang of three doesn't really talk but they seem braver when they are together. They try things which they wouldn't do alone and Simon shows remarkable patience, pushing the little girl on a swing for hours on end or working out some very complicated way that he and the deaf boy can race each other up the climbing frame. I think both these kids are a bit younger than him, but it's weird to think of Simon being nine. I've always thought of him as about six or seven.

So as well as these two kids and their mums and dads, there's also Robert and his wife and kids, and J and M's other son Leon was there as well. I haven't seen Leon for over a year coz he now lives in Canada, where he has this job inventing animal feeds. But he's over for a month coz he's here for business and then staying around to have a bit of a holiday and catch up with the family. Leon brought his new girlfriend, who's called Stacey or Tracey or something which I didn't quite catch. She's a bit older than Leon and she has this eleven-year-old daughter from a previous relationship. I know they say kids can be a bit demanding when their parent gets a new partner but this girl was way off the Richter scale. She had this constant pout and icy stare and she never said anything except whingeing and saying she didn't feel well, or wanted to be inside when everyone was outside, or complaining that the food 'tasted funny'.

And Lucy and Nathan and baby Ruby were there – and Rob's three boys squabbled about taking turns to hold Ruby, which was really sweet. And ancient Mrs Stoker, who's lived next door since before J and M bought the house, turned up with a tray of flapjacks and had some whisky in her tea. And Mr Aldwen, who's a music teacher, turned up, coz he's one of the few people who Simon really likes at his school and he'd especially wanted to ask him. And Mr Aldwen brought his little niece who's six and was dressed like a butterfly.

Ryan was sort of there in the background, but he kept disappearing to do stuff with the Xbox. But when he did come down for a bit, Rob's boys were all over him and wanted him to play football with them in the garden. And Leon got dragged in as well and then Nathan and Sean also wanted to play. So me and Lucy ended up like WAGS standing on the side (Ruby was asleep on Mrs Stoker's lap) and shouting rude comments or encouragement at the boys, and not joining in coz we were wearing our posh shoes. But we did pose for some group photos which Leon's girlfriend took – while her sulky daughter tried to persuade a very unwilling Boots to play with her.

I think Simon enjoyed his birthday party. He spent most of it with his two friends from the club, and the butterfly girl, chasing some balloons and doing silly things with the streamers that come out of poppers. There were a few tears and a few scenes, but that's usual at these times and Jane and Martin are so good at taking that all in their stride. (Jane told me later that the adoption agency had forwarded a birthday card from Simon's mum. I thought she was in prison or something, but I guess you can still send cards. She's not allowed Simon's address but the agency sent it on for her. Jane said Simon looked really upset when he opened it, like he was going to cry. And then he asked, sounding really anxious, if his mum was coming to the party. Jane said he looked a bit relieved when she explained that no, his mum wasn't coming. (But Jane wasn't quite sure whether he'd really wanted his mum to come or not.))

Me and Sean stayed behind to help clear up the mess, along

with Leon and the girlfriend and the Spoilt Brat. And then Martin opened a bottle of fizzy wine – so we could drink a toast to him and Jane who have been married for about a thousand years and are celebrating their wedding anniversary tomorrow. But then Lucy went to put Ruby to bed, and Nathan had to go and do something down at the cricket club, where he's helping out at the moment. And Rob and Mrs Rob (her real name's Carol but it's been this joke since one of our foster kids got her name wrong – and it's sort of became her nickname) took their three hyperactive boys home. I wonder how long it was before they got them into bed!

After we'd cleared away we sat out in the garden and drank the last of the lemonade. And Martin asked if anyone was still hungry and of course Sean and Ryan and Leon said they were. And Simon then said yes as well. But we women – Jane and Stacey/Tracey and me – said we were much too full up with crisps and cakes but when the men started looking at the Chinese takeaway menu, we couldn't help but add a few things to the order. I think the Brat said she hated Chinese but she'd said she hated almost everything by then so nobody seemed to be paying her any attention. Except Martin, who'd disappeared into the kitchen to place the Chinese order and came back out with a plate of very plain looking cheese sandwiches, which much to everyone's surprise the Brat actually ate. OK, so it was in a corner by herself and she scowled all the time, but it shut her up from whingeing for a bit.

We stayed out till it got really dark, eating sweet and sour prawns and egg fried rice and sticky ribs. Martin opened another couple of bottles of fizzy and we all toasted Simon's birthday and the fact that he was getting adopted very soon. (And we drank a toast to Lucy even though she'd already gone to bed, along with Ruby.) Even Simon wanted to taste the fizzy stuff, which he did very slowly and seriously like he was putting something into his mouth which might be poison. He sipped really carefully and made a big swallowing motion. And pulled a face and gave a little shudder. He handed the glass back to Jane and said 'stingy' which was, I think, the only word I heard him say all day.

And Sean held my hand in the dark and drew soft, tickly patterns on my palm. And we slipped away from the table for a few minutes to go and look for Boots, who'd last been seen chasing some small defenceless creature at the bottom of the garden. And under the only apple tree (which produces horrible, sour fruit) Sean took me in his arms and told me that he loved me more than anything else in the world. And although he knew I didn't want to make any plans yet, he'd marry me tomorrow if I'd only say the word. And I told him not to be so silly, but gently, not in an unkind way because tonight I really felt that one day – not now, but some time in the distant future – I would think about marrying him.

Sean drove me home but he couldn't stay all night. He did stay for an hour or two, and I felt like he was making love to me in a dream. It was like we were the only two people in the entire world and every kiss and every touch was so meaningful and so special that it felt like the most beautiful moment of my life. I guess maybe it was the effect of the cava, or just the result of such a perfect afternoon and being out in the moonlight until it was really late.

So why am I awake now feeling a bit strange? I wish Sean could have stayed but his mum wants him to go and visit his gran and she'd made him promise that he'd be home tonight so they could set off early in the morning. Sean says they probably won't leave till midday coz she has to have at least three cups of strong black coffee, and she'll want to do half an hour on her exercise bike and then she'll decide to change the colour of her nail varnish – but she'd been moaning that he'd done nothing but spend time with me since he came home and he hates it when she moans.

(If there's one good reason not to marry Sean then it's his mother. OMG – she would be the mother-in-law from hell! I must make sure she keeps her promise to go and live in the South of France when Sean's dad retires. But then no doubt we'd be expected to go and visit them every holiday. Still, the South of France wouldn't be too bad – the light is meant to be fantastic for painting.)

After Sean left I had this strange, strange dream. I dreamt that it wasn't Sean but James who made love to me – except I didn't realise at first and I thought it was my boyf. And when I realised it was SB I was shocked at first but then... And I also realised that we weren't using condoms (I have an implant in my arm so I don't get pregnant, but I don't want any nasty STDs or things like that). And then Spider Boy smiled at me – this really evil smile and I realised that he had fangs. And he bit into my neck...

I woke up and found I'd fallen asleep with my necklace still on and the pendant Sean gave me for Christmas was digging into the side of my throat. Which explains why I thought someone was biting me. But it doesn't explain why SB was in my dream. I can honestly say that my Sean is so much fitter than SB. Sean is tall and thin like SB but there's more of him to get hold of. And he's got lovely soft skin for a man. And I love the smell of him. SB smells of nicotine (which I absolutely hate) and he's a bit sharp looking, kind of angular and rat like, although lots of the girls and some of the boys at college think he's dead sexy. And I really, really don't like anything about him. He's so into himself and he's rude and arrogant, and his art is so pretentious. Why would any sane person want to be with him when they could be with my lovely Sean? Those girls at the gig would give their right arm to be me tonight and yet I go and have this stupid, stupid dream about a boy I absolutely can't stand.

Anyway I'm going to read that boring book about the amazing Botticelli now. That always helps me fall asleep. I think I shall write about him myself one day. He deserves a lot better than that rubbish...

MONDAY 26 JULY
Martin and Jane's wedding anniversary (Wish I had something to celebrate!!)

3.50pm on the bus

I've lost my job. I can't believe it! I don't know whether to cry or smash something, I'm that livid.

I was doing my bit with the conifers when Sleazebag wanders up, all cocky and flirty. Asks me how the gig went and all that stuff. I'm polite but make it clear I'm dead busy. But he keeps on hanging around. So I ignore him and go on doing the potting Marje has asked me to do.

Then just as I'm folding up the last of the compost bags, someone says my name. And there's my little bro standing there – looking all shaken up and miserable.

'Who's this then, your boyfriend?' Sleazebag asks, all slimy and disgusting.

'It's my brother. Ryan this is Kevin, Kevin this is Ryan... and if you wouldn't mind – I'd like a word with him.'

'Sure, go ahead.' Sleazebag's still standing there.

'In private,' I say. Why can't the stupid idiot take a hint?

'You're supposed to be working,' Kevin says. 'You can't go off talkin' at the moment.'

'I wasn't "going off" anywhere,' I tell him. 'I was going to talk to my brother *while* I was tidying up the heathers. Unlike some people I don't hang around all day doing nothing.'

OK that was a stupid thing to say to the owner's son, but I'd just about had it with him. He'd watched me tipping up heavy pots for most of the morning and never lifted a finger to help.

'Whatever you say, your majesty,' Sleazebag shot me a really nasty look. 'But if I catch you slipping off to be with your boyfriend here, there'll be big trouble...'

'He's my brother!!' I snapped as Kevin slunk off to find someone else to pester. (Do I look like the kind of girl who would go out with a spotty adolescent? I think not! And even a wall would realise this was a sensitive situation – my brother had clearly been crying.)

'OK,' I say as soon as me and Ryan are alone. 'What's been happening?'

Ryan tells me that he's had this text from Luke. A really nasty text saying that Luke would never have hung out with him if he'd realised he was gay. And that Ryan better not be anywhere in the holidays that Luke might come across him or he'd smash his stupid face in (teenage boys have such a wonderful way with words!).

Then Ryan had found another text from this boy called Gareth, who he knew Luke was now hanging out with. It simply said:

We r watchen u!

I told Ryan that he had to talk to J and M again and maybe get them to call the head. Luke and Gareth are both pupils at his school – they could be warned or something.

But Ryan doesn't want to do this. 'Luke's never gonna forgive me if I do that,' he insists.

Honestly, why would he care what that loser thinks? Luke has hardly proved himself the greatest friend ever. 'Forget him,' I say. 'He's got nothing to "forgive you" for. You don't need people like that in your life – they drag you down with all their negative stuff...'

'Easy for you to say,' my poor, sad brother tells me. 'You got hundreds of mates Hol. An' I can't see you forgettin' Lucy if this happened with you and her...'

'Yeah but Lucy wouldn't be such a prat. If she, like, found out I was like a lesbian or something she ...'

'Are you a lesbian, Holly?'

'No – and that's not the point. What I'm saying is that friends stick with you. They don't ditch you coz of some stupid little thing like whether you fancy boys or girls...'

'So you haven't told Lucy you're a lesbian?'

Why are teenage boys so exasperating? 'No, because I'm not. But if I was, then she wouldn't think any different of me. I mean she went out with some utter dweebs before Nathe but that didn't make any difference to us being friends. Who your mates date shouldn't be like some big issue...'

'Unless it's your boyfriend.'

'Well yeah – but I think that's a completely different issue. I mean, that's about being loyal to your friends and not cheating and ...' (OMG I start feeling guilty as I say it. Sean's my friend and my boyfriend and I've been cheating on him in real life – *and* in my dreams.)

Ryan looks at me like I've got two heads. 'You talk such total rubbish sometimes, Hol,' he says, sighing.

'Look – it's not about whether I'm a lesbian or you're gay. It's about friendship and how our friends treat us ... Can I help you Kevin?'

How long has the slimy toad been standing behind me? He must've heard quite a lot of what I was saying. Just what I need!

Ryan's in no hurry to hang around and I have to follow him almost into the car park, to make sure he has enough money for his bus fare home. On my way in I found Sleazebag waiting for me.

'Was that an official coffee break?' he asked, with a dead sarky look on his face.

I kept my calm. 'More of a short toilet break – I was only gone two minutes…'

'I'd say more like ten… So what does your mum say bout your brother being a ponce and you a lesbo? Oh I forgot, you don't live with her, do you? Your brother in a kiddies home too, is he? S'pose that's where you get all those pervy ideas… '

I'd never wanted to hit someone so much in all my life, but violence achieves nothing. 'Kevin,' I said forcing my voice to sound as relaxed as poss. 'Has anyone ever told you what a disgusting human being you really are? You're a bigot and the biggest perve I've ever met… hanging around girls a third of your age and making a total nuisance of yourself!'

Then I just turned and walked away. But I heard Kevin saying behind me. 'Pity about that brother of yours though. Pathetic looking kid. I bet he's a real target for paedos and the like…'

I don't know why that made me snap. Maybe it was coz of all the dreadful stuff my brother's gone through in the past. I just swung round and slapped Kevin's stupid mug. Not hard – just a gesture. To show what I think of him.

Nessa and another new girl were passing. I heard them gasp before they hurried off.

Kevin muttered 'you'll be sorry' and slunk off. I shouldn't have let my temper get the better of me. But he really did have it coming to him. You have to stand up to people like him or they'll never change.

Half-an-hour later Nessa came to tell me that I'm wanted in Marje's office. No big surprise there. Ness is really worried for me, but I tell her I'm able to look after myself.

'I thought you were such a nice girl, Holly,' Marje told me sadly, 'But we can't have behaviour like that… '

'But I was only...'

Marje cut across me. 'There's no excuse for it, young woman... if Kevin catches you sneaking out during work hours, then he's every right to tell you to come back in... And slapping him in the face... What were you thinking of?'

'But I was...'

'And I heard about that incident the other day – when you were rude to a customer at the desk.. Kevin said I should ignore it at the time because young people like you probably don't get taught any manners ...' Marje was shaking her head and looking like it was really hurting her to say this stuff. I was desperate to make her hear the truth. But with those last words something inside me snapped.

'People like what?' I demanded. 'People who are in care? Is that what you mean?'

'No need to raise your voice at me, dear...'

'I'll have you know that "people like me" do have manners – and morals. We aren't lazy slobs with a big fat gob on them who go round telling lies about other people...' I could almost feel the steam coming out of my ears.

But Marje wasn't going to listen. Sleazebag had told her his version and goodness knows how many other enormous porky pies. And she was convinced that I had attacked her poor, innocent son in the middle of the shop. She said that if I didn't calm down she'd call the police – and Kevin would press charges for assault. I said that I didn't care if the police were called because then I could tell my side of the story.

'Oh yeah?' Kevin demanded. 'Then I'll be tellin' them about how I saw your bruvver pocketing some of those fancy pens on the counter, when he first come in...'

I don't think Ryan would do that. OK, so he's done some daft things in the past and he can be a bit weird when he's upset about stuff. But stealing from the place I work – I really don't think so.

But to make his point, Sleazebag sticks his nasty sweaty face in mine. 'Not sure how that would go down, are you? Police sniffin' round your little brother, what with him already clearly in some kinda trouble... No smoke without fire they say... '

There are some things you can't risk. Any more upset and my little brother might just tip over the edge. Like our mum. So I didn't say anything.

'Good – shut up now, have you?' Kevin was clearly enjoying this. 'So here's what we'll do. You leave quietly now – no big fuss. But we don't pay you for this week, to make up for that stuff your brother nicked. And we never see your skanky face round here again, kid. Or that brother of yours. Coz this is a respectable place and we don't need scum like you...'

Marje had the decency to look a bit embarrassed, but she was never going to do anything to really upset her baby boy.

'Fine,' I said, keeping my dignity as best I could and speaking directly to Marje. 'But I hope you can sleep at night. Knowing you took someone's job away from them coz of a lot of lies, and this bully boy son of yours...'

Marje couldn't meet my eye. She looked away and then started to fiddle with pencils on her desk.

'I'm going now,' I told her. 'And I wouldn't mind betting you won't find any other mug who works as hard as me. But if you do, make sure they're ugly as sin, so that Mr Sleazepot here doesn't hassle them...'

I got my coat and picked up my bags. And I slammed my locker key down on the counter in front of a surprised customer. 'I wouldn't buy my shrubs here if I was you,' I told her. 'They might accuse you of nicking something.'

Nessa tried to speak to me, but I waved her away. 'Text me' I mouthed at her. I didn't want Kevin taking it out on her.

I've been fuming all the way back on the bus. Now I'm writing all this down so I remember every detail. Everything that happened, everything he said and I said. Just in case that Kevin does involve the police or something. I need as much proof as possible that I'm innocent.

Then I really must get my act together. J and M are taking Lucy and Nathe out for the evening – as a surprise. They wanted to take me too but I said I'd babysit and keep an eye on my little bro. It's nice for them to be a family sometimes, without us foster kids always around.

12·30 pm

Martin just dropped me off. Glad to hear they all had a nice time at the restaurant, even if Lucy fretted all evening and kept ringing to see that I hadn't dropped Ruby or washed her down the plug hole. Actually Ruby was good as gold. Martin had taken her out for one of his "exciting" visits to the park which he's rather good at (small kids always come back knackered and Martin comes back with a big silly grin on his face coz he's got to play swings and roundabouts), and Jane bathed her so Lucy could glam up. So Ruby slept like a log for most of the evening. She just woke up once and I walked her up and down a bit. It took about 20 minutes but she dropped off to sleep again. I wish I could believe babies were always that easy!

Ryan was out somewhere and when he came in he didn't have much to say. Just sat on the sofa watching TV with me for a bit, before heading to his room. Lucky that Martin had left me a pizza and banoffee pie for company.

Sean was dead sweet to me on the phone. He had this band rehearsal tonight and he offered to come over and pick me up from Jane and Martin's, but I said it was OK. I really needed a bit of time by myself.

Keesh rang to say she had some good news – which really cheered me up. She's been talking to the woman she met the other night, the one who's setting up a boutique in the city centre. She wants Keesh to meet up with some of her investors first, but she thinks Keesh is going to be perfect for the job.

So I'm not going to think about that bloody garden centre ever again. Not once. They can go and stuff themselves. I'm much too good for them anyway.

It must have been that conversation with Keesh, but I had this dream about clothes. In the dream there were all these frocks, and coats as well, with loads of layers to them, lots of different materials and buckles and flounces and beads and feathers. Some were made of silk and leather, some were rough cotton with lots of different seams, so that nothing was straight or simple but everything within the garment was all higgledy piggledy with sideways hems and patches of materials that were different sizes. And nipped in waists and big swirling skirts, and petticoats and lace-up bits and basques, and high stand-up collars and long baggy sleeves with button-up cuffs. They were colours like parachute silk grey and midnight shiny black, and the richest most royal purples and turquoises. They were clothes that models and diplomats and princesses could wear, but so could a girl from Corrington – like me, or any of my mates.

And in the dream I was designing these dresses and coats and skirts and selling them and people were saying, 'That Holly, she's creating artworks that people can wear.'

And that's what I'm going to do. And I'm not just going to design them for women coz men could look good in those as well. There was this New Romantics movement back in the day based on pirate stuff and things like that and men wore baggy shirts with lots of laces, and loads of eye make up and feathers and anything they felt like – and I'm going to kind of revive that but make it totally relevant for the 21st century by having the coolest and most trendy materials available. So along with velvet I might have that new spray on fabric they're using to create clothes, which I saw on telly. And there'd be denim in there as well as calico and rayon and sheer silk and taffeta.

Lucy rang and she clearly thinks I've gone a bit screwy. She said she was ringing to thank me for looking after Ruby last night but I think it's coz she's worried about me losing my job. She said the garden centre would go bankrupt or something or get bulldozed down coz they'd created all that bad karma. (She has quite an imagination that girl, when she puts her mind to it.) She said that I should come over and she'd bake cookies for me, and tempting as that was, I said no thanks, coz I have to start putting my ideas down on paper. And Lucy said good idea, but wouldn't it be a bit expensive buying all those materials and I said no, coz there were loads of charity shops in this city and I always know where to get a bargain. Of course I'm not going to get rich and famous overnight but I can start making stuff. First though, I have to get myself a sewing machine.

Then Luce says that Nathan has this mate who's a wizard at getting bargains on Ebay, so if I take a look and see what kind I want, he'll ask his mate to get me one. (I hope that means what he says and that I'm not committing myself to handling stolen goods, but I can't see Nathe as the criminal type.) And to be honest, today I don't care about anything much except how I'm going to get this business off the ground.

11pm

I spent the morning drawing and I have to admit – my ideas looked dead good on paper. I showed them to Keesh who had only just hauled herself out of bed.

Keesh was reading a fashion mag, painting her toenails and eating an enormous bowl of rice pudding, when I asked her if she'd mind giving me an honest opinion on my drawings.

'These are totally brilliant, girl!' she said, after studying my pictures for a few minutes. 'You got some serious talent, babes.'

I could feel myself blushing a bit. And I was sooo pleased. Keesh is a fab girl but she gives you honest opinions. If she doesn't like it, she says so.

'So maybe we could do this together, me an' you girl,' Keesh continued, selecting a hot shade of pink to tone with the purple stripes she'd already painted. 'We can create some cool outfits – yeah? Like you can design the stuff and I can turn it into patterns and then like teach you how to sew it, girl? I've got this sewing machine my first foster mum gave me.'

'We have to start small an' then we work up to bigger,' I said, getting enthusiastic now. 'Just a few bits here and there for now and we sell them on stalls or online or something...'

'Hey girl, you and me doesn't do small – we starts big and gets even bigger!' Keesha said, never taking her eyes off the very straight lines she was creating in Freakout Fuschia. 'An' we keep putting money back in the business, coz that's what one of my friends who sells handbags on the internet does. She buys likkle bits of stock and she puts the money back in. Then she buy bigger stock and she keep putting the money in – till she built up enough profit to start taking out a salary.'

I decided it was time to tell Keesha there was a small hitch with this idea. That I needed money asap coz I've just lost my job. She listened really sympathetically to my story and she cursed that Kevin and said she knew his whatsit would go manky and fall off.

'But, hey no problem babes – we can get you some work, girl, to pay the bills till you get your big break...You don't mind waitressing and stuff?'

That sounded good to me. People don't say 'no' to Keesh, coz she just turns on that charming smile of hers, and they give in. And if that doesn't work she throttles them til they say yes.

Keesh understands how important it is that I get some work. We knew when we moved into this flat that we could barely afford it. We get care leavers' payments from our council, which help to top up our student loans, but that isn't enough to live on and pay rent. We were both that desperate to get our own space. We'd both had a good time in the independent living place but when her friend Mel moved out to go and work abroad and Lucy was getting ready to move in with Nathan, the two of us felt we didn't want to get left behind. We could've stayed there and shared one of the flats but we both felt it was time to move on. It's what being in care does to you – you're dead keen to be as independent as possible.

'Anyway babes, you can come along next time I'm meeting wiv Davina. She bound to need another pair of hands launching dat boutique...'

That was so typical of Keesh – generous to a fault. She hadn't even been hired by this woman and already she was including me in her plans.

'Hey, no babes – you don't want to screw it up taking me along. It's you she wants to see...'

'Nonsense! You and me girl – together we can knock 'em dead. But no harm in taking along some of dem designs of yours, babes. Show her you know about fashion and stuff... Mebbe show her some of your ideas for the boys. She said it ain't so easy finding good stuff for the menswear bit...'

This was sounding better and better.

'And now to start your first lesson – using the sewing machine,' Keesh announced, giving her toenails a final once-over. 'I take it you used a sewing machine before babes? No? Hey, what did your carers teach you girl?! My foster mum taught me how to make my own clothes. OK – mebbe it was coz she was way too mean to buy me any new ones...'

So I spent the afternoon learning how to hem a straight line. Then a curvy line, then a really fiddly, wiggly line. But hardest of all was learning how to thread the machine. I thought I'd never get that right. You have to be careful coz you can really muck it up, or even break it if you don't do it right.

Keesh cooked us one of her wicked stews for tea – one of those spicy, fruity ones. Then she had to go to work and I did more practising with the machine.

I'm having an early night coz Keesh says she might get me some work for tomorrow and I want to look my best if I have to be interviewed or something.

Just a few pages of the boring old Botticelli book. Pity it doesn't have more pictures, coz his paintings are really cool.

4am

I do love my brother but I wish he wouldn't call me in the middle of the night. And I'm sorry he's having such a crap time. But just coz he can't sleep doesn't mean he has to wake me up.

'I just saw it,' was his explanation when I asked why he was calling at 2.50am. 'There's this stuff on my Facebook... '

'What are you doing on Facebook at this hour of the night?' I ask him. Sounding like I'm somebody's grandmother.

Ryan admitted he'd been lying awake wondering... just wondering and fretting what was going on. He'd tried not to look at FB for a few days coz the last time he'd looked there were still messages from kids calling him all kinds of stuff. And Jane had told him to stay away from the internet, especially till they got that hideous website taken down.

'But I just got this bad vibe,' he confided. 'I just knew sis, that there was something up there... something evil ... So I had to look.'

I knew that feeling. If I'd been in his situation, I'd have done the same.

While he was talking I was opening up my laptop and logging into my account (which I hadn't done all day). And immediately I saw the messages. Three of them – from my brother. Except they weren't from my brother, coz they contained stuff he'd never have shared with anyone.

The first one I read said:

Mr Stephens knows I'm gay coz he saw it in my file. An I also fancy my best mate Luke, coz he's a foster kid like me. Him, me, Mr Stephens and that Rashan Gayle we could really get it on!

Scrolling back I saw the previous message:

And you know what. My foster dad Martin is a right jerk. He doesn't know one end of a football pitch from his arse.

And before that was a message that read:

Wanna know a secret? I got three dads. My real dad's a violent nutter and I got this other dad in America. But my dads all hate me coz I'm a queer.

I flicked back through the rest of the day but there was nothing more to be seen with my brother's name on it.

'Just three?' I asked. As if that wasn't enough.

'Just three,' my brother said. And I hear his voice cracking and I know he's at the end of his tether. 'It's all from stuff I wrote on that memory stick. Changed a bit but...'

I don't know what to say, so I decide to keep it practical. 'How did this happen?' I ask.

Ryan cursed me for my stupidity. He doesn't know how it

happened coz if he did he'd have stopped it.

'But you must have left your page up on screen ... not logged out or something.'

'Nope. Definitely not. I'm not a total idiot,' Ryan assured me angrily. 'Anyway I never open Facebook when I'm around other kids. Not since that ... Unless you're suggesting that Simon or Martin or Jane did this?'

That's about as likely as pigs flying. I don't think Si registers what the internet is, or what it does. And Jane and Martin looked like good responsible people, the last time I saw them.

'Then you told someone your password?' I said to him. 'You told Luke and he...'

'I'm not bloody daft,' Ryan snapped back.

'Then someone guessed it,' I said. And he was about to curse me again, when I said, 'Rashan Gayle!' and my brother stopped in his tracks.

'How the... ?'

'Easy,' I replied. 'It's a bit predictable. They've got the stuff on your memory stick and they try a few options. It's the first one I'd think of. You need to have a proper password, something that people won't remember...'

'Cut the lecture,' my brother snapped. 'That's like the last thing I need just at this moment.'

'We've got to get your FB page closed,' I told him. 'You must be able to cancel these things.' But I didn't sound very confident. I was pretty sure it's harder to shut down stuff on the internet than it is to open it.

'It doesn't matter now. Coz everybody will have read that. All the kids at school will have put it on their status or something... And ... OMG ...'

'What is it?' I asked, feeling a bit sick.

'That girl, Josie, from my primary school, the one that I told you about… when I lived with Bitch Aunt and Evil Granny – she's my friend on there… What if she like told someone or something?'

'Is that likely?' I asked, but my stomach was churning. 'I mean, if she's your friend and…'

'Yeah, but what if she said casual like to someone, "That Ryan who used to live round here, you know the one whose aunt lives at number 46, you'll never guess what he was saying on Facebook the other day…" and somehow it got back to her or my dad. They'd freakin' kill me if they heard about any of that stuff.'

'But they don't know where you live, do they? I thought the court order bans them from having contact with you, till you say you're ready for it.'

'Yeah but that's not the point – there's other stuff. This girl in my class said that paedos track down kids by looking at pictures of them – coz there's usually photos with them or their friends in their school uniform, or some sports team or something. And then they find them and…'

'You need to get it taken down – all your pictures. Everything. Soon as poss,' I urged him.

Ryan let out one of his biggest sighs. 'Don't be daft. If I take my stuff down, then there's all those other kids. Kids with pictures of me on their pages, the football team…'

'Then we'll have to get it all taken down. Everything. I'm sure the police can make people do stuff like that.'

'Oh Holly, sometimes you are so bloody naive,' my brother told me. And hung up.

WEDNESDAY 28 JULY
evening

I rang Jane this morning and she passed me over to Martin coz he's working at home today. And Jane thinks he knows more about the internet than she does (which wouldn't be hard). But I think both of them are out of their depth. Martin says he's still waiting for the police to do something about taking down the horrible website – but he'll get Jane to speak to them again. And he says he'll have a word with the IT guy at work and ask him for advice about Facebook.

Then Martin says he'll call Donald who is Ryan's social worker. Donald is the most sensible man on the entire planet, so this is the best news I've heard in ages. Unlike some of the workers I've had, Donald actually gets things done. He makes the system work – maybe coz he's both committed and difficult, at the same time. I wouldn't want to be a senior manager who said no to Donald when he's made his mind up about something.

And tonight Keesh and me did a night's work at this restaurant called Romano's. This Italian family Keesh's boyfriend knows have set up their own restaurant – really posh looking from the outside. But they've employed their own kids and their cousins, and most of them had pulled a sickie or knew absolutely zero about running a restaurant. There were plates piled up in the kitchen from the last night and a bunch of dead flowers floating in filthy dish water, and the chef was doing his head in when we arrived.

Me and Keesh went through that place like a whirlwind. We gave everyone a job to do – like helping stack the dishwasher or get through that mound of pots and pans in the sink. Then one of the waitresses, who is like this girl of about 14, threw a wobbly coz she said that one of the customers had been rude to her, and she had to be sent home. So Keesh and me took it in turns to work as waitresses (which I've been doing since I was about 13) and we cleaned up about forty pounds in tips.

We brought home about seventy pounds between us what with the night's wages and the tips. We took out a tenner each for bus fares and a tenner to get some food, but the rest went straight in the Bills box, coz there's an electric bill due any day now. The man at the restaurant said he'd probably call us again but you can never be sure, so you've got to act like this is the only money you have, and save everything you can.

Anyway I need to sleep now, coz tomorrow morning Keesh is taking me to meet with Davina.

8pm

I was just getting ready for the meeting with Davina, when the phone rang again. It was Martin, sounding a bit anxious. 'Hey, Hollybear,' he said, so I can tell immediately he's worried. Then he told me that he's still working at home and he'd just got this call from Ryan's last foster carer, Kitty (who Ryan sometimes speaks to on the phone, coz he quite liked her and she's a decent person). She'd been really keen to speak to Martin or Jane – and wanted to make sure that Ryan wasn't about.

'Apparently she'd got a phone call from someone she didn't know and they were asking if she had a current mobile number for Ryan – or his sister,' Martin explained. 'Of course she didn't give them anything – but she said that when she asked who was calling the person hung up. Of course, there could be some perfectly rational explanation, but it did occur to me that with everything else going on ...'

'The thing is that Kitty said the voice sounded strange... sort of muffled... like somebody trying to disguise their voice. But she thought it was definitely female. My worry, Holly, is that it could be Ryan's aunt… but maybe I'm just jumping to conclusions. And as the caller also mentioned you, I thought I'd better check first before I mention it to Donald. Can you think of anyone? Someone you met while you were visiting Ryan at Kitty and Carl's? I mean, there could be some very innocent explanation. Some lad who fancied you and asked his sister…'

My visits to Kitty and Carl's house were hardly occasions for picking up boys. Unless you can call taking your little brother out to the local bowling alley the opportunity for a hot date. And even if boys did check me out, I'm not the type to give anyone my number until I really know them, let alone the landline of my brother's foster carers.

'Nope – can't think of anyone,' I told Martin. 'And yeah, my instinct tells me the same thing. It has to be the Evil Aunt. Did Kitty think to dial the number back?'

'Err… to be honest Hols, I think Kitty's about as phone savvy as me and Jane. Much too old to get with the programme.'

We agree that Martin should call Donald and let him decide what to do. After all, while Ryan's fostered his local authority is technically his "legal parent" and has to make decisions. Well, until Martin and Jane get the OK to become Ryan's "permanent carers", which means they get more say about what happens to him. Martin and Jane were my "permanent carers" so it kind of makes sense for us to "belong" to the same foster family. But Ryan's dad and aunt don't like that idea and they've been making all kinds of fuss about it, so the court can't really do anything yet. Stupid really, coz they're not allowed to know where he lives, but they get to control what happens to him.

Later

OMG! OMG! What else can I say about Keesh's new boss! I guess

Davina is probably in her 60s or she could even be 70 something but it's hard to tell coz she's had so many facelifts. And her silver hair is swept up in a bun that accentuates her very long neck. She was a supermodel when she was young and she's still thin as a rake, and wears these amazing vivid colours and crazy styles, which is probably why she likes Keesha's style so much. She's been in the fashion world for 'simply ages'.

We got to meet the totally mad Davina in the place that's going to be the new shop. It's in this really cool bit of the city, where all the old warehouses are getting bought up to be boutiques and trendy jewellery and handbag shops. The shop is 'divinely fabulous' (to quote Davina). She also says it was 'incredibly cheap – going for peanuts, daahling,' but I guess she's used to prices in London, where everything costs a total fortune.

Davina has really strong ideas about what she wants. 'This is not right!' she roars, when she doesn't like something, but when she does like it she's full of enthusiasm. So it seems that everybody tries hard to please. I heard her yelling at some suppliers on the phone and she's even threatened to sue the decorators for doing such a bad job. Everyone is a little bit frightened of her. Even Keesh, who's never frightened of anyone, is clearly doing her best to stay on the right side of her. Today Keesh signed her contract and she's now officially "manager" of the clothing side of the boutique. The money-side of stuff is being managed by Davina's "boyfriend", who's this wimpy little man who used to be a poet. Or still is or something, but clearly needs the work if his scruffy clothes are anything to judge by. But Davina seems to dote on him and believe he's capable of doing anything. Crazy really from a woman who's clearly a really tough businesswoman. Personally I wouldn't trust him to manage his way out of a paper bag, but love does strange things to some people...

And Davina has a personal assistant called Carly, who's this beautiful tall girl with the longest jet black hair and a dead cheeky sense of humour. I think Carly gets a hard time from Davina. When we were in the toilets, she told Keesh that Davina was 'the worst boss ever – and the best boss ever, but never at the same time,' and she was only working for her till she could afford her place on a film course.

Anyway Davina thought she might have some work for me round the time the store opens. 'We can always do with another pair of hands, daahling,' she said. 'And these frock coats have definite potential... make this one up for me, daahling, so we can see how it hangs...' she said, stabbing with her green-painted nails at the most complicated of all my designs. 'And who knows, we might consider getting them professionally made up. No promises of course, daahling...'

I'm dead excited by all of this. And that fab girl Keesh has promised to make up a pattern for the frock coat and tell me how to sew it. Although she's gonna be travelling all over the place for Davina in the next few weeks and she's gonna be crazy busy.

Sean just rang to say he's on his way with fish and chips. It's his b'day tomorrow so we got plans for a really special day together. Bye bye diary, me and my boyf are going to get all loved up.

Oh yeah – and I tried to ring my brother again, but he didn't answer. He just texted me back to say:

Am fine. Quit fussin sis.

Yeah well, it's easy for him to say. But J and M would let me know if anything seriously bad was happening. That's if Ryan told them, of course. But he wouldn't keep secrets from them, would he? He's too sensible for that these days, isn't he, coz he knows they're dead keen on getting that bullying stuff stopped? Hell! Now I'm really worrying again...

About 3-ish in the morning (in the kitchen with a mug of Horlicks)

What just happened? I was all snuggled up next to my boyf and I fall asleep and dream about Spider Boy!!! I'm at this party and there's no-one I recognise and I can't seem to find Sean or Keesh or any of my mates. Then I see Spider Boy standing all alone – and he's looking at me like he wants to eat me. And he says, 'There you are, Beautiful. I been looking for you all night,' like he owns me or something. And he gets hold of my hand and he leads me into this room where it's all dark and he pushes me down on the bed... And I'm saying "no" with my voice but my body is saying "yes" and he doesn't care anyway, coz he's going to get what he wants. And I realise that I'm in a film or something and that I'm supposed to pretend I don't want this, so I kind of struggle a bit but inside I'm feeling kind of excited coz I secretly do want this. And then the door opens and there's Sleazebag Kevin standing there and he's looking down at us, and he says, 'See, I knew you were a slut, Holly Richards.'

Why did I dream that? I don't know and it's bugging the hell out of me. Which is why I'm writing this down so maybe I can analyse it later. No fear that Sean's going to wake up coz he's sleeping like a dead thing. He was helping his dad in the garage all yesterday and he's that knackered.

I wish I could tell someone about the SB thing but I daren't. So you have to keep my secret, diary. They wouldn't understand and they'd think I was being unfaithful to Sean – which I'm not really. I do love Sean. I know I do.

FRIDAY 30 JULY

No time to write you properly tonight diary. Me and Sean just got back from dinner and he's just taking a shower. And I've put on my hottest PJs...

Last year for Sean's birthday, we went out for a posh dinner, which his dad paid for, and we had this bad argument. This year was much better, really romantic. It was one of those two for one special offer things and we went halves on the bill. But we held hands when we weren't eating our pizzas and we shared a cocktail with two straws. And the restaurant put a candle on Sean's piece of chocolate cake, coz I'd told them it was his birthday.

OK subconscious – no dreams of SB tonight. Just me and Sean and my fab new clothing range.

SATURDAY 31 JULY

Sean left early coz his mum wants to take him out for this "family day", with his dad and some of his other rellies. (Funny how his mum never thinks to ask if he wants to take his girlfriend along on these cozy little family outings.)

Today me and Keesh hit the market stalls. She's turned my men's frock coat design into a paper pattern and she said I had to get it started, soon as possible. We found this gorgeous material that was totally perfect but it was way out of my price range (specially when I'd just lost a whole week's wages). But Keesh said that the material had to be right or it wouldn't look good, and she said we could just about afford it between us if we lived on baked beans for the rest of the week, which was dead nice of her. She also cut the material out for me, which was brilliant. Coz I was terrified I'd cut the wrong bits.

Now it's evening and Keesh is out somewhere with her DJ boyf, and my boyf is having a Chinese meal with his parents. (He sent me this photo. His mum looks a real nightmare in pale yellow. It clashes something hideous with all that fake tan.)

So I'm sitting here trying to sew the material like Keesh showed me, and I nearly hemmed the wrong bit coz the phone rings...

'Nice pictures,' Ryan announces sarcastically, as I answer his call.

'Yer what?' I reply, balancing the phone against my shoulder, so I don't have to stop what I'm doing.

'What's that noise?' Ryan asks.

'A sewing machine,' I tell him. 'What pictures are you talking about?'

'That girlfriend of Leon's – with the whiny kid – she posted these pics on Facebook. You look like you've just seen a ghost and Jane looks like a hippo, and Martin's doing a fair impression of an orangutan with a banana up its bum.' Ryan chuckles unpleasantly. 'But me and Sean look pretty cool so that's OK. And Birthday Boy looks like a startled gerbil.'

'Ah,' I say, pleating the material between my fingers and manoeuvring a tricky seam (Why have I gone and included so many curved panels in my designs?). 'You mean photos from Simon's birthday?'

My brother sighs as though I'm the slowest person on the planet. 'No dumbo, they're pictures of the Queen's garden party.'

But two can play at that game. 'Oh, that's nice,' I said 'Was Jane wearing a big hat and a flowery frock?'

'It's not re...' then Ryan trails off, realising I'm winding him up. 'Yeah, Simon's party. Remember that? Or can your ancient brain not manage back that far?'

'Well, I think I can remember...' I say, concentrating on a bit of fiddly pleating. 'Wasn't there a garden and a house, and some people and some food? Or maybe I'm confusing that with the street party we had at the end of the last War...'

My brother swears softly with exasperation and changes the subject. 'I got some good news sis,' he says, sounding brighter than I've heard him in ages. 'You know that thing with Luke and his mates telling me to keep away from them?'

'Yes,' I said, picturing for a minute some kind of cosy reunion.

'Well this kid – he's called Gareth – has really messed those guys over and they've started this thing against him, sending him texts and the like ... and I saw Luke the other day and he like kind of looked at me without getting all narky with me, and he said, "Gareth has to die – I'll text you his number".'

'Hang on a min,' I said, 'I can see it's good maybe that Luke is talking to you again but there's some other boy getting bullied here, so you can hardly...'

'It's all good,' my brother interrupted. 'Coz it's him, not me... Takes the heat off me, if you see what I'm getting at.'

Yeah, I see what he's getting at. My stupid little brother doesn't care who gets hurt so long as it's not him.

'Ryan Richards,' I said, 'Sometimes you totally shame me! I hope you're not thinking of joining in this text bullying stuff?'

My brother made a non-committal noise.

I see red. And the next minute the words are tumbling out of my mouth. 'You are such a selfish pig,' I yell at him. 'I've just lost my job coz I stood up for you – and you don't give a toss about anyone else! You came into my work and you stole stuff – and like an idiot I didn't believe them. But now I do... I think you'd do anything just to look after Number One.'

There was a long silence at the other end of the phone. Then Ryan said very slowly and deliberately – like he's speaking to a little child. 'That's a bloody lie – I never stole nothing.'

I want to believe him but I'm that mad with him. 'Oh yeah?' I challenge him. 'Is that really the truth? Coz sometimes little bro I don't know who you are any more.'

I heard the silence and knew he'd ended the call.

I need to get on with machining the coat coz it's not going to make itself but I had to write that down, coz it was bugging me so much. Sorry diary. I'll try and write some happy stuff tomorrow.

2pm

I'm all awake and agitated. And it's not like I'm not dead on my feet, coz I did another night at Romano's. (They didn't call me till nearly teatime, saying they needed me and Keesh again, but Keesh couldn't make it coz she's got this cool date at some posh club where her fella is DJing.) It was even more manic at Romano's coz it seems that last night they sacked nearly all the cousins, but at least I knew what was what. And me and the chef, Armando, he's got this professional attitude and him and me got things buzzing tonight. I made lots more tips than last time and split most of them with Armando and this girl they brought in to do the washing up, coz we did all the work.

I think I'm worrying about Ryan if I'm honest. I was hoping I'd find a message from him when I finished my shift but there was nothing. So I texted him again from the bus. But nothing. So I had my shower and thought, let it go, coz he's a moody little B when he chooses to be. And anyway, Jane or Martin would let me know if anything was seriously up with him. It's just that I've been looking out for him all my life and even when we've had big bust-ups in the past we always make up pretty quick once one of us says "sorry". And I've been very grown up about this. I let my temper cool down and then I texted him and said:

Soz I yelled at u. I believe u that u didn't steal. But u can't be bullying that kid – not when we done so much to try n stop it happenin to u. Call me. Love u. Yr Bossy Big Sis

And when I got into bed I just laid there, checking the phone every minute or two to see if he'd replied. It's not like I'm seriously worried he's going to run away again or anything. He wouldn't do that. Not now he's living with J and M.

I got up to check if he'd put any message on FB but there's

nothing. He's not posted for a while now, since he put up a message saying:

Some jokers are putting up stuff that's not from me. Very funny guys. Goin' offline til they grow up.

But I see something there that makes me really worry. Someone's put up some more messages. Again there are three – and again they are full of crazy stuff I can't imagine my brother ever saying:

I knew this bird called Josie. (You fit, Josie, like your pictures, babes) But when she said she'd give me one, I said freak off, coz my heart belongs to Mr Stephens

My real dad's called Dave and him and my aunt they beat me with this belt. But I like it coz I'm pervy like that

Guess what? My mum's a dirty slag and she never got out of bed. That's why they put me in care. That and coz I was a queer.

I wondered if Ryan had seen these. And I wondered who that girl Josie was. Was she some other girl he'd turned down with all the subtlety he'd used with that girl Natalie? Just how many seriously peed-off girls were there out there? And were they now ganging up to get their own back? I took a look at this girl's profile and yes, she was really pretty. But she looked about three years older than my brother and there were pics of her with a guy who looked like her boyf. Then I saw she was from Newcastle. Which is where Ryan's real dad lives. And the totally crazy aunt and granny.

Coincidence or what?

There were also some replies on Ryan's page. Some kids were laughing at him but some were saying supportive or friendly things. Among these was a message from this Josie:

Hey Our Kid! What's goin on???? Call me coz I fink we need 2 talk

Personally I think it's time my brother cancelled his FB page but I guess that would be hard. I heard once that for someone under 16 to have their phone or FB page stopped is like having their arms or legs cut off. Thank god I'm an adult and not hooked on this stuff.

I sent Ryan a message saying:

Saw the FB stuff. You need to talk about it, little bro? Who this Josie?

And while I was checking my own FB I saw those photos that Ryan was telling me about, the ones from Simon's party. Yeah, Ryan is right. Him and Sean are about the only ones looking good in the pics. I definitely look like I've seen a ghost and little Si does look a bit like a gerbil. But I'm not sure those pics of Si should be up there, although he's almost adopted now. But Ryan's pics shouldn't be up there coz he's definitely still in foster care. And Leon's girlfriend's gone and tagged most of us and written this stuff about how it was Simon's birthday and the party being in Corrington and everything and how there are rellies and foster kids in the pics, and how it's all cool... And my little brother needs info about him on the internet like a hole in the head at the moment. But I guess that Tracey/Stacey doesn't know these things coz maybe the law's different where she comes from.

Then I found this message that completely freaked me. It's a friend invite from Spider Boy. Like I'd want to be his friend! But if I turn him down then it might look a bit weird. But what if he sent me some suggestive kind of message and Sean saw it? I don't want to have to lie to Sean. I just don't want him to know anything about it. I guess I'll ignore it till tomorrow or something. I don't have to decide now.

Nothing for it – I need some of that brandy Keesh has in the cupboard from when we made those cocktails. Maybe I'll have it in some hot milk like I used to have when I was a kid.

Woke up to a message from Ryan that read:

Chill out, Hols. I knew bout those new messages. I don't give a monkey's... Josie is that girl I knew when I was living at my aunts. I tole u about her a million times

Which makes me worry even more. I hate it when my brother's trying so hard to pretend he doesn't care.

Sewing all day long. And Keesh helped a bit this afternoon. She met Davina at the shop this morning and she was full of stories of how Davina hates the shade of lilac of the tissue paper they've got for wrapping clothes in. And how Davina thinks the door handle shaped like a sea serpent is 'so wonderful' she could 'simply die'.

This evening Sean picked me up and we went over to Lucy and Nathan's for a big pot roast thing, which was way too spicy and a bit burnt (Nathan is an awful cook) but we ate it coz we were hungry. After Lucy put Ruby to bed we all sat down to watch this DVD which a mate of Nathe's at the summer camp had lent him.

'The guy said dis was dead funny,' Nathe said, uncertainly after we'd spent ten minutes watching a lot of American college boys running round making stupid jokes about their private parts.

'We can watch *Love Actually*,' Lucy offered, opening one eye. The boys just groaned.

Nathe flicked through a range of TV channels until we eventually agreed that MTV was one of the better options.

'When we gonna see you on there, mate?' Nathe asked Sean, as we watched a band that sounded a bit like The Static.

'Probably not ever,' Sean shrugged modestly. 'We're just small time.'

'No you're not!' Lucy said, stretching like a cat. 'You're big – an' getting bigger.'

Sean shook his head laughing. 'I wish.'

'She's right, mate,' Nathe joined in. 'You got dem fan websites now ... and all dose girls are goin' mad for you.'

'What websites?' I asked. What was I missing here?

Lucy turned to stare at me, but the effect was ruined by a big yawn.

Nathe waggled a finger at me. 'You mean you don't know, girl!'

'Coz those girlies are gonna eat your man alive...' Lucy teased.

So of course I insisted I had to see these websites. And there were two of them. 'Fans of The Static' and 'Static Reaction' as well as the band's official website, which the drummer's dad manages.

'See – girls drooling over him,' Lucy said, waving a hand at a screen full of silly gushy comments and some almost frankly indecent suggestions from women who should know better.

I flicked through the comments, but there was nothing there to suggest that any of these women had actually got their hands on my boyf. Then I clicked onto the photos page and got a bit of a shock.

'What am I – we – doing on there?' I demanded, as a blown-up picture of Simon's b'day party appeared on screen.

'Oh yeah – I meant to tell Mum about that,' Lucy said. 'I don't think Ryan and Simon should be on there.'

'You're so right! Did you put this up there?' I glared at Sean.

'What? No, I just saw it for the first time.' Sean looked very uncomfortable. 'Fans are so clever, Holly – it's something I've been realising since we got a little bit famous... They've got this way of finding out so much about you. I saw something they'd found the other day – some pics of me at my cousin's party, about two years ago... Fortunately I wasn't snogging anyone or anything you'd disapprove of...'

'Glad to hear it!' I replied. 'And this pic of Ryan and Si has to come down,' I said, and Lucy nodded. 'You can't go putting up pics of foster kids like that. You don't know who could see it...'

'Yeah – but how?' Nathe shrugged his shoulders. 'I mean my social worker did her nut once when someone put some pics of the school concert in the local paper and nobody checked dat me and Keesh was allowed to be in it... But dis is Facebook – and the pics was put up by someone from your family, Luce.'

'That woman isn't family,' Lucy told him, stiffly. She's always been a bit iffy about her brother's partners coz she spent so many years being their spoilt little sister. 'Mum an' Dad will have to speak to her. She's got to take them down.'

'Sure – but dem pics could be anywhere,' Nathan shrugged. 'Half the fans could've downloaded dem and put dem on their bedroom wall...'

'Oh god, Holly, I'm so sorry,' Sean turned to me with anxious eyes.

But it wasn't really his fault. 'Don't let's panic,' I said. 'What's the likelihood that Ryan's dad or that mad aunt or granny of his go anywhere near this website? Honestly I don't think they even own a computer.'

'Yeah but people can trace you – like through addresses and website mentions and stuff. I read this thing about some people dat traced their long-lost nephew to this likkle village in Scotland where he'd got adopted …'

'That isn't helping!' Lucy gave Nathe her best cross voice. The one she uses when Ruby holds onto her nose and won't let go.

'But you got to think of it from de parents' point of view,' Nathan continued. 'They don't ask social services to take their kids away – so it's no wonder they go lookin' for their kids.'

And Lucy nodded wisely. 'Yeah, I don't know what the big fuss is all about,' she said. 'I mean it's not like Ryan's dad was a psycho or anything, was he? Mum always says it's good for kids to have contact with their parents… even if the parents haven't always been saints.'

'It's complicated,' I told Lucy. 'The thing is that Ryan really doesn't want to see his dad or the mad aunt or his granny, not at this time in his life because, well, because it brings back bad memories. And he's dead afraid that his dad might kill him if he finds out he's gay.'

'Yeah but surely he wouldn't?' Sean was joining in the conversation now. 'My dad's brother always said he'd disown any kid of his who turned out to be a "poof" – his word, not mine – but when he found his eldest boy had been living with this bloke for two or three years, well, his first question was, "Why didn't you tell me about it son?" '

'My mam threatened all kinds of stuff whenever we done anything she din't like, but she never done it,' Nathan offered. 'She used to say she'd kill us if we did dis or dat. She was real strict. But we always knew she loved us…'

Keesh and Nathe were born in one of those countries in Africa that's always at war (I can't remember which one coz I was never any good at geography but I think it was near the Congo or some place like that). Their mum brought them to England when they were really little. Their village was overrun by a local army and a lot of the women got raped and horrible stuff… and their mum decided it wasn't safe to stay. But soon after she came here she found out she was HIV positive and she got more and more ill, which is why the two of them spent most of their childhood living in care. Then she died when they were about ten years old. They hardly ever spoke about her coz it was too painful, but Nathe told me about her once, when he was feeling really down about it.

'Your mum was a good person, a really good person, Nathe...' I found that a lump was forming in my throat as I said this. 'She loved you and your sister so much ... I think deep down my mum still loves me and Ryan, cept she's too ill to show it. But not everyone's got parents like that...'

Nathan shrugged. 'I guess dat is true. But you sayin' Ryan's dad don't love him coz he act a bit crazy sometimes? Dat he's better off without his dad?' Nathe wasn't picking an argument, coz he's not the type. He just genuinely wanted to understand why Ryan was so keen not to see his dad. 'Isn't it better to have a dad like that, than no dad at all? Least he wants to see Ryan, take the trouble to go to court and all dat stuff.'

Now it was my time to shrug. 'I really don't know,' I replied, giving Nathan the most honest answer I could. 'But I do know that Ryan's genuinely scared of his dad – and his aunt, and that barmy old granny. And that's enough for me. I don't think anyone should be made to see someone if they're really frightened of them. And I don't understand why Ryan's aunt and dad are so crazy to be in touch with him, when they never have a nice thing to say to him. Maybe it's just possessiveness or being in control of kids or something. After all, they used to hit him, and all that.'

'Surely you've got to admit that some parents are just monsters?' Sean said. 'Look at those parents of poor little Si's. Half of them in prison for violent crimes and the other half waiting trial for armed robbery or whatever... if what you told me is true, Holly?'

I felt a surge of anger towards my boyf. 'I hope you include your own mother in the monster category!' I snapped at him. I shouldn't really have told him anything about Si's family coz a kid's family history is private stuff, but it was the best way to explain why Simon was so strange sometimes. But Sean also had no right to start judging other people's families. He's never been in care and he has no idea how it feels to love your parents and be mad with them at the same time.

Sean held up his hands in a gesture of apology. 'Sorry Hols,' he said. 'I probably shouldn't have said that. And yes – my mother is definitely in the creature from the black lagoon category.'

'Yeah well,' I said, coz it's hard to stay cross with someone like Sean for long. 'At least your mum's got fire in her belly. That wimpy dad of mine just slunk off to America and forgot about me.'

I rang Jane this morning and gave her the latest updates on the photos and stuff. And I've decided I'm not going to worry any more. I've done everything I can. If Ryan's family really want to find him they probably could anyway. I read in one of those fostering mags of Jane's that some parents whose kids have been taken away from them put up adverts on the internet saying their kids have been abducted and has anyone seen them, and showing photos of them. Then people think it's a real kidnap or something and they start looking out for the kid, and in some cases someone spots the kid and tells the birth parents.

Anyway I've got things of my own to worry about. I've had Dan on the phone half the morning wanting my advice about whether he should get back together with Rani. I told him not to be so daft coz she's really not his type and he was better off without her. But he'd bumped into her when he was out with his mates last night and his heart had done this little bound when he saw her.

'An' she had this guy with her,' Dan told me, sounding completely outraged. 'This bloke I'd never met before. She didn't introduce me or anything... and he was just hanging around... it wasn't till she was leaving that she said it was her cousin.'

I was about to say that meant nothing coz in some cultures it's considered fine to marry your cousin, but I didn't think that Dan would appreciate that. Neither is it really any good me telling him that he'd be much better off with a girl like that nice Kelly, who's always hanging around him and clearly thinks the sun shines out of his bum. She's cute and nice and a good laugh to be with, and she doesn't have pushy parents or always need to be the best at everything. But she isn't Rani.

'Rani gave me her number – her new mobile number. I mean she didn't have to do that, did she? It must mean she at least still wants to be friends, doesn't it? ' Dan was almost pleading with me on the phone.

'And do you really want to be her friend?' I asked, wondering why men are sometimes such fools. 'I thought you said you'd have nothing in common with her if you didn't really fancy her.'

'I also heard from my mate Keith that that James – the one you call Spiders Legs or whatever – had asked her out but apparently she said "no". You'd think he'd be just the right type for her: ambitious, pushy – all that stuff. Do you think that's coz she's still got a bit of a thing for me?' Dan asked me hopefully.

I felt a brief twinge of something which I couldn't identify. 'Those two deserve each other,' I said sharply, but then regretted it. 'Look, Dan. If you really still think you like Rani, then why don't you arrange to have a drink or something? Meet her at the pub for a cosy little chat.'

'She doesn't go to the pub. Her family don't allow it.'

'OK, then a coffee – or before you tell me that her family doesn't allow caffeine either, then a sparkling water or a nice cup of herbal whatsit... But the point is, Dan. Do you *really* like this girl?'

'Not as much as I like you, Holly,' Dan replies. And there's something in his tone which freaks me out. I love Dan dearly but he's just a mate. We've always been clear about that, haven't we?

I think Dan sensed my reaction, coz he laughed. 'It's OK Holly, I'm not getting all loved up about you, if that's what you're thinking. It's just that you're my mate and I really like being with you and I don't like Rani half as much as I like you... But I've kind of got this thing about Rani and I can't get her out of my system.'

So really I was none the wiser about anything. Anyway it was all too much for a Monday morning and I told Dan this. But he only promised to get off the phone after I agreed to go with him to Amber's party coz he knew Rani was going to be there. I think it's next week some time. I better check it in my diary.

And today I got another text from SB. It says:

You haven't accepted my FB request. R u avoiding me, Beautiful?

I don't have time for this craziness. So I just text'd back:

Ha ha

OK, it wasn't clever and it wasn't funny but I didn't know what else to say.

I then got this call from Romano's asking if I could do tonight and tomorrow, and I wanted to say no coz I've got to finish this coat and it's like taking forever. But Keesh said something the other night about Romano's recruiting proper new staff, so maybe this temp work won't be going on for ever. Anyway they might take me on and I don't want to ruin my chances by not showing up. And anyway we've hardly got any food left in the house and I really need some money.

It was a bit quieter than the last time coz nobody much goes out on a Monday night, but there was this big family there celebrating a wedding anniversary, and they drank a lot and left a really big tip.

And on the bus coming home I got another text from SB:

I'm waitin babes. When will I c u?

I wanted to text back 'never' but that's daft coz I'll have to see him next term anyway. So it's not like I can ignore him altogether.

But I'll think of something funny or clever to say tomorrow. For now I'm going to sleep and I'm not thinking or dreaming about anybody tonight. I'm way, way too tired.

Night, night diary.

TUESDAY 3 AUGUST

I spent most of the day on the coat, sewing on some more of the trimmings and the binding. It's almost finished now – I've just got some really fiddly machining bits still to do. I'm so proud of what I'm making. OK, Keesh helped me a lot with the pattern and the sewing and stuff, but the idea behind the design was all mine.

And I sent pics to Sean who said it was 'genius' and told me that I was the most amazing girlfriend in the world, and how much he loves me. And Lucy sent me a text saying, *Babes – u r sooooo clever.*

But Ryan sent me an out-of-credit message asking me to ring him.

I called him straight away, with a sinking feeling in the pit of my stomach.

'I know who it is,' my brother announced, soon as he answered the phone.

'Who WHAT is?' I demanded, irritated but mainly coz of the butterflies in my stomach.

Ryan did one of his dramatic sighs. 'Him – my cyberstalker! The guy wot set up the website. An' stole Mr Stephens's phone. An' all that stuff.'

The bottom of my stomach stopped its stupid dipping stuff. 'So?' I asked, 'who is it?'

'Gareth,' my brother replied. 'And before you say "Gareth who?" he's the kid that Luke says has gotta die. Seems Luke knew well before me who was doing that creepy website stuff.'

'Ah,' I said. 'And just how did you find this out? D'you know for sure it's really him?'

'Sure. It's definitely him. Cos Tiffany told me.'

'And Tiffany is... er, I do remember you mentioning her before but...'

Another sigh from Ryan. 'Yeah but your elderly brain can't hold it all in sis. It's OK we know that... Anyway, Tiffany is the best friend of that girl Natalie. She's the one who told me I was in for it and they'd get me...'

OK, I was following this so far. But why, I wondered aloud, was Tiffany telling Ryan about this now.

'Coz Gareth is Tiffany's cousin and she got him to do this stuff – coz he really fancied Natalie. Seems he was that jealous of me coz Nat made it clear she fancied me. And coz I got some brains where he's a total no-brainer,' my brother announced smugly. 'Anyway, seems he's also a thief, coz he nicked my memory stick – hoping he'd like find something he could use on me...'

'And then you went and slagged off Natalie on Facebook – and No-Brains Gareth uses his lack of brains and the info on your memory stick. To create an untraceable website and nab Mr Stephens's phone,' I remarked. But the irony seemed lost on my brother – who continued...

'But recently, Tiff and Nat had this major row – and Natalie's gone and told Luke about the website and stuff. Coz she's now going out with Luke.'

OMG – these teenagers. One minute they're like worst enemies with someone and getting their friends to trash them on websites. They they're going out with one of them and dropping their other friends in the crap, coz they've had a bit of a falling out. Sometimes I'm so glad I'm not young any more.

'Yeah, but there's still something I don't completely understand,' I told my brother, knowing I'll risk an even bigger sigh this time. 'Just why did Tiffany tell you all this? What's in it for her to diss Gareth to you?'

But Ryan didn't sigh. Instead he told me smugly, 'Coz Tiffany apparently fancies me. And she was only pretending to be mad at me coz she wanted to stay friends with Natalie.'

'Please tell me you haven't gone and put something awful about Tiffany on FB?' I pleaded with my brother, remembering the tactful way he'd handled Natalie's declaration of fancying him.

'No. Actually Tiff is alright. She thinks that Gareth is a real loser... I mean it's not like I fancy her or anything but she's pretty cool. She's got this room at her house with a pool table and all these computer games. And her dad collects old-fashioned slot machines and stuff. So I said we might hang out together sometime. I'm not a total idiot you know, little sis!'

Good to hear it little bro! I just hope it stays that way.

After Ryan rang off I went online and took a look. The vile website had vanished and there was no new stuff on Ryan's FB page. Incident over. Well, at least I hoped so.

Only bad thing was that Romano's cancelled because they said they found a permanent waitress. Oh well, even more time to spend on my sewing.

WEDNESDAY 4 AUGUST

Romano's rang this morning to say the new waitress didn't work out and they'd told her not to come back. So could I do this evening? I needed the money so I said yes.

I was planning a fairly laid back day, doing a bit of reading and painting and finishing off the frock coat, so I could show it to Davina. Then about 4.15pm I get a frantic phone message from my brother.

'It's all kickin' off – me and Tiffany was hangin' out in the shopping centre and then we saw 'em. Luke an his mates. An Gareth was wiv them...'

'What? But I thought Luke hated Gareth coz of the website?' I really couldn't keep up with these teenage politics.

'Yeah but that's coz Gareth told Luke that he only made the website coz he wanted Luke to know what a "poof" I was and how I had these pervy ideas about him...'

'And Luke believes that!' These kids are even stupider than I realised.

'Yeah – well, maybe. I dunno for sure. But the thing is that Luke and Gareth say they're gonna kill me. Luke said he got a knife...'

'They said WHAT?' My stomach was doing painful gymnastics again. 'Where are you now? I mean – I hope you're well out of that place. Shouldn't you call the police or...'

'Shut up Holly. Just listen to me!' My brother sounded pretty desperate, so I did what he said. And he told me that he and Tiffany were stuck in Carphone Warehouse – with a whole gang of boys outside, just waiting to get them. Seems they'd made a run for it and some security guy had stopped Gareth going into the store. But they were holed up in there, like rats in a trap.

'An' Luke an Gareth keep texting me stuff – like how they're gonna stick me in the guts. They say Tiff can go free an' they won't harm her – but if I call anyone like the police or her dad, or Martin and Jane, then they'll get both of us. Maybe not today, but some other time – and Tiff is dead scared coz she says that Gareth always does what he sez he's gonna do... I really don't know what to do Hol...'

And to be honest I was finding it hard to think clearly myself. Which is probably why I said, 'Hang on Ryan. I'm comin' to get you.'

I heard a silence from the end of the phone. 'You still there?' I demanded.

'Yeah sure – but I was thinkin' sis. I mean I don't want you getting involved in this. Best you don't come here. And I think Tiff should go now... coz whatever happens someone's gonna get hurt – so probably best if it's just me.'

And then I was so proud of my brother I thought my heart would burst. 'Yeah, let Tiff go – but maybe tell her to get her dad or something. Or her parents could call the police,' I suggested. Even I wasn't naive enough to think the police would take much notice of a few kids calling to say they thought someone was going to knife them if they left a shop.

I heard Ryan laugh, a hopeless kind of laugh. 'Not gonna happen,' he replied. So I guess Tiff's family probably aren't exactly on speaking terms with the police. And I did remember Ryan saying that Tiff's dad had a bit of a rep for drug dealing or some other criminal stuff. Maybe that explains the flash games room they've got.

'Look – just stay there, I'm coming. I'll get a taxi or something... Maybe I can find a policeman or something when I get there.'

Ryan told me not to bother, but I was out of there immediately. The money I had in my purse was for food and bills but there was no time for the bus, so I spent it on a taxi fare. On the way, in the cab, I did try to call 999 but the reception was crap. And when I got through to an operator she started asking really difficult questions – like what did these boys look like and was I absolutely sure this wasn't someone playing a pathetic joke. I tried to make her realise it was serious, but I guess they get quite a lot of hoax calls. In the end I gave up coz the cab was at the shopping centre, and time was running out. It was nearly 5pm and Ryan would get chucked out of the shop any minute. I kept glancing around to see if there were any police – there are always police around when you don't really want them. But just my luck, I couldn't see any today. Oh well, if it came to it I'd have to get some of the security guys from the shops involved. I could always bat an eyelid or something. It was the only plan I had.

There were several gangs of kids hanging around in the marketplace outside Carphone Warehouse. They were all trying to look cool and a bit menacing, in that scowling, hands in the pockets way that teenage boys are so brilliant at. But I hadn't any idea who my brother's potential "attackers" were. I saw a boy – about 16ish, tall and kind of pretty in that arrogant way some girls find cute, who I guessed from my brother's descriptions could be Luke. And this kid who looked a bit like a weasel and a computer nerd rolled into one, who might be Gareth but I couldn't be sure. I hoped he might be coz he didn't exactly look like he'd be much cop in a fight.

I decided to walk straight into the shop and find my brother and then make a plan. Maybe ask the security bloke if there was a back door he could let us out through. But before I got more than about 20 yards near the shop, I saw my brother walking out. His head held high, his hands thrust in his pockets. Trying to look all kind of nonchalant.

And as he comes out I see the "buzz" starting to form in one of the clusters of kids. The tall guy is stepping forward – so I'd been right about him being Luke. And there's also another kid moving out from the group. Not the nerdy kid but a solid, chunky kind of boy with a nasty smile on his face, who has to be Gareth.

And I see something else as well. A flash of brightness by Luke's side, something that catches the light as he moves. He hasn't been lying about carrying a knife. And Ryan continues walking calmly towards him.

I want to scream at my brother 'Run!' but the words stick in my mouth. I've heard that many knifings happen in seconds, before the victim realises what's happened. So as the hot blood is pumping out of their bodies, they're standing there thinking 'Did someone just hit me?'

Meanwhile my brother just keeps walking straight towards Luke. And Luke has a look about him, a look of such certainty. The total madness of someone who believes it's OK to mercilessly stick a steel blade into the warm flesh of another human being. All those thoughts go through my head as the slow-motion drama plays out before me. My brother walking so calmly, Luke standing so confidently, Gareth hanging around a bit to the side, full of swagger. But less certain.

'How can you do this?' I'm screaming inside my head. My words meant for Luke and Luke alone. 'You're one of us. You're in foster care. How can you turn on one of your own?'

And my brother is now standing before him, a look on his face that I can't really describe. It isn't exactly resignation, it's not bravado – just the calm look of someone who is facing up to something because they've run out of options and can't think of anything else to do.

I can see the glint of the blade Luke is holding by his side. I know he only has to move once – just once – and my brother could be lying in a pool of blood. And still I do nothing but stand and watch, as the slow-motion film story plays out before my eyes.

Then I see that my brother is speaking. And his eyes are clear and his chin is raised. This is the bravery of the cornered animal, who fights back because there is nowhere else to run. And I can catch some of the words as they tumble angrily from his lips. And he is saying, 'I wouldn't fancy you Luke Watson if you were the last bloke on this planet! So don't bloody flatter yourself...'

And Luke is just standing there, motionless with amazement. He knows the joker Ryan, the quirky, ducking and diving Ryan who slips and slides his way through life, walking close to the wind but never stepping into the gale. But he's never seen this Ryan before. My brave, mad brother facing up to him. My crazy, crazy brother, who any moment now could get a knife stuck through his ribs.

And then my brother turns and now he's aiming all his spite at Gareth. 'And as for you,' I hear him rage, 'You know what you are? You're a bully and a coward. I know how you used to pick on the really little kids when you was in primary school. Everyone knows about how you hit that little lad who was only half your size... smashed his glasses while he was still wearing them, so he got glass in his eye and nearly went blind... And nobody dared tell on you coz they thought you might do it to them. And didn't you think it was hilarious! Think you're so clever, just coz you know how to do some stuff on the computer? Well listen up, Gareth No-Brains – you're not as freakin' clever as you think.'

I'm waiting for something terrible to happen. For Gareth to punch out with one of those meaty fists he's clenched by his side; for Luke to slide in, blade in hand; for my brother to be injured, killed... and I know that I must move and do something, anything to stop my brother getting hurt. But my feet won't move and it's like I'm only a spectator watching from the front row. I can't step into the film set because it was filmed in another time, another place.

Then I see the look on Luke's face, a look of amusement and mild surprise. And I see him slip the knife back into his pocket.

'Oh my, Gareth Brown,' he says, directing his scorn at the boy beside him. 'You really are as pathetic as they say you are!'

What is he trying to do? I wonder if he's hoping that Gareth will lose his rag and flatten my brother. Do the dirty work for both of them? But then I see that Luke is turning away. 'OK folks,' he says, addressing the other kids, who are hanging around uncertainly. 'Nothing more to see. Fraid the show is over. Time for a ciggy break and then maybe some light shoplifting before the supermarkets close. We need some booze for tonight's party...'

And then Luke and his posse are gone. And it's just Gareth and my brother standing in the market place and my brother is now calling Gareth every obscene name under the sun and Gareth is just standing there in a daze. Like he can't believe this wiry boy is standing up to his bulk. And the whole scenario is being watched idly by some of the other kids from other groups who maybe hope there's some more entertainment coming.

Enough, I think, and my feet start moving again. I march straight up to my brother and grab his arm, pulling him out of Gareth's reach. And now I turn on Gareth. 'And you,' I tell him, venting my relief as much as my anger. 'You are in the biggest trouble imaginable. Cyber bullying is against the law and I'm reporting you to the police... and you'll be lucky if you don't end up getting sent to a remand home, or something... '

Gareth snarls something obscene at me and walks off. Or should I say slopes off. He reminds me of a puppy that's just been smacked for raiding the biscuit tin.

I hug my brother before I shake him. I don't know whether I'm proud or furious with him for taking such a stupid risk. But it doesn't matter. He's alive and breathing and that's all I care about.

We got chips and went and sat in the park. Ryan was ravenously hungry but I could barely eat. We didn't say much because there wasn't much to say.

Then I took him back to Jane and Martin's and I told them what had happened. Jane took notes and said she would 'deal with it' and she was ringing the police station when I left. I had to get home and change before going to Romano's.

It wasn't a good evening or a particularly bad evening at the restaurant. But I was glad to be busy. On the way home I got a text from Ryan saying:

Fanks sis, 4 comin 4 me. You wont belv what hapnd!!!! Luke sent me this mesag sayin i ws braver than e thort. An wld I be his mate agen? LOL!

I text back to say I hope my brother isn't going to be such a fool. But he texts me back to say he just textd Luke to say '*lets wait n see*' which is rather a good answer really. My brother is more of a diplomat than I give him credit for.

THURSDAY 5 AUGUST

The most delicious news ever!!! I got this text from Nessa which said:

You might want to buy a copy of the Gazette. Ring me when you've read it.

We've been texting a bit since I left the garden centre but just gossip, like how Sleazebag had been really miffed that his mum appointed a bloke to replace me. Guess he was hoping he'd get another girl to hassle.

I rushed out to the shop and there it was – on the front page.

'Local man arrested for role in national vice gang'

And there's this picture of Kevin's ugly mug, all smug and leery. I think it's one from the garden centre website coz I'm sure I've seen it before.

I bought the paper and treated myself to breakfast in the local café, so I could read it in peace.

Not only was Sleazebag mixed up in some money scam, but he'd also been involved in a vice ring – where they bring these poor girls over from Eastern Europe and tell them they're coming to a better life here, then make them work as prostitutes. The police had done some raids and there was all this stuff on Kevin's computer. Funny really, I couldn't imagine Kevin having enough of a brain cell to be involved in something like that. Shows you can never judge people by their looks.

Then there was a quote from Marje saying, 'I just can't believe it. My son is a good boy, he wouldn't get mixed up in things like that.' But then there were quotes from a couple of local people, like this guy in the pub who said, 'He's always been a bit of a dark horse. So no one's really surprised to hear this.'

I rang Nessa straight away and we had the best gossip! She should have been stacking pots but Marje wasn't around (probably trying to find a solicitor who's grubby enough to defend her baby boy) so there was nobody to tell her to get on with the job. She says that Marje is really cut up and some of the staff feel a bit sorry for her coz she's old and Kevin's the only family she's got left. But I don't feel sorry for her at all. She knew I was a hard worker and I wasn't a liar, but she chose to believe her lying slug of a son instead of me, so I can't waste my sympathy on her.

Tonight Sean picked me up from Romano's in his dad's car. He brought some wine to celebrate the news about Sleazebag. OK, some people might say that was mean but I don't care. We're celebrating the fact that there is still some justice in the world.

So all in all another good day – apart from just one thing. SB has been pestering me again. He's sent me a text saying:

See you at Amber's party tomoro

To be honest I'd almost forgot – or I'd thought it was next week or something coz time has gone so fast. Amber is this dead nice girl on our course and everyone likes her. And she likes everyone. So all my college friends will be there. And I think I promised Dan I'd go with him.

So I textd back to SB to say:

Sure. Me and my boyf wl be goin

But when I told Sean about the party he said he was sorry but he wasn't gonna be around. He and the band are performing at a gig in London tomorrow night. I have this feeling he told me about it but with everything else on my mind I'd completely forgotten. I felt dead guilty and I said I'd go with him if he wanted, but he said there was no room in the car and besides, they were staying at the drummer's uncle's place. And I shouldn't waste my money on train fares to London, coz they'd be performing round here again soon and I could see him then.

And that made me feel a bit uneasy coz I started thinking about that girl who said she'd got it on with Sean at one of the gigs and I started wondering if maybe that was why he didn't want me around. But he's right, I can't afford to waste money on the fare, not with my phone bill to pay and those new course materials I have to order...

It didn't help when SB textd again and said:

Ha ha ha – sure he is, Beautiful!

If I hadn't promised Dan I'd go with him, I'd cancel. I swear it.

SATURDAY 7 AUGUST

This is like the worst day of my life, ever.

Yesterday was like a good day to begin with. Keesh was celebrating that she's started working full time for Davina, and her boyf came over and he brought a bottle of vodka and orange juice and we made these cocktails...

Then about 8 o'clock they said they had to go as the boyf is DJing at this celeb party tonight, and did I want to go with them. But Dan rang me earlier to tell me he'd got his hair cut coz he knows Rani likes it when he's just had it done and he was all excited about seeing her, so I couldn't really let him down.

I didn't make that much effort dressing for the party, coz it wasn't like I had anyone to impress. I wore that short leather skirt of Keesh's that she sometimes lets me borrow and my red boots, and I put my hair up in this kind of bun thing, with bits falling down the back. And I tried not to think about Sean and whether some girl was feeding him olives on sticks. (Yeah that was silly, coz Sean doesn't even like olives but that's the kind of thing I picture those groupies doing.) And then he sent me a text saying:

Its so cool here Hols. The audience look awesome. Can't wait to play for them. Love u heaps

And instead of feeling reassured I decided this meant there were plenty of hot girls in the audience, and before I'd even got into Dan's mate's car I was picturing Sean snogging one of the olive-feeders who had curly blonde hair and great big blue eyes and a chest you could rest a tea tray on. (Actually I don't think he even likes girls like that.)

At the party I tried to stay out of SB's way, but he spotted me almost as soon as I arrived. He kind of nodded to me but didn't come over, so I just pretended I hadn't seen him. And anyway I was too busy psyching Dan up to decide when he should go and talk to Rani (but she came and spoke to him first and they were standing really close and she was leaning on his shoulder, and I wasn't surprised to see that very soon they were snogging the tonsils off each other). I ended up hanging out with some of the girls on my course and we were having a bit of a laugh and I broke my resolution not to drink any more and I had this big glass of wine which I told myself I would make last all evening, but somehow it got topped up a few times, and I didn't really notice...

I felt his breath on my cheek and his hands as he moved my hair. And his lips touching the side of my neck. I wanted to shake him off and tell him not to touch me, but the weird thing was that I was really liking the feel of his mouth against my skin. And before I knew it I'd turned to face him, and we were clasped together, kissing each other like we were sucking the oxygen out of each other's lungs. And all the time the alcohol was singing in my head and nothing felt real, except the idea that somewhere Sean was snogging a girl with blonde hair and huge mammary glands.

I don't know when I left the party but SB got us a taxi (I think he's definitely got rich parents coz he doesn't seem to have a summer job). And we went back to his bedsit and I don't remember very much after that. Well, I do remember but I don't really want to – except that I was trying not to think and it was kind of exciting and dangerous and totally unreal. And although he's not really that good a kisser, he had this way of undressing me that was like something in a film, and it made me feel kind of giddy with excitement. But I remember when he took his shirt off I looked at him and thought, 'You're not really my type' and everything after that was a bit of a disappointment.

Waking up with a hangover and a guilty conscience is bad enough. Waking up beside a boy who you don't really fancy is a million times worse, especially when he's all grey and peaky in the sunlight, and his hair is a total mess coz he normally gels it so much and it's now just sticky and flat. And when he reached out an arm and tried to pull me towards him I remembered what a poor lover he was and how Sean was so much better and more considerate, and I realised then how much I loved Sean. And I hated myself for being there.

I said I had a job to go to and had to get home. But SB just laughed and said he didn't believe me and that I couldn't go now coz he was "all hot" for me. I said that wasn't the point and that I needed to leave. I was halfway out of the bed when he turned over and grabbed my wrists. He kind of half dragged me back onto the bed and he was lying on top of me. He's a skinny boy but he's still a boy and his bones are bigger and heavier than mine, and I panicked as I felt myself trapped underneath him.

'Get off,' I told him, like I was pretending this was some joke or something. 'I really have got to go… or I'll lose my job.'

But he just laughed and tried to kiss my neck, still holding my hands pinned to either side of me.

I squirmed to move my head away from him. 'Let go of me,' I said, very firmly this time. 'I have to go to work.'

SB laughed, a really arrogant kind of laugh. 'No one goes to work in a skirt like that,' he said nodding towards Keesh's leather skirt, which I'd managed to hang on the back of a chair (she'd kill me if it got damaged).

'Yeah well, I got to change first,' I said. 'I need to go home and shower and dress and ...'

But SB wasn't listening. He covered my lips with his and his breath stank of fags and stale beer. He shoved his tongue into my mouth. So I bit it. Not very hard, just enough to make my point.

'Bitch!' SP was staring into my eyes, looking totally furious. 'Why did you do that?'

'Because you're pinning me down and I have to go home. I haven't got time for this nonsense...' I hoped I sounded braver than I felt.

'You didn't think it was "nonsense" last night,' the boy lying on top of me said, with a nasty little smile on his face. He was still holding my wrists and it was beginning to hurt where he was cutting the blood supply off.

'Yeah but that was last night – and things were ... different. I'm a bit more sober now. And I want to go home.'

'And you can go home ... but not just yet. Coz I haven't finished with you yet, Holly Richards...' And again he tried to kiss me.

But I struggled really hard this time. I rolled sideways and caught him on the chin with one of my elbows. 'Just get off me and let me go home,' I yelled at him, still sounding much braver than I felt.

He took his hand away for a moment and rubbed his chin. Before rolling his full weight onto me again and pinning my arm even harder than before. 'That really hurt,' SB said, sounding almost shocked that I could do such a thing to his precious face. 'Lots of girls would give their right arm to be here, now with me. You should think yourself lucky.'

'First, I'm not lots of girls... and second, you don't have any right to force me to do anything.' I replied, shoving against him with the whole weight of my body. 'You have to let me go!'

'Or what?' SB was laughing into my face. 'You can hardly claim that I'm trying to rape you... No court would believe you coz we already did it. There's a room full of people who saw you leave with me last night without any kind of struggle... and you certainly didn't say "no" when I brought you here last night. You could have left at any point during the night if you felt I was keeping you here against your will...'

'No!' I said, my spittle flying into his face. 'That's where you've got it wrong. A girl has a right to change her mind – even if she's done it with the guy before. Last night was last night, but today is different...'

'Yeah, yeah, yeah – tell that to a court... or any of your friends. They'd just laugh at you...' SB was grinning, so pleased and smug with himself.

That's when I brought my knee up really, really hard. As he lay howling on the bed I scrambled out of his way and grabbed for my clothes. 'I will tell everyone how I tried to leave – but how you're too stupid to understand a few very simple words like "no" or "I want to go home now".'

I ran down the stairs still clutching my clothes in my hand. A door opened on the landing and a woman's head looked out. She took in my naked state straight away and she must have registered the panic on my face. She threw the door wide. 'Come in, luv', she said, 'Get in here and let me call the police.' And she took off the dressing gown she was wearing and made me put it on.

The woman, who looked in her mid-30s, led me towards the sofa and made me sit down. She was athletic looking, strong and capable – like she wasn't afraid of anyone or anything. 'You want some hot sweet tea first? Or you want me to ring the police now?'

But I realised then that this wasn't what I wanted. Not because I was scared of what would happen. What I realised was that more than anything in the world I didn't want Sean to know about last night. Because if anything good had come out of that horrible experience it was realising that I really and truly do love my boyfriend. Not just because he's kind and decent and because I know that he would never take advantage of a woman – and not because in my heart of hearts I know he hasn't ever laid a hand on any of the girls who throw themselves at him – but because he's my Sean and he's the only one of him in the whole world.

And if the police got involved then Sean would have to know what happened. And after that he'd never quite be able to believe me when I say I love him. He'd wonder if maybe I really liked SB and if things hadn't gone wrong, whether I'd have left him for that revolting idiot... And he'd never know whether it was just because I was so grateful to him for taking me back and understanding everything, and being so nice to me (which I knew he would be). That he'd always believe that was the main reason I stayed with him.

So I told the woman that I didn't want her to call the police and she asked me if I was sure, and I said I was sure and that I hadn't actually been raped, and that she needn't worry because I wasn't letting the pig upstairs get away with trying to rape me. And I told her that he was on the same course as me and I could make life very, very difficult for him – in all sorts of ways. And then she said that she wasn't going to have a brute like him in the same house with her and she'd be talking to him herself later on, and telling him that unless he left straightaway she'd be calling the police and speaking to the landlord, and all kinds of things which I believe she'd really do.

'I'm a kickboxing instructor,' she told me. 'I teach self-defence classes to women and I've got some contacts with the rape crisis centre. Shall I give you their number? You might want some support later on. You don't have to involve the police, but you could still talk to someone. I know you say you feel OK now, but later on... That's when people often start to experience the shock.'

The kickboxing woman wanted to know who she could call for me. I was really tempted to ask her to call Jane but I know Jane would insist I call the police and I'm not sure she'd understand why I was so scared of Sean finding out. She's known me drop Sean for the tiniest reasons and I don't think she really believes that I love him. (I wasn't sure myself till today.) And if I called Lucy she'd say that we ought to call Jane, so maybe that wasn't the best option either. And I'd seen Dan leave with Rani and I didn't want to spoil his happy little love reunion, and besides there are some things I tell my male friends and some things I'd rather not... In the end, I decided that the best person would be Keesh, coz she's probably got the wisest head on her shoulders. So I just prayed that she'd be home and not still in Manchester or wherever it was her boyfriend was DJing last night.

I was in luck. Keesh was in and her boyfriend drove her over and they took me back to the flat, and Keesh listened to everything I said to her, and she didn't ask any difficult questions like why was I so stupid to get drunk and go home with a boy I despised. She just ran me a long hot bubbly bath and then wrapped me up in blankets on the sofa and sat with me all day long, and told her boyf to go away and that she wouldn't be going out with him tonight, coz I really needed her.

And when Sean rang this evening to see how I'd been, I said I was a bit under the weather and thought I had flu. And he said how was my night and I said OK, the party was a bit dull and I slept round a friend's house coz we all drank a bit too much. And he just believed me and didn't ask any more questions. And I've made a promise to myself that that's the very last lie I will ever tell Sean – except maybe when I'm trying to hide his Christmas present and I have to tell him it's only a bag of vegetables or something.

And Sean said he loved me and although the gig was really good he'd missed me and got irritated with Kyle and Alicia who were all loved up, as it made him think about me. And he was staying another night in London coz the drummer's uncle's car had an electrical fault and it was still in the garage. And I believed every word he said and I told him I couldn't wait til he came home, and I'd cook him a special meal.

'Hols, don't be daft,' he said, 'You're the one who is ill. I'll come round and see you when I get back, and bring us a takeaway.'

SUNDAY 8 AUGUST

I slept most of today. Keesh phoned Romano's and told them I had some hideous stomach bug thingy and it wouldn't be safe for me to be near food. I realised how tired I was after all those late nights sewing and waitressing and worrying about my brother. And I'm still pretty shaken up from yesterday. But I did something this morning which made me feel better.

I texted the following message to SB:

I'm not afraid of you, and I know what really happened. If u come anywhere near me again I will call the police. And speak to the head of our course. Next time a girl says no remember that she means no.

He didn't reply but I was hardly surprised.

Sean came round this evening with my favourite chicken chow mein. I think he'd have liked to stay but he took the hint when I said I wasn't feeling too good.

MONDAY 9 AUGUST

Keesh wanted me to take another day off but I want to get back to work. I'm worried they might find someone else for my job and besides, the more I stay in the more I keep thinking about what happened. Like this mixture of anger and guilt keeps going round and round in my head. I've always been one of those people who thinks girls are stupid to go out and get drunk and go home with some guy they hardly know. And then I go and do just that – just coz it felt like a bit of an adventure. I don't think I was ever really suspicious that Sean was cheating on me. It was just my excuse to let Spider Boy hit on me, coz I wanted a bit of fun. But I shouldn't have got drunk and I should never have gone to the party, and I should never, ever, ever have let SB persuade me to go home with him.

And even when I got there I could have changed my mind at any point. Like when he took his shirt off and his body was all scrawny and weedy (not like Sean who is skinny but quite muscly at the same time) and I should have said, 'No thanks mate, you really aren't my type,' and walked out before anything happened. I didn't have to sleep with him that first night just coz I went home with him. But I was a bit curious then – and way too drunk – so I just let it happen. The only thing I have no regrets about is that I made him use a condom.

What he did the next morning was wrong, coz men have to listen to women when they say no. But I was pretty stupid to let myself get into that situation in the first place. And the old Control Freak Holly can't really believe she let herself do that. And then I start beating myself up again for being such an idiot, which I've got to stop doing coz it's not achieving anything. Keesh says that we all make mistakes sometimes and I think she's probably right. She says that when she was 13 these two older boys in her children's home grabbed her and made her do stuff to them, and they threatened to cut up her face if she told anyone about it. So she didn't say anything. But then about six months later they raped this other girl and hurt her really bad, and this poor girl killed herself a month afterwards. And Keesh said she felt dead guilty that she hadn't reported them in the first place. But she had to forgive herself coz she was just young and scared…And she's learned from it and no guy is ever going to make her do something she doesn't want to do, ever again.

Going in to work was good coz it kept me busy. It's nice to be the head waitress even if it means spending the whole shift hassling the younger kids that they've started employing again. What is it with these Italian families and their loyalty to each other? (I thought that was just in *The Godfather*.) Carmeena told me she never wanted any of her sister-in-law's kids back on the premises again but Roberto is an old softy and when his brother came round begging him to take them back on, he gave in almost straight away.

How many times do you have to say to a 16-year-old boy, 'Take the bread to the table when they first arrive', 'Don't forget to offer them the wine menu' and 'Tell them that the dish of the day is absolutely delicious and freshly made' (even if you suspect you've just seen it being reheated in the microwave). That's bad enough but you should definitely not have to say, 'Do NOT pick your nose in view of the whole restaurant!' and 'Don't mumble swear words at the clients if they only leave a small tip – especially when you spilt soup all over them.'

At least I made some decent tips today, especially for a Monday. It's good to come in all smiles after young Roberto (I think everyone in that family is called Roberto) has just fallen over with the tray of Tiramisu, and offer them complimentary coffees as an apology. The customers see you as a bit of a hero and they quite often press a £10 into your hand for being so nice to them. Especially if you trot off to get their coats for them and make a big thing of helping the ladies into theirs.

After work I went to the chemist. Keesh said I should do something to make me feel good about myself, especially something that makes me feel a bit different, so I've brought some hair colour. (Yeah, I know I can't really afford it.) Holly Richards is going jet black for the first time in her life. Like the princess she always wanted to be when she was a little kid. When her mum kept saying how lucky she was to have such lovely auburn hair.

I just had time to dye my hair before I got the bus over to J and M's for supper. Everyone is sitting round deep in discussion, when I arrive but they break off to welcome me. And comment on my hair.

Jane says it's good to have a change, but I'm not sure she likes it. Martin says 'nice hair' and gives me a big hug. Simon stares at me and says nothing, but that's not unusual.

My brother is a lot ruder. 'Honestly sis, you're a bit old for the My Little Pony look,' he tells me.

'I think it's very … you know… nice,' says Lucy, who is never particularly eloquent at the best of times. 'And Ruby likes it too.' Her evidence for this is that her daughter is sitting on my lap and holding on very hard to a fistfull of my hair.

'Be careful she not sick on you,' Nathan tells me with a grin. 'She been sick on everything today.'

'Watch out sis – your hair's enough to make anyone vomit...'

'Enough!' Jane says, pretending to swipe my brother with the oven glove, 'Leave poor Holly alone... I think her new colour suits her. Now Holly, we could do with your opinion on something.'

Martin leans across and gently takes the oven mitt out of my foster mother's hand. 'Now you know Holly's going to agree with me on this one... so don't try buttering her up.'

'Dad's right you know,' Luce tells her mother, gently. 'You always take on far too much... And look, Ruby agrees – she's nodding...'

'I think she's about to puke...' Nathan snatches up Ruby and whisks her out of the room with an anxious Lucy following on his heels. But they're back in a matter of seconds, announcing a false alarm.

'What exactly is going on?' I ask. 'What do you want my opinion on?'

'The thing is,' Ryan tells me, before anyone else can get a word in. 'Jane and Martin said no more foster kids and if we give in this time, it's never going to stop. The social workers are going to be phoning every five minutes going, "Oh pweese, pweese Mrs Brennan, we got this cute little boy who just murdered both his parents... Oh pweese Mrs Brennan he's only got 11 bruvvers and sisters and maybe he could bring them too...". '

'Since when does my brother make decisions about who gets fostered by this family?' I demand. (And OK, yes I do feel a bit jealous. When I lived with Jane and Martin we had loads and loads of other kids, but since they decided to long-term foster my brother and adopt Simon, they'd decided not to have any more "short-term" kids.)

'Well, he does have a point,' says Martin. 'You did tell Ryan and

Si that we weren't taking any more placements. And if we make an exception this time...'

'Then there will be kids in the cupboard and kids under the beds,' says Ryan cheekily. 'Not to mention babies sleeping in the bread bin (which is what Martin always said when we used to foster regularly).

'Yes but this is just ONE placement,' Jane says, very calmly, knowing that if she sticks to her guns, Martin will eventually give in. 'It's only for a week and these people desperately need a break.'

'And we,' said Martin, smiling as he pours Jane another glass of his homemade lemonade, 'are going on holiday very soon... And besides we already have quite enough kids under our roof.'

'I'm not a kid,' Ryan protests.

'No – you're a tyrant,' says Jane, and my brother grins. 'But honestly this one really is only for five days or so. Just so the foster carers can go and visit their daughter who's had a baby – she lives just outside Paris, and they can't take the little lad with them.'

'What? Coz he's so awful the French authorities won't let him in?' My brother is always in first with some hilarious comment. Not.

Lucy giggles but Nathan is wagging his finger at Ryan. 'Ryan, man,' he says, very earnestly. 'You know well as I do we foster kids cannot go out of da country wivout a passport – not wivout a lot o' hassle. Dis likkle boy is probably good as gold.'

'No kid is ever good as gold... though come to think of it, Nathe, you probably were...' Ryan teases Nathe, who just shrugs his shoulders.

'Actually he isn't really a *little boy*,' chips in Martin, who is looking worried. 'And he's not exactly the most straightforward of children... You know me, I'd never turn down a child who was really in need – but it is just before our holiday and I have a feeling this one is going to get complicated.'

'So what's he like then? You have to tell us, so we can make a proper decision!' my brother demands.

Martin shakes his head. 'You know I can't do that, Ryan. Just think how much you'd hate it if somewhere a bunch of strangers were talking about you over their supper table.'

This really hits the mark with Ryan, who says, 'OK – you got a point.'

'Oh come on – we've dealt with some really complicated young people before and we've never had any real problems,' Jane says, confidently. And Lucy starts laughing.

'Oh Mum – how can you say that! There was the boy who got onto the roof and we had to get the fire engine, and the kid who switched on the taps and flooded the bathroom. And wasn't there that girl who kept biting people and the boy who was forever getting in trouble with the police? And the lad who smashed all the downstairs windows...'

'He only did that because he was upset by something his family did,' Martin replies, always ready to defend any young person, however obnoxious or difficult the rest of us might have found them.

Seeing her father about to change sides, Lucy says quickly, 'Yeah, but the two of you had to be up all night coz the window repair people couldn't come until the next day. And that little girl we had that was always trying to run away – we had her then and you thought she might try and get out through one of the broken windows...'

I've never heard Lucy say anything like this before. She tolerated the most difficult children coming through her home and hogging her mum and dad's time with never a murmur. Being a mother has definitely changed her. She's much more confident these days.

'To be honest Mum, I really don't think you should do this,' Lucy continues, reaching over to take her wriggling daughter from

Nathe, so he can manage to eat something. 'You know they never just come for "five days" or "a week" or however long it's s'posed to be. You and Dad deserve this holiday and Ryan and Si are looking forward to it. Don't do anything which could mess it up...'

(When I last spoke to Ryan he was complaining about the idea of spending a week in a caravan with 'two oldies, a young loon and a loved up couple with a screaming baby' but he'd convinced himself that nobody would enjoy the holiday if he wasn't there, so he'd have to put a brave face on it.)

'I do wish you'd think about coming with us,' Jane says, turning her attention to me. 'I'm sure now you're not working at that horrible garden centre you could manage a few days away. And Sean, you could come too.'

'Thanks Jane,' I say hurriedly, 'but I've got this new job at a restaurant and they're pretty busy this time of year... It's an OK job and I don't want to risk losing it.'

(I can't let on to Jane how broke I am at the moment. She would think I wasn't managing my money properly and would worry about me and probably try and give me some money. *After* she'd given me a long lecture about proper budgeting.)

I've almost forgotten about Simon who had been sitting next to me, silently arranging his shepherd's pie into smaller and smaller squares between gingerly putting tiny amounts of it into his mouth. But I feel the brush of his fringe as he leans against me to whisper, 'I wish you was coming, Holly.'

Immediately my eyes fill with tears but fortunately nobody else notices. Ruby has taken that moment to try and pull Lucy's nose off and in trying to stop her, Lucy has upset the lemonade jug all over the table. Which has dripped all over Sean. Fortunately Sean is used to meals at Jane and Martin's so he takes it all in his stride.

'Sorry Si,' I whisper back. 'Maybe another time.'

And then Simon whispers something else. 'I want that boy to

come.' And without really thinking I say, so everyone can hear, 'Simon thinks that boy should come here...'

Martin puts down the cloth he's using to wipe up the table and smiles at Simon. 'Is that really what you want, Simon my lad?'

And Simon nods, just once before continuing to make geometry patterns in his dinner.

'OK,' Martin says, catching Jane's eye. 'It seems our minds are made up for us. I withdraw my opposition.'

And Jane grins and says 'Well – I can't argue with Simon.'

'Lummin' Norah,' says Ryan (I think he got that expression of some old TV sitcom). 'Here we go again...' But he doesn't really look that fussed. 'But he's not having my room. He'll have to share with Simon.'

'Actually he'll have the spare room, as it's only for a few days,' Jane says.

'Well just make sure the social worker knows that,' Lucy tells her parents firmly. 'Coz otherwise we'll be hanging around with the car packed and this boy will still be here and his social worker will be texting to say, 'Sorree, I'm stuck in traffic and I'll be there in ten minutes,' which will really be like 47 hours later...'

Who stole my friend Lucy and replaced her with this new person?!!

Sean brought me home and stayed for a coffee and a cuddle. I think he was hoping for more but I made some excuse about really needing to catch up with my sleep. He left without any awkward questions but I could see a hurt look in his eyes, coz I think he guesses I'm hiding something from him. Maybe he thinks I've got bored of him and I'm wanting to break up. So I've just sent him this text:

Love u loads. Night night H xx

He's just texted back to say:

Love u too. U know u can always talk to me, dont u? S xxxxxxx

Anyway it was good to see my little bro looking cheerier again tonight. He told me he's started hanging out with these twins from his year. He says they were nice to him all the time when other kids were giving him a hard time about being gay. There's a boy and a girl and they're not identical at all, he says. The girl is 'a bit like you sis' he tells me, which I'd like to take as a compliment, but know I probably shouldn't. And the boy, he says, is 'dead laidback'. They get teased a bit by other kids who think they're EMO or something coz they dress differently, but Ryan says they've got good taste in music. And support the right team. And that's what really counts.

TUESDAY 10 AUGUST
9am

Just woken up and feeling all agitated, which is annoying because I was meant to be having a lie in. I'm not working today coz Tuesday is supposed to be the day the restaurant stays shut, but sometimes they forget this and open anyway. But we've got some kind of wedding party tomorrow night so Roberto says the staff need to be 'fresh as daisies'. I'm not sure if he realises his nephews are going out on the booze tonight, but at least me and Keesh will be there to keep them on their toes. Keesh is working full-time for Davina now, but she's agreed to do some occasional nights in the restaurant. 'You can never put all your eggs in one basket, girl,' she tells me. 'Sure, I got me some fancy job ... but we livin' in a recession, girl. Davina just might go bust and leave de country. You never know what is round de next corner.'

Now I know Lucy would say this is negative thinking but Lucy doesn't know that much about real life. Me and Keesh know that while some good things happen in life, so do some really bad things, so you've always got to be prepared. You seize the good opportunities and you give it all you've got, but you cover your back – just to be on the safe side.

8pm

OMG – the most awful thing just happened and I've only got myself to blame.

Sean rings to say there's a party on tonight and do I want to go, but I say I'm still feeling a bit "off colour". He asks if I want to go to a film but I say I don't much fancy that coz I'm feeling tired. Then he gets all concerned about me and says maybe I should go and see my doctor, coz this isn't like me… And I say 'maybe' but I probably didn't sound very convincing. And I can hear Sean taking a deep breath at the end of the phone.

'Is there something wrong? With us?' he asks me, and he sounds so worried that my stomach is filled with guilty knots.

'Nothing – honestly nothing,' I tell him hurriedly. 'I'm just not feeling too good. I think I might have got a bit of a virus.'

'You're not…' I can hear him pausing, embarrassed. 'You're not thinking you might be pregnant or something, Hols?' he asks eventually.

I start to laugh and then stop, coz I realise that sounds dead insensitive. 'No – definitely not,' I say, 'I can feel the most horrible period ever just about to start.' (Which is kind of true. I do have a bit of PMT and I keep thinking about chocolate.)

'Sometimes women still get periods even when they are pregnant,' Sean says. (For a man without a sister he's way too informed about girls' stuff. I think he listens to all those late night programmes on the radio where people ring in and talk about their problems.)

'Yeah – but I'm not,' I assure him. 'I know my own body and I'm telling you that the implant is doing its job properly.'

But Sean isn't going to let the subject rest. 'OK, I believe you, but I want you to know I'd be there for you Hols. Whatever happened.'

And I know that – and I believe he means it. But could I really say the same thing to him? I know that I really love him but does loving someone make everything OK? I suppose if he got arrested for something he didn't do or lost all his money or got thrown out of college, I'd stand by him. But I wouldn't be there for him if he killed or injured someone intentionally, or did what SB tried to do. And I'd never forgive a man who let me down badly. Or hit me.

'You've gone very quiet,' Sean says after a while. 'You freak me out Hol when you do this. Last time it was when you were getting ready to split up with me...' I can hear there's real pain in his voice. 'Just be upfront with me Hol – tell me what's going on, coz I'm tearing myself apart here wondering if ...'

I hear myself saying something I really don't want to say. I'm asking him, 'Would you really stick by me, whatever I did? If you knew I'd like had an affair with another bloke or something?'

Now it was Sean's turn to go dead quiet. Then he says, 'Have you, Holly... Have you been seeing someone else?'

And I wanted to say no because it wasn't really like that, but instead I just said 'Yes' in a tiny, tiny voice because I want to be so small that I can crawl into the ground and hide. 'But it didn't mean anything... It was a stupid, stupid, stupid mistake. I love you Sean, I really do.'

But Sean cut the call.

I'd just burst into tears when Sean calls back. 'I love you Hols,' he says, 'But what you said hurts me like... like you've just torn my guts out. But there's something you don't know and something I need to tell you. So I'm going to come over to see you right now, so we can sort this thing out.'

I'm writing this now while I'm waiting for Sean to arrive and my insides are churning round and round like they're in a tumble dryer. Where's the old Holly who was always so cool, so totally in control? She'd have known what to do in this situation and she wouldn't have been crying her eyes out like a baby.

But would she? Really? The old Holly probably would have pretended she didn't care and got all aggressive. She'd have told Sean that he didn't own her and that he had no right to cross-examine her. She wouldn't have gone blurting out some confession on the phone. And would that be better or worse than the new Holly?

WEDNESDAY 11 AUGUST
morning

I've got to write this down while it's still in my head. Otherwise I won't be able to get through that hideous wedding party thingy tonight. A wedding is the last thing I want to be around, feeling like this.

Sean says he loves me, he's always loved me but sometimes he doubts whether I really love him. There were times, he says, when I was finishing my end of term project when I didn't contact him for three days. When he'd phone me and I wasn't listening or he'd text me and I wouldn't text back. And he started to think I was bored of him or maybe I'd met someone else.

She was just one of the girls who came to the gigs at college, he says. She wasn't as pretty as me and she wasn't especially funny or cute or anything. It's just that she was always there. She hung around with some of his friends and she'd been coming to gigs since the band first performed. She was always in the front row – and he'd kind of got used to looking out for her.

He wouldn't tell me her name because he says she's 'nobody important' and 'it doesn't matter any more'. But because I've been so honest with him, he feels it's only fair to be honest with me.

He says he doesn't really know how it happened but one night she was the only person left in the union bar and they were both walking home the same way, and she asked him in for a coffee... After that he only slept with her one more time coz he knew he didn't really want to be with her.

'I think I was doing it to punish you Hols,' he told me. 'Because you seemed to have forgotten I existed. It was like I was proving something. But then I realised I wasn't proving anything – except that I didn't want her and I only wanted you. So I told her that I couldn't see her again, and she broke down and cried and cried and said she was going to kill herself. And I believed her Hols, because when I first met her someone told me her older sister used to be here at uni, but how she starved herself to death... and how Annie – yeah OK, that's her name – wasn't very stable. But I'd kind of forgotten about all of that.'

Sean said that he didn't know what to do, so he did the only thing he could think of. He stayed with her that night, just to keep an eye on her. And from then on it got into a bit of a pattern. He kept on insisting that they could only be friends but the girl kept saying that she couldn't be without him, so he was spending more and more of his time with her. And everyone thought they were going out and nobody believed him when he said it wasn't true.

'And she started getting so thin,' Sean told me, looking terrified. 'I felt like I was personally killing her or something. And I really, really didn't want to have anything to do with her, because I was so sick of being around her... and then one day she said she was pregnant.'

My heart, which had been breaking into tiny little slivers of pain, now started pushing against my ribs so painfully that I thought I couldn't breathe.

'But of course it wasn't true – I knew really that it wasn't true. But I panicked when she first said it,' Sean told me, nervously stroking my hair. He was holding my head against his chest because neither of us could look each other in the eye any more. 'And all I could think was "no" because I knew that the only person I ever wanted to be the mother of my kids was you, Holly.'

I'd already confessed my own sordid story to Sean and he'd listened, crying a bit but also clenching his fists while I told him exactly what had happened with SB. So he knew that my acting "strange" wasn't coz of any immediate likelihood of there being any little Hollys and Seans.

'But I pretended I believed her, just to get her down to the uni doctors. And when we saw the doctor I said everything – like how I was dead worried she was anorexic and suicidal – but that I really couldn't cope with it any more, and that they had to take care of her for me.'

At first the GP had thought Sean was a cruel, uncaring boyfriend but they'd soon realised that Annie needed professional help. 'So I left her there. And I got my own life back... And I know that sounds kind of really callous, but all I wanted was to be with you, Hols.'

'So what happened to her – this Annie?' I asked. Not that I really cared, but I was curious.

'A friend told me she'd gone home – that her mum came down to London and took her home. I guess that was probably the best thing for her...'

'Definitely,' I said, sounding so much calmer than I felt. 'And so you just picked up from where we left off?' I sounded very angry and very bitter but I was surprised when Sean pulled away from me, his eyes blazing with outrage.

'Actually, no I didn't! You were still so busy wrapped up in your own life that I might as well have stayed with Annie, coz at least she appreciated me! But instead I went back to waiting and hoping you'd remember I existed – just like before... Stupid loser that I was...'

'You should've said something,' I replied. I hate it when people just suffer in silence. 'Anyway, you knew what that college project meant to me...'

'Yes I did, which is more than I can say for the way you've been about the band! For months you just acted like the band was nothing – some little toy I was playing with that meant nothing at all...' but Sean broke off, his anger now turning to tears.

He pulled himself together then said, 'OK, I'll grant you that you've been really nice about the band for the last month or so – but it took me going on the radio and dedicating a song to you before you actually sat up and took notice...'

'I'm sorry,' I said, 'I didn't realise...'

'That's the trouble with you Holly, you never do realise.'

'Well, maybe if you weren't such a total doormat and let me walk all over you...' I knew that was really spiteful, but I have a right to put my point of view.

And then instantly regretted it. 'Look, sorry, I'm sorry I said that,' I tried to touch Sean but he pulled away.

'And then you go deciding I'm seeing some other girl – just so you can justify seeing this Spider Person, who sounds like a right head case, which he clearly is. I'm not saying for one moment that you deserved what happened to you but c'mon Holly, if you play with fire you must expect to get just a little bit burnt.'

What was he saying? To me it sounded like Sean had just said that SB trying to rape me was some kind of punishment for me being unfaithful. And I wasn't going to let him get away with that.

'Get out!' I spat at him. 'Just get out and stay away from me! You men are all the same. You can do all kinds of stuff yourself but you always blame it on us women. We tempted you or we made you do it. It's the old Adam and Eve story all over again... but I'm not listening to your lies! Nobody deserves to get raped, or nearly raped, whatever you might think!'

'That isn't what I'm saying...' Sean had a really desperate look in his eyes now. 'You know that isn't what I mean... Please Holly, we have to sit down and talk all this through, without getting so upset with each other.' He was plucking at my arm, trying to get hold of me.

'You were the one who started getting upset – and then you come on all high and mighty saying that I deserve everything I got... when you've been playing round even more than I have. You chose to have that relationship with Annie but I didn't exactly choose to get involved with James. He was just bloody stalking me!' I was shouting at Sean now and pushing him towards the door. 'Just stay away from me! This relationship is totally over!'

We were still shouting at each other in the corridor when Keesha let herself in through the front door. 'Hey... guys,' she said, her eyes flicking anxiously between the two of us. 'Why don't you both come and sit in da kitchen wiv me – and we can try and sort things out?'

'There's nothing to talk about,' I snapped at Keesh. 'Sean just said it served me right that I nearly got raped – and I've nothing more to say to him.'

'I didn't ... you know I didn't mean... Oh for freak's sake Holly, please just let's talk about this...'

'No,' I said. 'You've said it and you can't unsay it. Just get out.'

And I turned my back on both of them and slammed my bedroom door.

I heard Sean and Keesh talking quietly in the kitchen for a bit. I was so angry with both of them. Keesh had no right to take his side against me. She's my flatmate not his, and she's supposed to be one of my best mates. Eventually I heard the front door close behind him. And Keesha came and knocked on my door. But I pretended to be asleep.

'OK Hols girl, I know you awake in there. When you ready to talk, Keesh is here for you.'

Like I'd really want to talk to her, after she'd taken sides with Sean!

I thought I'd never sleep but I guess I was worn out with the whole thing. I had the most confusing dreams. I was back in that bedroom with SB but this time it wasn't him sleeping beside me, it was Sean. And I was scared because I knew that when he woke up he was going to do something to hurt me. But also a bit of me knew that Sean would never really hurt me. I got up and I tried to get away but the door was locked and I couldn't find a key. And I was pounding on the door and shouting and yelling for someone to let me out ... but then the dream changed and I was somewhere else, and I don't remember what happened then.

I slept through to almost 8am and after that I was totally wide awake. There was no sound of Keesh and to be honest I was glad to avoid her. I made my tea and brought it back to bed. I'm sitting here now drinking it and writing this diary. I can see there are messages on my mobile but I don't want to read them. I'm going to text Dean and some other college mates, and see if someone wants to meet me in town for a coffee or something. I know I shouldn't spend the money but I've got to get out of here. Before Keesh wakes up and it turns sour.

10pm-ish

OMG – what is happening to my life! I can't believe myself any more. What did I do but go out to the pub – and get drunk as a skunk. Dan tried to tell me I should slow down but I wasn't listening to him. He's so freaking loved up with Rani again and all he wanted to talk about was her. But I had plenty of sorrows I needed to drown and one of Dan's mates was trying to hit on me, and kept buying me cocktails. And I kept drinking them. It's good

I've got such a downer on guys at the moment or I'd probably have slept with him too, coz he was quite good looking in a smug git kind of way.

Then I thought I'd better come back to the flat and have a shower and maybe a little nap so I'd be fresh for work later. But then I forgot to set the alarm. And when I woke up there were hundreds of messages from Keesh – which I hadn't heard coz I'd turned the sound off so Sean couldn't call me. She said that when she realised I wasn't going to show she'd told Romano's that I was still a bit under the weather from that bug thing I had, and she'd suspected I felt awful and hadn't been able to get out of bed. But they hadn't been impressed. Anyway, more important was that I was OK. Would I please phone or text her as soon as I got the messages just to let her know I was still alive.

So I sent her a text saying:

Yeah I'm still alive. Sort of

Middle of the night

Keesh got in about one o'clock and she came straight and banged on my door. She didn't wait for me to answer. She just walked right on in.

'Girl, what is goin' on wiv you? You look like you been dead, buried and dug up again!' she demanded, hands on hips.

'It's none of your business,' I told her, 'Just get out of here.'

'Hey, hey, hey … slow down there… You getting mighty fond of throwin' people out your room…'

'That's coz I don't want traitors in here, people I can't trust.' OK, I knew I was sounding like one of those crazy women on *EastEnders* but I couldn't help it.

'Babes you *know* you can trust me. I'm not your enemy. And neither is Sean if you'd only listen to him. You cheat on him and he cheat on you – but you both sorry now.' Keesha was trying to sit down on the edge of the bed, but I really didn't want her near me just now.

'I don't know who I can trust any more,' I said. Shifting over so there wasn't enough space for Keesh's curvy bum. 'Not after what he said...'

'Babes he didn't mean anything by it. People say mixed up stuff when they feelin' emotional.'

'Yeah, but that doesn't mean I have to forgive him. And I don't see why you're taking his side.'

'Girl I ain't takin' nobody's side – well nobody but yours really. You tole me how you knew you really love dis boy and now you want to chuck him away. You two is good together babe. He'd never hurt you on purpose.'

'It didn't seem like that last night... You didn't hear what he said!'

'I know what he said babes, and he didn't mean it like that. He was just saying that you'd both been muckin' about wid other people and you both knew it was wrong. An' when you tried to say he was more guilty than you, he got real hurt. I mean, he'd never hurt you like dat other slimeball did.'

'You don't know that! You weren't here when he said it. If you think he's such a perfect boyfriend then why don't you go out with him?'

Keesh sighed, 'OK, OK, I not gonna argue wiv you coz I'm dead on my feet ... but you know where I am if you need me.'

I'm crying now. That seems to be all I ever do these days. I feel like I'm losing everything – and everyone I care about is against me.

THURSDAY 12 AUGUST

My baby brother is 15 today! I called and wished him a fab day (even though I feel like hell on legs). He says Jane offered to cook him a special meal but he said that Charlie and Ella's mum is taking them all out for dinner, somewhere posh. Good job that Jane has a thick skin, coz if I was her I'd have been a bit upset bout that. Anyway, it means I don't have to go over there today.

And just as I'm bout to end the call he says, 'Oh and thanks for the card sis. How old do I have to be before you send me a proper shop bought one, 'stead of this handmade stuff?'

Nothing happened. I stayed in my room all day. I don't want to see anyone or talk to anyone. I kept my phone on silent and hid it in a drawer so I can't see it. I should've gone to Romano's again tonight but I don't care. I don't think I care about anything any more. Well, maybe a bit for my brother... but he doesn't need me. He's got his own life. Wish I could bounce back the way he does. You'd think the way he carries on that half the school hadn't been bullying him for the last couple of weeks. He's, like, so cocky again, going on about all the places he's going to with those twins he's so thick with. I don't remember Jane letting me go off to day festivals and stuff when I was only 14 but Jane says she doesn't remember me ever asking.

FRIDAY 13 AUGUST

Guess I wrote that too soon. Ryan rang me this morning totally
freaking. He said Jane took this call from the head, when he
was having breakfast. Apparently someone's sent a letter to the
school and it has my brother's name on it – and it said URGENT.
The school secretary was in checking the mail and she says the
postmark's a bit blurry so she can't see the date it was sent, or
where it was sent from. The head was trying to say that maybe
it was nothing to worry about, but he thought he ought to let
Jane know 'just in case'. Of course Ryan overheard the whole
conversation coz he knows that trick all us kids know, that you can
hear through the walls of Jane's office if you put your ear against
the plaster... And when he asked Jane about it afterwards, and
when they could go and get it, she shook her head and gave a big
sigh. 'Honestly, your headmaster has less brain cells than a gnat,'
she'd told him. 'He's asked the secretary to forward it to you –
wasn't even sure she'd definitely send it first class, but suspected
she probably would... And then he has the nerve to ring and check
he's done the right thing! I've tried to ring the secretary but she's
no longer there... Why didn't the stupid man ring me BEFORE he

told her to post it...'

'Jane was all red in the face, really furious with Mr H...' Ryan told me. 'An' that worries me the most...'

I can imagine Jane being really angry. There's only one thing that really makes her lose her cool. It's adults who do stupid things that upset children.

I tried to assure Ryan that it was probably nothing to worry about. And tomorrow morning a letter would arrive telling him he'd won some poetry competition or something. Or a place on a football camp...

'One, I'm getting a bit old for football camps, and two, I don't write poems, and three, I'd never do anything as gay as send one off to a competition!' my brother informed me.

I can't believe my brother just used the word "gay" like that, after all the stuff he's been through. But I decided to keep my lecture about it til another day.

'And four – and this is a really big four – I just know that this means the crap hit the fan... it's got to be my aunt tracking me down coz she's found out something... threatening me with something truly evil... Maybe that Josie... '

'I thought you said she'd written on your wall, said she wasn't saying a word to your aunt or your dad or anyone, and how she'd try to hush stuff up round the town if she heard anyone saying anything ...'

'Yeah – she's cool, that Josie... but I mean, she's got this younger sister and what if her sister or someone looked at her stuff? It happens, sis. You know how gossip spreads in small places...'

'Of course I know that,' I snapped back. (I'm going through enough of my own problems not to need Ryan's just at this moment.)

I told my brother not to panic too much. There could be all sorts of reasons for someone sending a letter to his school. And if – just if – it was his aunt, then what really could she do to him?

'That woman could do anything,' I could hear the shudder in Ryan's voice. 'She used to beat me with these things and...'

'Yeah, but you're not a kid now Ryan, you're probably taller than she is. Not to mention a lot stronger. She's a woman, who's got to be at least 50 or something old like that, and she's probably not getting any fitter... And the mad granny – she must be nearly 80 these days. I thought you said she was housebound or something...'

'You met my aunt, Hols,' my brother reminded me. 'You KNOW what she's like. She'd get my dad or one of her cousins or someone to beat me up, if she couldn't do it herself.'

And I do remember meeting Ryan's aunt. Just the once, on some contact visit I went to with him. She's this big bruiser of a woman with these great meaty arms, and one of those gruff voices you could grate cheese on. I heard from someone that she used to be a real tearaway as a kid, and she got into a lot of trouble in her early 20s. But then she got sent away and she "saw the light". She came out of prison with a mission to save everyone from their sins. Which she did with all the fierceness she'd once put into mugging old ladies (or whatever). And she was sure as hell that her only nephew wasn't going to become a 'bad lad who'd burn in the fires of eternal damnation'. Even if she had to beat the devil out of him, which apparently she needed to do several times a day... until he was taken away from her.

'Ryan, you're older now. You have Jane and Martin and Donald to support you, and the law on your side. She can't really do anything to hurt you,' I tried to reassure him.

'That woman could do anything... anything she set her mind to,' Ryan repeated. And I felt so sorry for him. That aunt is like the monster under the bed. When you're a little kid you *know* there are only slippers and some snotty hankies and bits of fluff between the mattress and the floor, but you still believe that a monster with 100 sharp teeth is going to bite your ankles as you climb into bed. So even when you're really old enough to know better, you never like to look too closely at the shadowy bits where the duvet doesn't quite meet the carpet...

And hey, I know how that feels at the moment. So I'm gonna pull the duvet back over my head and stay in the safe zone. And the world can bloody well go away and leave me alone.

SATURDAY 14 AUGUST

Today was pretty much the same as yesterday. I watched a lot of crap TV in my room. Cept Dan and Luce tried to call me a couple of times. But I just ignored both of them. I don't want to connect with anyone at the moment. I need my space. Keesh knocked on my door a couple of times but I pretended I was asleep. She pushed a note under my door saying

Girl you gotta come out!

But I haven't got to do anything. I'm a free agent.

SUNDAY 15 AUGUST

2pm

SB was in my dreams again last night, and Sean too, but I don't remember what happened. I've got better things to do than waste my time on them.

Woke up feeling guilty and that I maybe ought to go and see Ryan, coz I know he's fretting about that letter. I can tell from the very jolly texts he's been sending me. But I don't think I'm any use to anyone at the moment.

Jane tried to ring me but I just texted her and said:

Not feeling great so lyin low. Be in touch soon. Let me know what's happenin wiv Ryan.

I've never been one of those people that goes off the radar coz they've had a little bit of a crisis or just don't feel like talking. But I've got nothing to say to people at the moment. I feel dug out and empty inside. So I'm still in bed and watching crappy TV.

midnight

I've been dead brave. I looked at the messages from Sean. And they made me cry. First of all he was saying stuff like

Talk to me Holly – please

But then after a bit the tone changed and he wrote this amazing email:

I love u Hols, and I prob always will. but I'm not yr doormat. Annie only hpnd coz I needed 2 try and break yr spell. But it didnt work coz u r kind of hooked round my heart – like it sez in that song I wrote 4 u. Its like torture 2 know u slept wiv another guy – just 4 a laugh. Coz thatz how it seems 2 me. But what he did 2 u was wrong. Nobody deserves that and if u thought I ment that then I understand why u so angry wiv me. Sometimes words just come out wrong. I'm sorry if I hurt u – in any way. U v hurt me so bad that I can't think str8 right now. But plez can we try n sort things out. No rush. Let me know when u redy to talk. S xx

That's the thing with Sean, he doesn't force anything. He's respectful of other people, which is one of the many reasons I still love him.

Yeah, I just wrote that – and I mean it.

I cried for a long time but eventually I text'd him back:

U r a good person. We'll talk soon. H xx

I'm going to try and sleep now coz I'm all wrung out.

MONDAY 16 AUGUST

Today I woke up knowing I had to get my life sorted, otherwise I'll end up like some of those care leavers you hear about who get into a right mess. Debts and depression and too much booze, and all kinds of stuff. I'd always vowed I'd never be like that. I'm Holly Richards, I'm strong and I won't let other people mess up my life for me. I started a new painting this morning and that made me feel so much better. I kind of expressed all my anger and my pain and my frustration. It's a very violent kind of painting but it's how my soul has been feeling. Now it's down on paper it feels like it's not inside me any more.

I sent Keesh a text and I said:

Babes how ur job goin'? H xx

And she text'd back:

Its cool. An I got some good news for u. K ☺

So I text'd back and said:

You want I shld make us some supper?

And she replied:

Sounds good 2 me xx

There were other messages on the text but I'm still not ready for them. But then I saw a missed call from my little bro. So I rang him straight away.

'Hey sis, where you been? I been trying to get through to you for ages. That new kid, Liam, arrived last night and he is one *barbarian*!!'

'So he's a bit wild then?' I asked. I couldn't help smiling at my brother's description.

'Wild is not the word, man. The boy's an animal!'

'Guinea pigs are animals,' I said, 'And the worst they do is run around squeaking.'

'A guinea pig would be fine. A guinea pig would be totally acceptable,' my brother said, pausing for full dramatic effect. 'But this kid is like one of those mad hyena things – he laughs like he's about to tear your throat out. 'Cept he's not a hyena coz hyenas don't climb and this boy is climbing – climbing everywhere and on everything. He got on the top of the wardrobe in Jane and Martin's room and he wouldn't come down.'

I had this sudden image of J and M poking the boy with a broom and coaxing him down with pieces of chocolate. Or a banana. And I laughed. For the first time in ages and ages.

'I'm tellin' you sis, this is not funny! He's been up on my cupboard too and he opened up all my stuff. Then he threw it all over the room. And he was laughing while he did it...'

'That does sound kind of creepy – and annoying,' I said. 'D'you think he's got some kind of condition or something? You know like that Hyper Active thingy that some kids get if you feed them too much orange juice?'

'Well, we haven't given him any orange juice, coz he doesn't like it. But that's not the point sis... poor old Si is hiding in his bedroom and whimpering like a puppy and Jane is having to spend time comforting him, when she isn't chasing this kid round the house. He was running out onto the road earlier. Just opening the garden gate and running out... Jane tried to shut him in the playroom for a bit but he climbed out of the window. It's like he's not scared of anything.'

'How old is this child?' I asked. 'And why did nobody tell Jane this? Surely he must be just as bad with his other foster carers. You'd think they'd have warned them...'

'Yeah well – Nobody got any sleep last night coz the boy was up and down all night. An' he's nearly eight. If they stopped watching him for a second he was climbing up something, or running out the doors ... I heard Jane on the phone to the social worker when I was having breakfast... you know how she thinks no one can hear her when she closes the door but if you sit at the table and put your ear to the wall, you can hear it all. She was really mad with the social worker and saying she couldn't understand why nobody had said anything about this before.'

'She deserves to be furious,' I said.

'Anyway, it seems the social worker said they didn't know. They really didn't know that the boy was like this. Seems he used to be like it when he first went to the foster carers but that was like three years ago – and the foster carers put bars on the windows and things to keep him safe but they thought he'd properly grown out of it... '

'And did Jane believe them?'

'Seems so. She says the social worker is pretty new and hasn't known the kid or the foster family very long. So when the foster carers said he was "a good boy" they just believed them...'

'Hmmm,' I said. Someone was clearly to blame here but it was hard to know who. 'And how's you?' I asked changing the subject.

'Me's fine,' Ryan replied sounding chirpier than I'd heard him for a long time. 'That Luke is like "You want to hang out with me mate?" but I'm not so sure now. Just coz we both foster kids doesn't make us buddies. And me and Ella and Charlie got more important things to do...'

I didn't know whether to ask him about the letter. But I guess he's probably trying not to think about it. When it turns up he'll let me know. Just hope it's soon coz it would be worse to go on holiday worrying about it.

This afternoon I went down to the shops and I found some things that were just reaching their sell-by-date, and were reduced to like a third of the price. So I got these chicken breasts dead cheap and some potatoes and some carrots. And there was some little lemon dessert things where you could get two for the price of one, and I got those as well. I wanted to get some wine or something but I hadn't got enough money for that and the fare back. Need to leave enough to top up my mobe when it runs out.

Later

Keesh came home bursting with news. Davina wants me to work in the shop tomorrow. She's still not happy with the job the decorators have done and she's decided the walls need brightening up with some "real art". And I've got to do a bit of carrying and cleaning and unpacking boxes and stuff, but I don't mind that. Keesh says if I make a success of it they might keep me on for a Saturday job and other things.

Me and Keesh are back to normal, like we always were. She said nice things about my cooking and I asked millions of questions about how she was liking her job. Before she went to bed (she's into early nights coz she needs to be in the shop dead early) she gave me a hug and I told her I'd texted Sean and she said, 'Good for you, babes.'

When I came back to my room I did a really soppy thing and got out all my photos of Sean and then went and looked at the websites. There's so many pics of him and the band up now. The pic of him with Ryan and Si is up on the official one, along with some of him and me which are on the fan site. And there's this discussion going on between some of the fans about whether I'm his girlfriend or not – and one of the fans says she saw me with him at the gig in Corrington and that she knows where I live coz she's been doing a bit of "detective work". Which is dead freaky – but she's not that good a detective coz she clearly thinks it's the old address where J and M live. Still, it's pretty creepy and I don't like it. What are these girls planning to do to me? Kill me or something?

But when I look through the site, it seems that they just collect info about all the places where you might see Sean – like where his house is and stuff like that. And it doesn't sound like they really mean to turn up there or anything. They're just silly fans who need to know as much about him as possible. Do they really get a kick from knowing that his first hamster was called Mr Fluffy or that he won a table tennis competition when he was nine? That's pathetic! I bet they'll never know that when he was four he had an imaginary friend called Timmy Tomkins – which was really his toothbrush. And I shan't be sharing that with them.

All these girls would give their teeth to be in my position (although I can't imagine Sean fancying girls with no teeth) and it makes me realise that I'm lucky to have him. He is fit and he is talented. And I send him another text which says:

We'll work it out. I love u 2. H xxxx

'Need to get away from that Liam who is seeeer-iously doin' my head in...' my brother announces as I answer his call. 'Ella and Charlie say I can move in with them but I fink Jane and Martin really need me here.'

I imagine Ryan spends more time grumbling about this Liam than giving Jane and Martin a hand. 'You could spend some time with Si – make sure he's doing OK,' I suggest.

'Naah – Si's gone pretty weird. Well weirder than usual. Jane says she thinks it's coz he watched me opening my birthday cards ... you remember how he freaked when he got that card from his mum on his birthday? No – coz you weren't here at breakfast that day. Anyway, Jane says it's a delayed reaction or summat. Personally I fink it's just this crazy kid we got on the premises. Why does Jane always have to have some big psychowhatsit explanation for everything? Our Si's just peed off coz there's a bigger loony than him in the house.' Again, Ryan doesn't mention anything about the letter and I don't bring it up. I've got stuff of my own to focus on.

Before me and Keesh set off for work, I rang Romano's. I was expecting to leave a voicemail coz it was far too early for anyone to be in, but Roberto answered the phone. He sounded tired and rather sad.

'I'm disappointed in you Holly, I must be honest with you. You were such a good girl, so reliable, so good at the job. But then you let me down so badly... I could not trust you again.'

I felt really angry to hear him criticise me like that – he had no idea what I'd been through. But then I realised that was exactly why he was cross with me. He didn't know what was going on in my life. He just thought I was a typical young person having a good time, who hadn't turned up for work coz of a party or a hot date. And if I was in his shoes I'd probably have thought the same thing.

'There were reasons,' I said, but I decided not to go any further. 'I'm sorry Roberto. Sorry I let you down.'

'That is OK. But you are a clever girl Holly. You must not spoil your chances by being unreliable. Take care of yourself – and come in and have a cappuccino sometime if you are passing.'

It was all go when we got to the shop. It might only be 9.30am but Davina was pacing up and down outside, smoking, sipping from a steaming mug of black coffee, and giving someone a right ear-bashing on the phone she had tucked against her shoulder.

'The caterers have crossed her,' Carly tells us, with a wink, as we follow her through to the back of the store. 'Apparently they want to replace the asparagus spears with celery bites coz they can't get any really nice fresh asparagus at the moment. Davina has told them that it's not her problem and she simply has to have asparagus for the opening... That she simply can't do without them... '

'Girl, you have soooo got to have asparagus spears for a posh opening!' Keesh giggles. 'If you don't, then no customers are going to buy a thing from de shop...'

'Exactly! No point having an opening if you don't have

asparagus spears,' I join in. And we giggle like silly schoolgirls.

I help Keesh and Carly with some pricing and labelling until Davina sticks her head around the door and beckons to me.

'Are you ready to be totally creative, daahling?' she asks me, with such an anxious look on her face that I'm tempted to say, 'What me? No, I'm just here to read the meter.' But I don't, of course. It might be fun to see Davina explode but I don't want to be the one clearing up the mess.

Davina waves her arms at some walls that look perfectly fine to me, and goes on about what an 'appalling disaster' the painters have caused.

'Create me some street art or something a bit graffiti, darling – and make it totally wonderful,' she implores me, with her hand on my arm.

I feel a bit nervous and I don't like to tell her that grafitti isn't really my thing, but I pride myself on being able to adapt. I'm a real artist after all.

I come up with this idea – of painting eyes and clock faces on the walls. And Davina says she's thrilled by the idea. 'Very retro, very early 70s daahling,' she says.

However, she didn't really like the first ones I painted so I had to paint them out and start all over again. Then she wasn't sure about the second ones, so again I had to start over. But fortunately she liked the third ones and after that I had a bit of a style to follow and she said it was 'utterly perfect'. Until I painted a slightly larger clockface on one of the walls and she said it was 'utterly wrong' because she needed to have a display cabinet in front of it.

Anyway, it was really exhilarating working for her coz you never quite knew what would come next. At one point she took a look at a box of clothes that Keesh was starting to unpack and burst into tears. Then she was on the phone calling someone all the names under the sun, and saying they had 'totally and utterly betrayed' her by sending the wrong designs. And that she 'utterly hated the dresses and would probably throw up all over them, unless they were removed. Immediately!'

And she smoked like a chimney. And she always wanted someone else to go and stand out on the fire escape with her while she did it. I had the feeling it wouldn't be long till Keesh, who – good for her – gave up smoking so we could share a flat together, would be tempted back into her old ways.

But Davina was also generous to work with. Although she never seemed to eat anything herself, she rang the local deli and got the most amazing picnic sent round for us: smoked salmon, crusty bread and lovely soft creamy cheese and yummy chocolate brownies and gallons of fresh orange juice. She also got a bottle of champagne delivered and promised that everyone could have a glass when we finished work for the day. Which didn't happen till about 8pm.

By then my painting was almost finished and most of the storage units were complete. Keesh had spent most of her day hanging clothes on rails in one of the back storage rooms, well out of the way of stray splashes of paint (not that I do splash paint around, coz I'm dead neat, but you can never be too careful). Carly went off somewhere to try and soothe the caterers, who were seriously threatening to pull out after Davina had rung them back and called them 'incompetent buffoons'.

Davina's partner Michael arrived during the afternoon with this ultra-swanky briefcase. He did a lot of scuttling about and looking at price labels, and writing things down in an ultra-expensive looking leather notebook. It seemed to take him forever. And he did a lot of crossing out. I had no idea poets could be so limp. I always imagined they'd be passionate, energetic kind of people. I suppose he's quite good looking in a 40-something, pale, nervous kind of way, but his way of hesitating every time he goes to say or do anything would drive me crazy. But Davina seems to be dead fond of him, and he gazes at her with the eyes of a dog that's totally besotted with its master. So I guess they must be very happy together.

When we were all seated on the packing boxes, we drank a toast.

'To Divine Inspiration – our splendid new boutique!' Davina raised her glass. 'And thank you my daahlings for all your hard work. I couldn't have made it through this terrible day without you...'

'And to our dear Davina, our very own divine inspiration,' Michael replied. He pronounced it all very carefully, in a stuttery, pretentious way that made you want to throttle him. 'Without you, my beloved, we would be nothing.'

'Bottoms up,' said Carly, grinning, 'And here's to Keesh, who has survived more than a week with Davina and is still alive...' Except she said it very quietly while Davina and Michael were locked in a noisy, slurpy kind of embrace.

'To Keesh,' I murmured. 'Coz she's fabulous!'

'Dat is so true, babes, so true,' Keesh raised her glass to both of us, smiling.

I have to stop writing now coz there's stuff I still need to do. I haven't phoned Luce for a few days and from all the texts she's sent me, I know she's bursting to tell me about something new that Ruby has done. I also need to phone Jane and see how she's coping with this wild kid. And whether poor Si's come out of his bedroom yet. And if the school secretary has remembered whether she sent that letter first or second class. Or whether she actually remembered to send it at all.

But before all of that I think I'd better ring Sean.

WEDNESDAY 18 AUGUST

It was weird waking up in Sean's arms again. But weird in a really nice kind of way. We haven't done a lot of talking yet, but it's good to be together again. I think both of us are treading on ice a bit round each other, being real careful not to do or say the wrong thing. I had to leave early to be in work on time, but he had to go early too coz he's driving for his dad again. Funny how he's this big indie frontman one day and the next day he's the delivery boy. But his dad says you have to keep your feet on the ground. He had this mate who was in a band when he was Sean's age. Got really famous – for five minutes. He now works in a call centre.

The sun shone today, which was almost unbelievable. This is one of the worst Augusts I can ever remember. When I was a little kid Augusts were hot and sunny all the time. But they said on some programme on the telly that apparently everyone thinks that. So people who were old when I was a little kid were looking at the weather and going 'It's not like it was when I was young'.

Another crazeeee day in Divine Inspiration. Today some men arrived to put up the sign on the front. It's all fancily done in this black lettering and I heard it "cost a king's ransom". Pity Davina didn't know about me back then. I'd have done if for her, much better, at half the price. Davina spent most of the morning checking up on these two quite fit young guys who took their shirts off almost as soon as they arrived. Every five minutes she'd say, 'Just what are they doing now? They're going to rrrr-uin my shop front!' and rushing out to wave her hands at them. But she also took them out a lot of tea and biscuits.

I finished the eyes and clock faces and then I did a bit of decorating in the changing room area. Davina liked my idea of shiny sun faces. 'So fitting for the theme darling – very ancient Egyptian sun god... How clever of you to think of that.'

Actually I hadn't thought of anything except how to paint something fairly simple that would tie in with the designs in the main shop. But I didn't say so.

Today it was just Davina and Keesh and me for most of the morning, but Carly arrived later with bags of goodies. Today we could sit on real chairs coz one of the reasons Carly wasn't around was coz she'd gone to collect them in a van she'd borrowed from her mates.

The chairs were made of iron and in weird twisty shapes. They're dead trendy but they're a bit chilly to sit on. Lucky it's such a warm day.

'These need cushions,' Carly announced after we'd finished eating. 'That big store up the road has some cool stuff. I could go and see what they've got in stock.'

'Something simple darling – black silk or maybe grey...'

'Brown fake fur cushions – or maybe dark green,' I said, almost without thinking. Davina clapped her hands and declared this perfect. And Keesh gave me a high five.

Tonight we didn't finish till just after 9pm. Everything had to be finished for the showroom and the changing rooms. Friday is the launch party and fashion show and tomorrow is the dress rehearsal and all the tecchie bits get done.

Everything had to be swept and polished from top to bottom, clothes had to be hung and priced, or arranged artistically on display units. With Davina it had to be perfect. She would spend 20 minutes deciding how a little silk cardigan should be draped over the edge of a shelf, or where to place a chunky handbag so the light caught it at the best angle.

I was getting worried we'd never make it over to Lucy's before bedtime. I'd promised her I would call in and see the 'amazing new thing' that Ruby could do, and Keesh was coming with me coz she hasn't seen her 'likkle bruvver' in ages. I'd texted a few times to say it wasn't looking good and we might not be able to make it tonight and Lucy texted back saying that Davina must be a slave driver to keep us so late – and we should tell her we'd had enough. But Luce's never done a proper day's work in her life and I don't think she understands what it's like. Besides, this was an exciting new project and our chance to prove ourselves. Davina was passionately committed to her new shop and expected Keesh and I to feel the same about it.

But when she finally announced that we were finished she was very generous. She pressed two £50 notes into my hand and called us a cab which she said would be 'on the company account' to take us wherever we wanted to go. And she also booked a cab to collect us from there by 11.30pm to take us home for our 'beauty sleep' because we had a big day ahead of us. And she also said something which was better than any sum of money.

'I've been thinking about some of those drawings of yours, Holly. I don't suppose you have anything made up yet, do you daahling? We're a little short on the menswear … and if that collection from Paris still isn't here by tomorrow, we may have to think of some alternatives.'

Keesh was instantly by my side. 'She has one of dose frock

coats made up – the one you really liked, with de slanting pockets…'

'Oh daahling, that would be marvellous. Bring it in tomorrow and I'll take a look at it. We could show it as some kind of prototype and if customers like it… Well, let's just see how it goes.'

'What the hell were you thinking about?' I demanded of Keesh, as we settled into the taxi. 'There's hours of fiddly braid work still to do on that coat, and Lucy will kill me if I cancel now. I mean, I don't mean to sound ungrateful but…'

'Sure babes? You don't sound like you grateful to your Auntie Keesha, girl … Hell, girl, we not gonna let you miss this opportunity! We just go eat our tea at Nathe 'n Lucy, we tell dis cab to pick us up at 10.30 – then we gonna get home and sew. An' sew. Till our arms falls off, if we has to.'

'You're gonna sew it with me?' I was so grateful I gave Keesh a hug.

'Don't be stupid, babes!' Keesh said, patting me on the back. 'Dere's no way you could do dat on your own. You not good enough yet girl!'

Which is why I'm sitting up writing this diary while Keesh manoeuvres the material under the flying needle, steering dangerously round corners at breakneck speed. She's doing things it would have taken me a day to do, and I'd probably have needed to unpick most of it and start again. She's concentrating till she's cross-eyed. She told me I'm not allowed to talk and I can't help, so the only thing I can do is sit here and keep her company. And make her the occasional cup of peppermint tea.

Anyway – I've still got time to write about our visit to Lucy and Nathe's.

We must have arrived looking pretty pleased with ourselves, coz Nathan opened the door to us, saying, 'You two look like a pair of pussycats dat got da poor canary.'

'I hope you haven't eaten any canaries,' Lucy appeared at the top of the stairs, with a sleepy Ruby in her arms. 'Coz Nathe has made enough macaroni cheese to feed an army. I guess we can heat it up a bit.'

I was absolutely starving but the thought of Nathe's cooking was almost enough to take the edge off my hunger.

But clever Keesh came to the rescue. 'Likkle bruvver I hope you made this one good,' she said. 'You remember dose special ingredients Auntie Marcia use to put in, you got to put dem in or it taste like sick ...' And she headed into the kitchen to sort out her brother's cooking.

Lucy was eager to get me into the front room so I could see Ruby's new trick.

'She not a circus animal,' Nathe called from the kitchen. 'Don't you go makin' her do nothin' when she only half awake. She should of been asleep ages ago.'

Fortunately the "new trick" wasn't a very complicated or energetic one. Lucy nuzzled her nose into her daughter's blonde curls, and whispered her name while tickling her gently under the chin with her free hand. And Ruby let out a delighted little giggle.

'Tell me that isn't the cutest thing you ever heard!' Lucy said, beaming with pride. 'I don't think babies are meant to giggle this young ... but my daughter is going to be a genius. She's going to be prime minister before she's twenty-one!'

'Which is more than you can say for her mother.' Nathe appeared from the kitchen and kissed the top of his step-daughter's head. Before giving his girlfriend a little squeeze. 'Man, she still not sent in dat form for college. She wasting her talents – dat's what I tell her. You agree wiv me Hols, don't you?'

Luckily Keesh appeared just at that moment, wearing a kitten-patterned apron over her glittery purple top. 'Hey, you got to get out dere, Lucy. Life is for living girl! You can't sit here and wait for it to come knockin' on your door.'

'Talking of which,' said Lucy, craftily changing the subject. 'I want to hear all about the shop, from both of you. What's this about one of your designs goin' in the fashion show, Hols? That's fab – not that I'm not cross with you both for rushing off early. But this time we forgive you, don't we Nathe?'

'We forgives you anything,' Nathe said, taking Ruby from his partner and rocking her gently in his arms. 'Coz you Holly, and Keesh, you the feistiest girls I know...'

Just as we were going downstairs for our taxi, Lucy said something that made me stop in my tracks. 'So what do you think about this news about Ryan's other sister?' she asked me.

'You what?' I asked.

'Didn't he tell you? I thought he would have done. Sorry Hols. I ... Are you sure he hasn't called you or something? I've been waiting for you to bring it up all night... coz I wanted to see how you felt about it. But I just had to ask before you go... '

I remembered then that I'd seen a message come up from my brother, just as I was finishing my coffee, and Davina called me to help her with some boxes. I'd meant to read it later but in the bustle of the day, I'd forgotten all about it.

I stopped on the stairs and read it then and there. When Keesh called to me from the pavement, I told her to ask the driver to wait a minute. Davina's bill wouldn't mind a few extra minutes.

Ryan's message read:

This is like unbelievbul sis. That letter was from this person called Susanna. Shez like my half sis. But shes older than us. 24 or something. Shes my dads dorter from this woman he knew before mum. But nobody knew she was born. Not dad or evil aunt. Till last year she found out about them. She hates them just as much as me Holly. But she says they tole her about me. An she's been looking for me. She met that Josie in the pub and they got talking...

Then there was a pause and the message continued on another text:

She sez that Josie like really grilled her and found that she ment no harm to me. So Josie told her where my school is an she looked up my address. And she sez shed like to meet wiv me sumtime. I tole Martin and Jane and L and N coz they were there when the letter arvd. And they say to tell you sis. Soon as poss but u not anserin ur fone coz I think u got some big thing on. R x P.S. This Susanna sez that evil granny is very ill and mad aunt is looking after her all the time. Dave has gone away coz he's fed up wiv them both PPS OMG, Hols!

I stood there on the stairs with the world spinning round. Lucy put her hand out to steady me. 'You OK Hols?' she asked.

A thousand thoughts went through my head. I could go round the front and see if Ryan was back from his night out with his mates. I could go and talk to Jane and Martin if he wasn't. I could ring Sean and ask him what he thought. Or I could stay here and talk to Lucy and Nathan about it. I was about to go out and tell Keesh to get the taxi without me.

But then I thought about my unfinished coat and the fashion show on Friday. I could ask all those questions I needed to ask some other time, I could talk to Ryan and Jane and Martin, and Lucy and Sean about it. And Keesh and Nathe too, coz they also feel like my family.

'I'm OK,' I told Lucy quickly. 'Please tell Nathe not to say anything to Keesh about it yet... I need to ... to think about this first. It's a bit of a shock. But Keesh's got this really big day tomorrow and we got something to finish first...'

I don't like keeping secrets from Keesh but I do need to think about this myself. And I need to have a conversation with my brother, face to face. So I just made some excuse about why I'd got held up on the stairs. I'll tell Keesh soon as the shop launch is over.

But now she needs some more peppermint tea coz she's working like a madwoman to get this stuff done for me. I owe her something really nice as a thank you present.

And after it's made I'm going to think about what to text back to my brother. Coz he is my brother. He's always been my little brother. And no new half-sister coming on the scene is ever going to change that.

THURSDAY 19 AUGUST

Keesh and me sat up till about 4am, till she was satisfied the coat was perfect. It looked pretty bloody amazing to me, but she kept finding things that weren't quite right and sorting them out. 'Dat's why I work for someone like Davina,' she told me. 'Coz I got an eye for detail – and for quality. Not everyone got dat, girl.' But this morning she's still up before me, making us strong coffee. 'We sleep when dis is over, girl,' she tells me. Pulling me from my bed and pushing me in the direction of the shower.

On the way in I look for a reply from Ryan but I guess he's not awake yet. But there's a message from Sean saying he'd really like to see me tonight. And do I want to go out for pizza (on him). I'm all ready to text back and say I'm way too busy but I remember what he'd said. About me never making time for him. So I text him to say, 'Sure' but I will have to make it early coz I'm knackered and have a long day tomorrow. He says that's cool and he'll see me at the pizza place at 7.30pm. I think it will be good to talk to Sean about this "new sister" thing. Maybe before I talk to Ryan. Sean knows me so well. He'll understand why I'm so shocked by this news. He'll help me think of the right things to say, so Ryan won't guess how jealous I feel about this new person.

Me and Keesh arrive to find there's a right palaver going on at the shop. (When isn't there?)

'The caterers have definitely given Davina the boot,' Carly explained to us, watching her boss, pacing and waving her arms outside the front window, dragging deeply on her usual ciggie, and creating cancer-inducing clouds of smoke as she roasts someone at the other end.

'More problems with the asparagus?' I asked.

'Oh, no, much worse,' Carly tells us, soberly shaking her head. 'Something much much worse…'

'The celery is out of season?' I suggest.

'De celery got lost in de post wiv Je T'Aimes fashion samples?' Keesh volunteers.

'No, no, no,' Carly says, swishing her mane of beautiful black hair and faking a very serious look. 'Much much worse… So terrible you're not going to believe this…'

We suggest that maybe Michael has run off with the catering manager. Or one of the cooks has told Davina she can stuff her asparagus where the sun don't shine. And at last Carly gives in and tells us the Terrible Truth. That the caterers were planning to use paper plates.

Keesh and I faint with shock. Never in all our years in care have we heard anything quite so awful. ☺

'So now Davina is insisting they provide china ones but they won't,' Carly shrugs, trying not to smile. 'They told me yesterday that they were at the end of their tether with this whole thing, and if they heard another peep out of her they were pulling out. Don't know why I'm laughing really because I don't know where I'll find someone else at such short notice. No peace for the wicked…'

Being in a such a busy atmosphere gives you such a buzz. Phoning a man about 60 fold-up chairs may not be the most exciting task in the world, and going out to buy soap and toilet paper isn't exactly glamorous, but I was dead happy to be part of the whole process.

But in the afternoon I got a really good job. I was a bit nervous at first when Carly asked me to help her, but I turned out to be pretty good at it. I had to ring round lots of fashion journalists and ask very nicely if they were definitely coming to the show tomorrow. At first I just called a few of the local papers but when Davina called Carly away to sort out another "disaster", Carly asked me to call some of the fashion editors on really top magazines. I was sure they'd tell me to go away, but much to my surprise many of them said, 'Ah, Davina's do – yes one of us is definitely coming.' (Although you could tell that they thought Corrington was the backend of nowhere and I suspect some of them were wondering if they needed to bring bodyguards and emergency supplies.)

'How do you get to be a fashion editor?' I asked Davina, when we stopped for a cup of tea and some fancy French pastries, which Michael had just delivered.

'A total passion for fashion, daahling – and lots of very hard work,' Davina replied, sipping her weak cup of tea without milk and nibbling the tiniest piece of pastry imaginable. 'And you have to be prepared to do *absolutely anything* to get into the magazine world in the first place – making the tea, working on reception, doing advertising sales, anything to get your foot into the office in the first place.'

'But can anyone do it? I mean, do you have to have a degree or something?' I asked. 'Did you have to come from a posh family or have lots of money or…? '

Davina threw back her head and roared with laughter, like I'd said the funniest thing in the word. 'Daahling, I grew up in a back-to-back terrace in this city, just round the corner from here.

There were eleven of us in a house with only four rooms... And when I was a child we never had enough to eat and I was growing faster than a giraffe. Everyone teased me because I was so skinny. But then I reached 17 and being skinny was suddenly all the rage, and I was spotted by a photographer from *Vogue* magazine... but before that I worked in the mills like my sisters... Then one day, I started writing some little bits and pieces myself. They didn't take me seriously at first because I was a model and everybody thinks models have no brains, but then I was offered my own little column in a local lifestyle magazine. And I worked my way up from there – and had a few lucky breaks. And eventually I got to be editor of one of the best fashion magazines in the country...'

I could see Keesh's surprised reaction to all this. Like me, I think she'd assumed that Davina had always lived a glamorous and privileged life, swanning around with the London fashion crowd.

'And always being prepared to give it everything you've got... That's what my friend Mitzy always said. She said that both her marriages failed because the job always had to come first – but she was totally obsessed... And now daahlings, I need everyone's help for the next hour or so. The caterers Carly booked have let us down so badly and we need to find a replacement.'

That's when I made my suggestion. 'Do we really need caterers?' I ventured, a little hesitantly. 'What if we bought some posh food from some of those local delis... And we could maybe rent some china plates and glasses. We've got the kitchen where we can heat stuff up.'

Davina shook her head. 'Daahling – you have no idea how difficult it is to cater for 60 people...'

'Actually, I do' I said, being quite cheeky now. 'I organised our first term party at college and I did all the catering for 120 people. I just roped in a few people to help. Much cheaper than paying someone else to do it.'

'Goodness,' said Davina, a trace of sarcasm in her voice. 'You are a resourceful young woman.'

'Actu-alleee Daveena,' Michael was speaking in his irritatingly slow voice, 'I think this young woman has a jolly good point.' (He never remembers anyone's name.) 'We will never find a caterer of sufficient quality who is available at such short notice. In fact, I could drive her to the shops myself. I have nothing too demanding on my time just now. Perhaps one of the other young ladies could come as well...'

'Certainly not. We have far too much to be doing here... and these young girls wouldn't have a clue what's appropriate for an event like this!'

'What about ...' I got in hastily, 'If you made a list and I asked my boyfriend to take me there in his dad's van. We could do the shopping on the way in tomorrow, so the food stays fresh?'

I could feel Keesh's eyes on me as I said it. I hadn't told her I was seeing Sean tonight. And I kind of hadn't told her he'd stayed over the other night.

'Fine,' said Davina, relieved that the worst threat was avoided. 'I will make the list – when I have time...'

'Er ... I will need the list by six o'clock, coz that's when I'm meeting my boyfriend,' I told Davina. I wasn't really meeting Sean till 7.30 but I know what Davina's like about time, so I had to give her some sort of deadline.

'My boyfriend will of course need paying for his petrol and a fee for the time he spends,' I said quickly before I lost my nerve. 'He can also stay on and help with getting the food ready, he's very practical. It's a lot cheaper than paying a fortune to caterers... And he'd make a pretty good waiter if you needed one.'

Davina didn't look too happy about this. 'Well, I mean... I mean does he know anything about mixing with these sort of people...' (What she was really wanting to know was whether Sean was some "oikey" lad who'd belch in the faces of all her fancy guests. And pinch their bums while going 'Like a bit of rough, lady?' She might have grown up in a slum, but Davina was still a first-class snob.)

'You can take my boyfriend anywhere – he's very polite and friendly – and women find him very attractive,' I told her, confidently. 'He's actually a lead singer in a band and some of the younger guests might recognise him... ' I'd already opened a link to The Static website and I had my phone ready to hand to Davina.

As she studied Sean's photos I could see the look of approval creeping across Davina's face. 'Yes, a very... yes, a very presentable young man. I wonder, could he sing or play the guitar or something for us tomorrow? Just something melodic and atmospheric – nothing loud or raucous. We've been let down by the musicians, I'm afraid. Such unreliable people... ' Carly had told me earlier that the musicians were friends of Michael's. They were very nervous souls who bumbled around gently and couldn't cope at all with the demanding Davina. When she'd tried to organise them to come to her launch, they'd chosen to go to a wholefood festival in the Outer Hebrides.

'And another thing,' Davina continued. 'I don't see why he couldn't wear that delightful coat you've created. We could put him in the finale perhaps. If he was up for that, of course. Do you think £300 would be an acceptable fee for him?'

'Three hundred pounds?' Sean looked at me in amazement, when I met him at the pizza place. He arrived late and a bit sweaty, looking much more Mr Van Man than the cool singer I'd just sold to Davina. 'That's more than the whole band gets paid for some of our gigs.'

'Exactly,' I told him. 'Which is why you've got to say yes.'

'Course I'll say yes,' Sean replied grinning. 'Now explain it to me again. Do I have to snog this daft old bird, for the money? Or just flirt with the female guests?'

I was about to say I sincerely hoped not, when Sean leant forward and cupped my face in his hands. 'Because I seriously never want to kiss anyone ever again. Except you Holly, 'cept you.'

We ate our pizza very quickly and we didn't hang about for pudding. On the way back to my place I told Sean all about the message from Ryan. He's good, Sean. He listens and asks all the right questions. He doesn't start telling me what to do, so I don't mind asking him for advice. He says he thinks that maybe I should just let Ryan take the lead, tell me what he needs from me. Coz he's probably even more confused than me.

I'm wary when I ring my brother but the first thing he says to me is. 'You're not upset are you, sis? Coz I'm that upset… I don't want any sister but you, Hols. You're the only sister I ever need.' And he says all this without a trace of the normal, too-cool-for-school Ryan. Which immediately brings tears to my eyes.

So then it's me trying to point out to him that it could be really good to have another sister in his life – someone else to call family. And maybe I could think of her as a sort of step-sister or something, specially as our fathers are such losers, and no good to anyone.

'Yeah – I mean, she does sound, like, quite nice, Hols. But I don't know what to do… I mean I don't feel ready to ring her yet. Jane says to wait and see. Not to rush anything,' Ryan tells me hesitantly. 'And if I do go to meet her Hols, you will come with me, won't you? I don't want to go and meet her on my own.'

FRIDAY 20 AUGUST

What an amazing day! I'm going to write it all down now in case I forget anything. I really should have a rest but I'm wide awake with excitement, and got a bit of time now till I'm due over at Jane and Martin's. Sean's had to go home coz it's his parents' wedding anniversary and his mum's invited all their friends over for a special meal.

But he brought me home and came in for a little while. We sat over cups of coffee in the kitchen and we talked about everything. We've agreed that the past is the past but you can't just forget it, so we're not going to try. We're going to make tomorrow the beginning of the next stage of our relationship. And we drank a little toast to each other with supermarket own-brand coffee – and congratulated ourselves on a happy ending, and a job well done.

And Sean and I really did do a very good job as the "catering staff". We got to the shops soon as they opened and we got everything over to Davina's by 10am. We were filling mini bagels with smoked salmon, making miniature cucumber sandwiches and heating lots of tiny quiches and vol-au-vents. We even found enough asparagus spears to keep Davina happy.

We unpacked and washed all the hired glasses *before* Davina could complain that they were smeary, we rang the people to see why the champagne was late, we rushed out to buy fizzy water when we realised that nobody had ordered any ... and we put out all the chairs *exactly* where Davina wanted them (which would have lasted all morning if Carly hadn't found a way to distract her with the arrival of the flower arrangements).

I also looked after the hairdresser who seemed to do nothing but complain that all the plugs were in the wrong place, and that there were no decent surfaces to stand anything on. And to ask for fresh coffee every five minutes. The make-up artist was much easier and she even shared a few professional tips after I fetched her a cup of tea.

Keesh was busy checking that all the clothes and accessories were perfect and alternatively encouraging and arguing with the hairdresser, who seemed determined to do whatever Davina *didn't* want with the models' hair, and Carly was checking the running order, while a strange man fiddled with the microphone causing it to make horrible screeching noises that nearly fried our brains. And Davina was panicking about everything, in between taking calls on her mobile from various friends, journalists and potential customers.

Finally the run-through happened at midday and apart from one of the models falling over a cable backstage, nothing went wrong. (There was a large notice by it which said MIND THE CABLE and Carly had already explained that they needed to be very very careful around it, until the proper cover thingy arrived.) The model had to be sent home with a sprained ankle and there was a frantic discussion about whether to replace her.

'Y'know I think Hols herself would be the best model for dat outfit – coz it kind of needs someone with long black hair and great legs like hers...' Keesh volunteered.

Davina clapped her hands with delight but I was a lot less happy. 'Actually I'd be awful as a model,' I said quickly. 'I tried it once in a charity fashion show at school and I was the laughing stock. I kind of freeze once everyone's looking at me.'

But Davina wasn't so easily convinced. 'Oh daahling, I'm sure we could teach you how to walk ... you just watch the professional girls tomorrow and you'll soon get the hang of it.'

I had a moment of inspiration. 'Y'know *who would* make a fabulous model,' I said. 'Carly would be terrific. She'd be just perfect.'

'She's not exactly model thin,' Davina said, dismissively.

'Exactly – and dat's de ting,' Keesh said, warming quickly to my suggestion.' Carly's probably a size 10 or 12 or something, but dat's perfect. She more like a real woman. We got de outfit in stock in dat size – and we gonna have customers of all shapes and sizes comin' to de show. We need dem to see that we are catering for *real women*.' (Keesh has the most stunning figure and she turns heads everywhere she goes but she'll never be a beanpole, so she's a real champion of curvy women.)

Davina looked uncertain. 'Well, 10 or 12 is far too large for a catwalk model,' she said. 'I really don't think we could have that...'

'And Carly is gorgeous – and tall and totally funky. Real women in da audience would realise she not a skinny ting but dey would also realise she's totally stunnin'... Did you see the way dose sign men couldn't keep their eyes off her? I fink the older one asked for her number when she was leavin...' Keesh, started on one of her favourite subjects, had suddenly found her fighting feet with her new boss.

A flash of anger appeared in Davina's eyes – I don't think she's used to people crossing her – so I said hastily, 'Y'know, I think Keesh has a good point. You're hoping to appeal to a whole range of women with this shop, not just the ones with perfect "model figures" like yours. A lot of the women in this part of the country have a bit of meat on their bones – coz it's probably colder up here than down south.'

And, much to my surprise, Davina held up her hands in surrender. 'OK, my daahlings you win – Carly shall go to the ball...'

Carly was thrilled to be asked to be a model. She's got such poise and confidence, and she looked quite amazing. She strutted her stuff and danced better than most of the professional models – in my opinion.

At 2.30 the guests arrived. Davina greeted all of them like they were her long-lost cousins and there was more daahlinging and mwah-mwahing than you would ever believe. I left Sean to pour drinks (and to the attentions of various middle-aged ladies who were fascinated to know where Davina had found such a handsome waiter) and went backstage to help Keesh put the finishing touches to the models. When I watched Keesha brush out a model's elaborately lacquered hair and sweep it into a loose knot at the back of her neck, I was very glad the precious hairdresser had rushed off half an hour ago to another appointment. But it did look sooo much better ... 'You have a flair for this,' said the make-up artist, grabbing Keesh by the hand and leading her off to ask her opinion about the colour of a model's eye shadow.

The show itself ran like clockwork. And we took lots of orders and sold lots of clothes. Davina was absolutely thrilled. She was also pleased with the small stir my handsome boyf created, strumming his guitar and singing softly, while Keesh and I handed round the canapés. 'What an amazing garment – and so beautifully made. I just adore the detail,' one of the fashion editors remarked, using this as an excuse to get a good feel of my boyfriend's upper arms.

Fortunately Davina happened to be passing at just that moment. 'Marvellous, isn't it daahling, so fresh and unique...' she gushed, stopping to kiss the editor. And run her fingers across Sean's shoulders. 'We are definitely going to be stocking some of these designs... A very up and coming young designer. And local too... Most exciting.'

By 5pm Davina had kissed the last guest goodbye, taken the last credit card order and finished telling Keesha exactly how to hang up all the dresses. She then came into the kitchen to supervise Sean and I who were finishing the washing up. 'Well done, all of you. I couldn't have managed without you my daahlings. Excellent work everyone. Excellent work.... It was all quite marvellous. Truly marvellous. Oh, do be careful with those plates daahling... those wretched people will charge us for any breakages.'

Then, like magic, Carly appeared at her boss's side. 'Come along Davina, it really is time you had a break. You must be utterly exhausted after such a triumph... and I bet you're gagging for a cigarette...'

At the word cigarette, Davina allowed herself to be steered away by her assistant. As they left we heard her saying, 'Daahling you were a most enchanting model. No real sense of rhythm of course, but I think the audience loved you for your naturalness...'

'Phew,' said Keesh, slipping into the kitchen and plopping herself onto a stool as soon as she saw Davina leaving for the fire exit. 'I'm that knackered I could die.'

I gave her an enormous hug then, forgetting to take off my rubber gloves and dripping soap suds down her back. 'Thank you sooooo much,' I told her. 'That outfit would never have been finished without you. I can't tell you how much ...'

'Yeah well, the important thing is that the boss lady likes it,' Keesh said grinning and lifting my dripping hands from around her neck. 'Some of those customers were simply droolin' over it. An' she was askin' me how soon I thought you could knock up another three or four, so she can sell them in de shop. I said it would take time – coz your seamstress needs a bit of a holiday.'

I can't wait to tell everything to Jane and Lucy tonight. I know they'll be so excited for me.

Hello diary – do you remember me? You must think I've forgotten you. But everything's been so strange lately. We only had the funeral today and I think I've been a bit like a zombie, just going through the motions coz it's the only way to keep going. You kind of need to keep busy coz if you stopped and thought about it too often, you'd just never stop crying.

I'm glad they needed me at Divine Inspiration a couple of times, and I've also done a couple of days at the garden centre.

I meant to tell Marje to get lost when she rang to offer me my old job back but it's a recession and there's not that many jobs around. Besides, she sounded so down and broken. She even apologised and said that recently she's begun to realise that Kevin was pulling the wool over her eyes about all sorts of things. And she'd come to thinking that maybe he'd lied about me too, coz I was such a good worker. 'You're a nice lass, Holly,' she said and I could almost hear her thinking 'despite being brought up in care'. Which is daft really when you think about it. Her son was his mummy's pride and joy and he turned out rotten through and through. I've made my own way in the world, admittedly with a bit of help from really decent people like Jane and Martin, but I could hold my head up and look anyone in the eye.

But I did make her put my pay up though, and she's promised to make sure I get all the money that was due to me from before. And it's nice to be back with Ness again. I'll miss her when she goes back to uni but we're going to keep in touch. She says that I must go down and stay sometimes, coz she's dying for me to meet Bea.

Why am I writing about this? It's so trivial really but if you don't keep the basic stuff going everything else will fall apart. You have to keep some kind of pattern in your life otherwise the sadness would just overwhelm you.

See – I'm still putting off writing it. But it's time to get it all down. I'll try to remember what happened as best I can, although I'd really rather just forget.

Diary – we are back to that Friday evening, two weeks ago. I was round at J and M's house and floating on air, and telling them all about my brilliant day. Jane was there and Lucy and Nathe and baby Ruby, who was fast asleep in her carrycot. And even my brother Ryan was in for once. He was a bit nervous about seeing me and I realised he was still worried I might be cross about him having another sister. He wanted to show me the letter – and of course I read it. It was dead friendly, really nice. This Susanna woman seems like she's got her head screwed on. And she genuinely wants to meet up with Ryan, but she says it's fine for him to do things in his own time. I liked the sound of her. I said to Ryan that maybe we'd better speak to Donald first – but Ryan said that Jane had already done that. Donald had suggested that the first time Ryan meets this Susanna, Jane should be there (as well as me) and Ryan seems to be OK with that idea.

By the time I got there Jane had already ushered both the younger kids upstairs – so I didn't get to set eyes on the-terror-that-was-Liam, but Si had slipped down to give me a little present he'd made for me. It was a drawing of Boots but it looked like a stick insect. I said it was wonderful – of course.

After we ate our supper, we sat around drinking tea and half-watching some crap programme on the telly. Martin was due back any minute, coz he'd been away for a conference down in Devon – and Jane was getting a bit edgy about where he was. But her mind was much too occupied by checking on the Liam-hazard. He'd stopped doing quite so much climbing and running out of the house, but he still needed constant watching. Ryan eventually offered to supervise Liam and Simon playing some fairly simple kind of computer game, but Jane kept popping out every few minutes to check they were all OK.

The phone rang while Jane was out of the room. 'Hi Dad,' Lucy said, picking up the receiver. 'Where you been? We're waiting for you.'

Lucy's face fell as she listened to the answer. It clearly wasn't good news.

'Can't they let you have any idea when they'll get out to you?' Lucy asked anxiously, after a few minutes. 'No idea at all? That's so unfair... You could be stuck all night... Ring again and let us know when you're moving... We all send love... Take care.'

'Poor Dad's broken down on the motorway and there's like this huge traffic jam because there's been a big smash up coz it's so windy... and they can't tell him when he's going to be rescued,' she announced to Jane, who was just re-entering the room.

'Poor man,' said Jane. 'And it's such a miserable night. I really must write to someone to ask what they've done with our summer. But I suppose it does mean we can eat his share of the pudding...'

'Oh Mum – you're terrible!' Lucy announced, but I noticed she quickly skipped out of the room and returned with the remains of the chocolate cheesecake. We were just dividing it up into four pieces when there was a terrible crash, and the sound of falling glass, close to the sitting room window. We all froze for a second, and then each of us leapt to our feet.

'The back door ... I think,' Jane said. And I guess me and Lucy were also thinking the same thing – that someone had just fallen out of an upstairs window. But Nathe was already halfway up the stairs. He reappeared about thirty seconds later with the boy, Liam, in his arms. He was a smallish boy with curly blonde hair and rosy red-cheeks. Quite angelic looking in fact if you went by first impressions. He looked frighteningly calm, almost pleased with himself despite the amount of blood that was pumping from his wrist and covering his clothes and much of Nathe's.

'I'll call an ambulance,' Lucy said immediately. As the daughter of foster carers she's seen her fair share of emergencies.

'Lay him down there, Nathe – and Holly – please fetch a lot of towels, and the first aid kit.'

The ambulance arrived remarkably quickly. By then Jane had managed to staunch the bleeding with a tourniquet, and we'd pieced together what had happened. 'He just stuck his arm through the window,' Ryan kept saying again and again. 'He lost the game, and then he lost it ... he just punched the window with this giant stapler in his hand... the glass cut him like... there was blood everywhere...'

Lucy insisted on going to the hospital with her mum. I wanted to go too but someone had to stay with poor Ryan and Si, who was terribly distressed and bewildered. And Nathe was going to stay with me so he could be there when Ruby woke up.

Eventually we managed to calm Simon down enough to get him to bed. Nathe and I took it in turns reading his favourite dinosaur book until he eventually fell asleep from sheer exhaustion. Ryan insisted on being given a drop of brandy to calm his nerves and somewhere past midnight he agreed to go to his room. Ruby slept peacefully through everything, much to our relief. Jane rang from the hospital to say they probably wouldn't be home till dawn as things were "complicated". It turned out the boy had some rare blood group and it was taking time to organise a transfusion.

'I'll sit up and wait for Martin,' Nathe offered. 'You get some sleep, Hols.'

I was going to say that I wouldn't be able to sleep when I suddenly realised how tired I was. I'd been on my feet all day doing fashion show things and the evening had been mega eventful. I bunked down under some blankets on Jane and Martin's bed and probably dropped off for an hour or so.

I woke up to the sound of breaking glass. At first I thought I was having a dream about what happened earlier, but even after I was fully awake the sound continued. The wind that had been whistling round the house earlier had dropped, so it wasn't caused by that. And the noise seemed to be coming from the computer room where Liam had smashed the window. (Me and Nathe had done our best to try and patch it earlier, but the sheets of cardboard we stuck up kept unsticking and falling on the floor.) Every now and then there'd be a small tinkling sound, like someone was carefully pushing out remaining pieces of glass. My immediate thought was that someone had climbed onto the utility room roof and was trying to steal the computers. Then I told myself I was just being stupid – it was probably Martin, arriving home late and throwing stones at the window coz he was locked out. But I wasn't convincing myself.

The noise went on and I hung frozen on the edge of the bed, urging myself to move. I'd nearly found enough courage to get up and take a look, when I heard another noise. A couple of dull thuds, followed by the creak of floorboards and the sound of cautious footsteps.

'It's just Nathe coming up to see what the noise is,' I told myself, but I knew it wasn't. There were two sets of feet moving and then I heard low, male voices whispering to each other. 'What bedroom should we go in first?' one of them asked.

Without thinking, I wriggled off the bed as silently as I could manage and propelled myself across the carpet, to hide, trembling, behind the large armchair that stands in the corner. It's always piled high with laundry that nobody's yet managed to put away, so it gave pretty good coverage. As long as nobody looked behind it.

The light went on. I thought I'd wet myself with fear. I could sense but not see two men standing in the doorway. My pulse was racing so fast, and my heart banging against my ribcage, that I thought they were bound to hear me. I was holding my breath, and shaking. And praying to any kindly force in the universe who might be good enough to save me.

'Nobody in here,' one of the men said, after what felt like an eternity. His hushed voice was deep, gruff and older sounding. And very menacing.

'Yeah but them covers is piled up, like... someone been sleepin' in here...' This voice sounded younger, probably somewhere around early 20s.

'We ain't playing ruddy Goldilocks,' the older voice growled. 'Whoever bin in here probably the one what's downstairs, and snorin' by the telly.'

The light went off and the footsteps started moving towards the other end of the corridor. I knew I had to do something before these men got to the other bedrooms, before they found my brother or Simon. And I tried to remember where Ruby was sleeping but I couldn't remember which room she was in. My brain had gone to jelly. I just couldn't form any sort of plan.

Then I heard a door slam, a high-pitched childish yell and the sound of more scuffling. This was followed by the sound of movement from below. Nathe's voice floated up from the foot of the stairs. 'What you boys doin' up? You should be asleep. What's goin' on?'

(I remember when bombs going off wouldn't wake Nathan from his sleep. Amazing how a few months with a baby had made him so sensitive to the slightest noise.)

I could hear the men whispering on the landing. There seemed to be some sort of argument going on. Then the sound of a door opening and some banging and shuffling going on. Then came the sound of Simon's piercing cry. 'Holly!' he wailed.

I scrambled out from behind the chair and was nearly at the door, when I heard Nathe running up the stairs and the sound of his deep voice demanding, 'What de hell is goin'...?' And behind him – coming, thank god, from a downstairs room – was the faint indignant whimper of a waking Ruby.

There was muttering and thudding on the landing. The sound of more doors opening. And my brother's voice saying, 'What the...!' More noises and more confusion, but I was still too petrified to leave my hiding place.

'Stay back Ryan,' I heard Nathe shouting urgently, 'Stay back in your room...' and to the men he said in a voice of velvet fury. 'Put de likkle boy down, coz I'm going to mash you up if you don't get out now.'

One of the men laughed – the older one. A dirty, sinister laugh. 'You what? You fink I'm gonna take orders from a black bastard like you? You must be bloody jokin! This is my grandson and I'm takin' him home...Where he belongs.'

'Yeah, him's my bruvver,' the younger voice said, deeply threatening. 'You got no right to keep him here.'

'Well, he don't look like he want to be wiv you!' I heard Nathe's furious response. 'Let him go coz you're hurtin' him!'

There were further sounds of a scuffle and again Simon's piercing voice cried out my name. And now my brother's voice joined in, yelling and swearing, scared and angry at the same time. He'd obviously come out of his room and was trying to help Nathan. Go back Ryan, I prayed, but I was also impressed that he was brave enough to be out there while I, his older sister, cowered, shaking behind the door.

I heard a bang and more swearing. Then there was the sound of feet running... and a cry of fury. It sounded like Ryan's voice. Then more scuffling and the sound of someone being dragged... and muffled noises – like someone had their hand over someone's mouth.

'Stop it you little bastard – you ain't goin' nowhere. We just gonna shut you in here, coz you causin' too much fuss. And if you don't shut up, we gonna have to hurt you...' This was the older man speaking. I guess the men had grabbed Ryan. I got the impression he was further down the corridor and that Nathan was between him and the room where I was hiding.

Suddenly there was another scuffle, a loud yelp and some very loud swearing. There was the sound of feet running down the stairs – young, agile feet. I was pretty sure my brother had made his escape.

'He's goin' outside and he gonna shout for help,' I heard Nathan saying. 'So if you stupid bastards got any sense you'll go now... Let go of de boy.'

'Not bloody likely, not when we took so long to find him,' the older man yelled back.

'My mate Roy spent weeks searchin' on that interweb – we not gonna leave now wivout him,' the younger man's voice had dropped now, to a sinister sneer. 'You jungle boy – you get out tha' way or I'll cut you... Maybe I'll cut you anyway just to teach you a lesson...' And there was a sound of bodies colliding.

I heard Simon's voice rise in a panicky wail. 'Don't hurt Nathan – Holly! Holly! Stop them!'

And then the terrible sound of Nathan roaring – with agony and rage.

Over the sound of all of this I could also hear new noises coming up from the street below – coming in through the open front door. Above them all was my brother yelling frantically, 'Get the police! Get the police!' and what I took to be neighbours' voices as they came out to see what was going on. And Ruby's desperate wail as she cried out for a parent who did not come.

Then there were heavy feet thudding down the stairs. I couldn't stay hidden any longer. I threw open the door and looked straight into the eyes of a terrified Simon who had wrapped his skinny body round the post at the top of the stairs. Below from the staircase, a figure whose face I couldn't see was tugging at the boy's arm. 'Holly!' the boy cried out to me and I knew I had to do something.

Now it was my turn to scream. I screamed like a banshee, blood curdling and inhuman. Like a mother animal that finds another animal about to harm its babies. And I kicked out at the face of the figure on the stairs, truly intending to do some serious injury. And the man let go of Simon's arm and ran down the stairs. And out into the night.

As I grabbed Simon up in my arms, I heard my brother shouting from below 'Don't let them go, stop them...'

I can't write any more now coz I'm that tired. And I've got to make sure that Keesha gets something to eat. That girl is eating like a sparrow and me and her boyf are having to keep a real eye on her.

I'll finish this tomorrow.

THURSDAY 2 SEPTEMBER

Martin had found me curled around Simon, my body protecting him from the sight of Nathe's butchered face, the hideous, scarlet gashes where the penknife had sliced his throat, his cheeks, his eyes ... (I've been seeing that face in my dreams, but that's not how I want to remember Nathe. I want to remember his slow kind smile, his lazy way of grinning. His round, kind face that made you feel that everything was totally OK.) I couldn't let go of Simon, who was sort of convulsing with shock but might any moment run away, jump from the top of the stairs, do something terrible to hurt himself. I knew I ought to carry the boy somewhere, get him onto a bed or something, wrap him in a blanket. But I also knew that someone had to stay with Nathan. I couldn't leave him alone, even though I knew he was no longer really there. I couldn't look at that dead, mangled face, so I reached for his hand – which was still whole, unharmed. A big, fleshy hand with the rough bits from holding a bat or catching a ball, working out in the gym and scribbling frantic notes in his tiny, cramped-up writing. I'd often teased Nathe about his "sweaty paws" but as I held that cooling hand in mine, I'd have done anything to make it warm again.

They called Nathan a hero at the funeral and he was. He was the bravest person I've ever met. But he was so many other things as well. Nathe was gentle and laid-back and kind... and one of the biggest-hearted, most generous people you could ever meet. He suffered fools when other people lost their patience. He gave someone the benefit of the doubt when other people made quick judgements. He smiled when other people would have frowned. He found kind things to say when other people were cruel. He was gentle when other people were hasty. You could rely on Nathe again and again. And he proved that – right up to the end. He wasn't a saint but none of us are, but he was a lot nearer to it than most of the people we know. The world has a great big jagged hole in it now Nathe is no longer here.

The mayor came to the funeral and the local MP, and the director of social services and the head of Nathan's college. And a whole load of friends and tutors from Nathe's year. Rashan Gayle came to the service with his model girlfriend and some other guys from the Corrie team, because they'd read about Nathan's story in the papers and they wanted to pay tribute to his incredible bravery – and his love of sports. Some kids came, too, from the sports camp where Nathan was working, and several of the staff and some of their parents. Some cousins of Nathan and Keesh's came who none of us had ever met before. They told us that Nathe was 'so like his fa'dder' and they told us how Nathe's dad got taken by the authorities because he always stood up for what he thought was right.

All sorts of people sent flowers and cards and messages – and the funeral was very beautiful, which sounds strange but isn't. Coz when people really put time into thinking who the person was, and what they liked, and what they would have wanted, then they come up with something that makes you feel that the person is almost in the room with you. And Keesh chose a dead classy coffin for her brother, and he was dressed in his football kit. And she remembered some hymns and songs her brother had really loved when he was little, and Ryan and I researched them on the internet and printed them out, so we could sing them during the service. And I designed a bookmark with Nathan's picture on it, in the colours of his favourite team. And Lucy chose a poem to go on it, which she said Nathan liked, although she couldn't really concentrate and she's never stopped crying since she first heard the news. And me and Ryan put the bookmarks on the seats in the church, so everyone could take something away, to remember Nathan.

I think I'm kind of cried out for the moment and I feel a bit numb now. The bereavement counsellor says it's not necessary to always try to be strong and it's good to let your feelings out. But I have to be strong for Keesh, who has lost her only brother and for Lucy who's lost her partner – and for little Ruby, who's lost the best dad a child could ever have. So I have to hold it together for all of them – just for now anyway. And I need to be there for my brothers – for little Simon who permanently walks around like the world's about to end, and for my brother Ryan who is trying to put a brave face on things.

In his own way, Ryan's a bit of a hero too. He gave chase to the two men who were caught by a couple of police cars, a few roads away. The police say that if Ryan hadn't followed for so long, they probably wouldn't have been able to track them down. Ryan made so much noise, yelling with rage, determined not to let them get away, that the men thought that half the neighbourhood was after them, so they just kept moving. They hadn't dared go back to the van they'd parked round the corner. So eventually they kind of ran into a dead end, which is where the police caught them. They'll stand charge for murder, which is what they deserve and I hope they get life. Nothing can bring back Nathe but, as I see things, the more of Simon's family who are behind bars, the better. It's terrible really that his family are like that, but thank heavens he has Jane and Martin, and Lucy and Ryan and me. I know we'll never be his blood family but we can do everything to make him feel like he's one of us. Ryan has a new sister and in a way, I now also have a little brother.

Martin says that it wasn't necessarily the photos on The Static's websites that led Simon's family to their house. It seems that some of the kids from Simon's school had pictures of him on their FB pages, with school uniforms and names and everything. Martin says that kids that young aren't really supposed to be on FB and maybe there's a good reason for it.

Coz of being fostered, Ryan couldn't have his picture in the paper but everyone round here knows what happened. The head rang and said they'd make a proper thing of it next term – a presentation or something in assembly. I think that's not a bad thing. After all the stuff that happened last term, it's kind of a way to give my brother a fresh start. Even really mean kids are pretty impressed when someone is that brave.

And it was good that some of Ryan's friends came to the funeral, to be there for him. Those twins are pretty cool and they seem to really care about my brother. And Donald came down for the funeral coz he's been Ryan's social worker a long time and he's good about coming to stuff that matters to kids. And that Luke came too and you could see he was deeply shocked by what had happened, and that he was really sorry for how he'd treated my brother. But Ryan has moved on now and I don't think he has any room for people like Luke in his life.

I don't think it's really hit me properly that we're never going to see Nathe again. But I know we have to keep on living as though he was still here. At the funeral, the minister said that we can keep people in our hearts and make them live on in our memories. She said that we can make a positive effort to live our lives to the full, and we don't have to feel guilty that the dead person isn't here to enjoy the things we enjoy. We can remember them when we're happy as well as when we're upset. I like that idea. A little bit of Nathan will always be in my life and I'm going to make sure it's a life he would have been proud of.

But I worry about Lucy who doesn't know what to do with herself. She cries all day and all night and wanders around the house with her daughter in her arms. It's good she has Jane and Martin and some of her school mates to be with her when I'm not, but I'm not sure she really registers any of us. She's a bit like a zombie at the moment, although I can see she's struggling to be there for Ruby coz that baby means so much to her.

Tonight me and Sean are going out with Dan and Rani. Sean and Dan met at the funeral and they seemed to get on well, and I think it's time that two of the most important men in my life got to know each other properly. Even Rani has been dead nice, ringing me and stuff, to see how I'm doing. I think I'll make an effort to get to know her a bit better when we go back to college.

And I'm so glad Dan's going to be there when the new term starts. I don't think SB will have the nerve to come back to college, but you can never tell with him. Sean thinks I should maybe tell Dan what happened with SB, so I've got a friend I can talk to if I get upset or anything. I think that's probably a good idea.

FRIDAY 3 SEPTEMBER

Today would have been the last day of the caravan holidays for Jane, Martin and the boys, and Lucy and Ruby, and Nathe – except, of course, they never went.

J and M got a massive bouquet of flowers and a letter from Liam's foster carers. They said they blamed themselves for his difficult behaviour. They said they should have realised he wasn't as settled and secure as they thought. Apparently when Liam was younger his first foster carers handed him to a new foster family and told him it was 'just for a few days', but he never saw them again. So he hadn't believed his present foster carers when they'd said it was 'only for a week'. They wrote that they were going to see if it's possible for them to adopt him or have a residence order or something – so he can feel properly secure in their family.

Ryan rang this morning, when I was at the garden centre. Marje knows about Nathe's death and all that stuff, so she says it's fine for me to take calls from my brother, even if I'm meant to be working. Ryan says he thinks that maybe he'll talk to Jane about making that phone call to Susanna. Maybe sometime in the next few days, before he goes back to school. I said I thought he should do whatever feels best for him. But that I'm behind him, whatever he decides.

Sean came over again this evening. I don't know what I'd have done without him this last week. He's been so supportive, so understanding. And he's been wonderful with Keesh, spending time just sitting with her when she needs to cry, or talking when she needs to talk. (Davina's been dead kind and said Keesh must take as much time off as she needs, but most days Keesh just goes into work. But she's not so good when she gets home in the evening.) And my wonderful boyf's also been running around in the van, helping with things like shopping, making tea and coffee, looking after Lucy when Jane or Martin need to go out, reading dinosaur stories to Simon, and just making sure everyone gets a bit of rest and a sit down every now and again. J and M say they couldn't have coped without him.

It's going to be awful when Sean goes back to uni, but there's still a while yet. The band's got a gig tomorrow night in Leeds, and although a gig's the last thing I feel like at the moment, I'm going with him. Sometimes you've just got to be there for the people you love.